Winter Magic
in
Port Berry

K.T. DADY

Port Berry Book 3

Choc Lit
A JOFFE BOOKS COMPANY

Choc Lit
A Joffe Books company
www.choc-lit.com

First published in Great Britain in 2024

© K.T. Dady 2024

Cover art by Dee Dee Book Covers

ISBN: 978-1781898208

Winter Magic in Port Berry

ALSO BY K.T. DADY

Understanding changes the world.

CHAPTER 1

Will

'I don't like pilchards myself,' Will told the kitten outside his grandmother's cottage. He used a booted foot to gently nudge away the empty tin the black furball was licking before retrieving and tossing it into the recycling bin.

The smallest of whines scolded him before the skinny thing scarpered into a bush.

Will chuckled to himself but dropped his smile as he faced the light-oak front door. He inhaled deeply as he knocked and rubbed his hands together to help alleviate his nerves, rather than warm them from the October nip in the air. With another steadying breath he ran his hands through his mousey hair.

He'd felt awkward when joining the Royal Navy at eighteen, too. He liked to think he had more social skills now he was forty-two, but what he was presently undertaking rattled more parts of him than any warship ever could.

The forty-year-old woman who answered the door greeted him with a cheery smile and happy green eyes. 'Hello, Willard Pendleton. Wasn't sure you'd be back again.'

He gently tipped his head. 'Said I would, Marie.'

'Well, you're in luck today. Come inside. It's a bit fresh out there. Although I guess you sailors are used to the wind in your face.'

'I retired from the navy two years ago,' he said with a smile, following her along the narrow hallway to the kitchen at the end.

'I'll pop the kettle on, then take you through. She's just watching her favourite gardening show.'

'How's she been?'

'Oh, good and bad days. The care home called. She moves in next week.'

Will sat at the small wooden table, resting his arms on top. 'What can I do to help?' He glanced around at the chipped cupboards and floral crockery on show. 'I can pack and transport.'

Marie looked over her shoulder. 'She can't take everything with her. Just a few personal bits.'

Will frowned. 'But what about her stuff?'

'You can sort that this week. Charity, second-hand shops, dustbin. I know it's a shame, but it is what it is. The person who bought the cottage is due to move in here a couple of weeks after Babs moves out, so we don't have much time to shift the lot.'

How sad was that? Will didn't own a lot himself, but even he felt a slight attachment to what he did have. How would Babs feel leaving so much behind? He was gutted on her behalf.

Marie sat opposite him, showing compassion in her gaze. 'She's lucky she has you now.'

Lowering his head, Will sighed. 'We don't know each other.'

'But you're here now. That's all that matters, and she's lucid today, so go say hello, and let's see if we can get you some answers this time.'

Marie was good at her job. A great care worker. He'd picked up on that on his first visit to this snug cottage in Port Berry.

Will stood, gazing towards the square window, taking in the view of the quiet backstreet not far from the harbour. 'Feels weird knowing this is where I came from.'

'Cornwall isn't too far from Wales. Give us time, we'll change that accent of yours to Cornish in no time.'

'Ah, it's not that strong anyway.' His smile faded as he entered the small living room. His grandmother sat upright in a beige wingback chair, cuddling a cream blanket.

Soft features diverted from the television and gazed his way. 'Ooh, hello, young man. And who might you be?'

Marie handed her a teacup half-filled with apple juice, then turned down the volume on the TV. 'It's Willard. He's been to visit you before.'

Babs frowned. Her dark eyes, so like his, homing in on him. 'I don't remember.'

Will sat on the sofa to her side and smiled warmly, unsure what to say. He'd only met her four times, and each time felt the same. He was so glad Marie was around to help. At least Babs looked alert and somewhat peaceful today.

Marie passed him a mug of tea as she plonked herself at the other end of the sofa. 'Willard here used to be in the navy.'

Babs smiled and nodded. 'Like my father.'

That was the first Will had heard about that. How strange. He wondered if the sea had always been in his blood.

Marie smiled softly. 'Willard never had a family, so he joined young, making his own.' She nodded at him. 'But now he's older, he's decided to find out who his parents are. Where he comes from, you know, that sort of thing.'

Babs sat up straighter, looking as though she was studying him. 'I loved my parents. Good people.'

Will warmed, pleased with the knowledge there were good people in his family. At least his grandmother seemed to have had a happy life.

Marie took a sip of tea, then cleared her throat. 'Willard did one of those gene test things that tell you who you're related to. He found some distant relatives.'

Babs perked up. 'What did you find, love?'

Will smiled softly. 'I found out I was related to you.' There was silence for a while, before he continued. 'Some distant relatives told me you're my grandmother, then I did some research. Birth certificates and all that, but I don't know much so far. I was hoping you might be able to fill in some blanks.' He steadied his breathing and waited.

'You okay, Babs?' asked Marie. 'Do you understand what this man is asking?'

Babs started to twiddle with the gold bracelet on her left wrist. Her thin lips twisted to one side as she assessed him from head to toe. 'I thought that was you as soon as I saw your face. I knew you would come back one day. I felt it.' She kept eye contact, not showing much emotion, more intrigue. 'You were adopted.'

Will shook his head. 'No, I wasn't. I was raised in and out of care homes for most of my childhood, then one foster mum took me in when I was twelve.'

Babs looked confused. 'My grandson was adopted. I was told.'

'By who?' he asked gently, not wanting to force anything, for fear of her clamming up.

'My little girl told me. Your mum. She couldn't cope, see. I tried, but I've always had bad health, and she didn't want you around so . . .' Her hand met her lips. 'Sorry, love. That sounded terrible.'

He didn't feel too great either, but he kept that info privy.

Marie stepped in. 'We all handle life our own way.' Her smile was sympathetic, but it didn't soften the blow Will had just taken to his solar plexus.

There was no way he was going to get a happy ending, by the sound of things, but he still had questions whirling.

'Why did she give up her baby?' he asked, thinking that a simple enough start.

Babs lowered her eyes to her bracelet again. 'She wasn't very well. Good girl, until she wasn't. It was that lad's fault.

He made her ill. Took my baby away, he did.' Her lips pursed as her eyes narrowed.

'You don't have to talk about it, Babs,' said Marie, and although Will agreed on some level, he wanted to know the truth.

Babs wiped her hands together. 'Done and dusted,' she said sadly. 'Gone now. Nothing I can do.'

Will shuffled forward, placing his tea on the coffee table. 'I'd like to know about her.'

There was a shift in the old woman's eyes as she turned his way. 'You look like my husband. He was a handsome chap as well.'

'Tell me about my mum, please,' he said gently, hoping she would take pity on his needs.

'She met a boy. He was no good. Got her taking all sorts. She was never the same. She had you, and he was angry. Told her to get shot, else she couldn't live with him. It was only me here, and she wouldn't listen. What did I know? I was just her daft old mother.' She breathed out a small laugh as she twiddled with that bracelet.

'So my mum was on drugs?' He needed the confirmation, as it seemed like that was what Babs was saying.

Babs glanced up. 'She had lovely skin. After him, she was such a mess. Broke my heart, Marie.'

Marie moved to her side to hold her hand. 'She's at peace now. Let that comfort you.'

It wasn't comforting Will. 'She died?'

'Long time ago,' said Babs. 'So young.'

'You could have told me, Marie.'

Marie shook her head. 'Not my story to tell, Willard.'

It wasn't shaping up to be the family reunion he was hoping for. When he'd started his search, he wasn't entirely sure what he would unearth, but dead druggie mother — harsh but that seemed to be the case — wasn't on the list. He wasn't quite sure who to feel sorrier for: Babs, his deceased mum, or himself.

5

He looked at his gran and realized she probably wouldn't even remember him tomorrow. He swallowed hard. He had to regain focus. *What a bloody mess!* Would his dad's line be able to answer more questions?

As if reading his mind, Marie asked Babs if she knew anything about the father.

'No. Mindy didn't know.'

Mindy.

'That lad was stabbed though,' added Babs. 'A few years after my Mindy passed away. Good riddance to bad rubbish.' Her eyes shot up to Will. 'He wasn't your dad. He had her sleeping around with other men for money before you were born. Mindy didn't know who she was half the time. And I will say, you don't look anything like the ugly rat.'

Will took a long steadying breath. And another for good measure. There was no way of finding out who his biological dad was. That was it. He'd reached the end of his quest. It had all seemed so light and easy in the beginning. Sure, he figured a sad story would come his way — but *this!*

And poor Babs. He observed her afresh; she really did look so frail, lost, and alone. How she must have suffered all those years, worrying each and every day about her daughter being used and abused. The thought made his blood boil. He realized he'd have loved the opportunity to get his hands on the scumbag who destroyed his mother.

A swirl of sickness hit his gut as it dawned on him he wasn't born out of love. And it appeared all this talk of her dead daughter was having a similar effect on Babs. She was having a lucid day from dementia. It needed to be filled with happy vibes, not some strange bloke sitting in her cottage bringing up terrible times.

For years he'd managed to live without knowing about his roots. Part of him wished he hadn't bothered. Just the thought of his biological father being some loser who paid drugged women for sex made him feel all kinds of weird.

'What a fabulous man your grandson grew up to be,' said Marie, beaming his way as though sensing his distress.

Babs smiled at Will. 'I'm so pleased you look like my husband. He was a good man. Died young. That's when Mindy met that horrible lad. Life wasn't the same after that. Been on my own for years, I have.'

'You're not on your own now,' Will found himself saying before he could think.

Babs patted Marie's hand. 'Go fetch my photo album, love. The one by my bed. I want to show my grandson my Willard.'

Will smiled. 'Your husband's name was Willard?'

'Yes, love. I named you, and I told him to watch over you. Keep you safe, no matter what. See, he did good by you. Tell me you've been happy.'

Lying wasn't something that was part of his set-up, but she didn't need to know how his heart ached for a family, how alone he often felt, how much he threw himself into the navy just so he could belong somewhere. How could he tell her how unloved he felt? How wary he was of falling in love in case his already broken heart got broken again. He'd never given relationships much of a chance, rejecting women before they could do the same to him. It was such a dilemma to want such closeness but be too afraid to have it.

Will tilted his head and nodded. 'I've been happy.'

'Here.' Babs waved him closer and removed her bracelet. 'You take this. It was your mum's.'

'Oh no, I couldn't—'

'Shush now, Willard. It belongs to you.' She slipped the gold into his palm and curled his fingers around it.

Will didn't know what to say or how to feel. He wasn't even sure if he wanted anything of Mindy's. 'Thank you,' was all he could muster.

Her fragile fingertips raised to lightly stroke his cheek. 'You're a good boy. Will you visit me again?'

A lump hit his throat. 'Every day,' he told her quietly, not wanting her to slip away again.

'Where are you living, love?'

'I'm staying at a B&B along Harbour End Road. It has a nice sea view.'

'I bet you're a good swimmer.'

He nodded. 'I am.'

'Do you have family?'

'Just you.'

Babs raised his hand and kissed his knuckles. 'We'll be all right, won't we?'

'Yep.'

'I'll look after you. You can move in here with me.'

It was crushing. She had no memory of her upcoming move to a care home, and his heart broke for her once more.

Will simply nodded and sat back on the sofa as Marie entered with the photo album, and Babs smiled widely as though no cares were to be had.

But Will knew the cottage would soon belong to someone else, her things gone, her memories hazy.

He smiled at the pictures of faces he didn't know while listening to his grandmother merrily natter away about her past. He had a gran, some understanding about his childhood . . . and nowhere else he had to be.

CHAPTER 2

Ginny

Three grocery shops later and Ginny still hadn't found the brand of strawberry jam her mother liked. It was time to give up, else she'd be late for work. She had given her most trusted member of staff, Annie, a key and the alarm code for the café so she could open up on days Ginny was running late. Today was definitely one of those days. Annie didn't mind, but Ginny always did. She hated being out of routine. Weighing up her options, she popped in one last convenience store to see if they had what she needed. Nope!

Ginny felt deflated even before she crossed the threshold of her mum's house.

'Did you get Birdy's jam?'

Ginny wrinkled her nose at her mother's care worker. 'I swear to high heavens, Suzanne, I blimming well tried. I told old Smitty he needs to get it back in stock, but he said he's been trying. I did consider making my own, but who makes strawberry jam in October?' She plopped the shopping bags on the kitchen table and huffed.

'Is that Ginny?' yelled a rough voice from the living room.

'Yes, Mum.'

'Did you get my jam?'

Ginny's shoulders flopped. She entered her mother's space, already knowing the reception she would get regardless of right or wrong conserves. 'Smitty said it's still not in stock.'

'Bet you didn't tell him it was for me,' she grumbled, slowly turning the page of her magazine.

'He knows.'

'Did you use my real name or nickname?'

Ginny silently sighed. 'He knows you're Yvonne and Birdy. He's known you for years. It makes no difference to his stock.'

'I'll have to call Lee. See if he can send me some.' She scowled at Ginny. 'Your brother works hard, you know. I shouldn't have to bother him with this stuff. It's not as if he lives up the road.'

'Speaking of work, I have to—' A black kitten rubbed along Ginny's ankle, catching her attention. 'There's a cat in here.'

'Well done, Sherlock. At least your eyes work. Shame they're not blue like Lee's. Hazel is such a boring colour, don't you think?' Birdy started making kissing noises, but the kitten seemed to prefer Ginny's leg.

'Who does it belong to, Mum?'

'It's mine, isn't it? Stupid.'

Ginny clenched her teeth, determined not to bite back. It wasn't as though she wasn't used to the name calling. She scooped up the skinny creature, then pulled back her face from its fishy breath. 'Where did it come from?'

'It's not an it. Her name is Lucky, and I bought her from Mary up the road. Her cat had kittens.'

'You can't have a cat. You're going in a home soon.'

Birdy slammed her magazine shut so hard, poor Lucky jumped and tried to wriggle further into Ginny's khaki dungarees. 'Why don't you come round here more often with your cheery statements?' Her brow creased. 'You can't wait to lock me away, can you?'

The last thing Ginny wanted was another argument about the care home. 'I'm not locking you away,' she said gently, ignoring the kitten nuzzling her earlobe.

'You've always hated me,' snapped Birdy.

That's rich!

'It's got nothing to do with me, Mum. You need help getting in and out of bed now.'

'I've got Suzanne. She's a good girl. I bet she wouldn't toss her mother out with the rubbish.'

'She can't do everything for you anymore. You need full-time care.'

Birdy flicked the magazine to the carpet. 'Then why can't you move in and look after me? You're only thirty-four. Got lots of strength left in you.'

'I have a full-time job running the café.'

'So, give it up.'

'I can't afford to do that.'

Birdy huffed. 'Of course you can. I know you're loaded.'

Ginny almost choked on her laugh. 'I'm not loaded.'

'Oh please. This is me you're talking to. I know how much that loser left you.'

Ginny hated it when her mum called her dad names, but she bit her lip, not wanting to stoke the fire.

Birdy wasn't done. 'Didn't leave me anything when he snuffed it, did he? Oh no. Just you. Didn't even care about Lee.'

'He didn't know Lee. Lee had his own dad. Anyway, he didn't know me either. He left when I was two.'

'Don't tell me about my own life. I was the one who lived it, not you. Left me alone with a nipper. Good thing Lee's dad did come along. He was so lovely.' She pulled a peach hanky from her cardigan pocket and sniffled. 'Look, you've made me cry now. Pleased with yourself? You know how much I loved him.'

Oh, she knew. Heard it all her life. Lee's dad this, and Lee's dad that.

'It's your fault your brother's dad left me.' Birdy scrunched her handkerchief. 'Didn't want someone else's kid, did he? Couldn't put up with you. But did I lock you away somewhere so I could live a carefree life? No, I bloody well didn't. You've always been selfish, just like your old man.'

11

Her mother's words failed to sting anymore. She'd heard them so often, she knew each line off by heart.

'Even when your dad died and left you everything he had, you still didn't bother giving anything to me, and I'm the one who raised your sorry arse. See what I mean about you.' She dramatically raised a hand to her brow. 'Oh, Ginny, why couldn't you just be different? You drain me, you know that. I gave up everything for you.'

'I need to get to work,' Ginny said softly, swallowing hard.

'You haven't even made my breakfast yet.'

'Suzanne's making it right now.'

'Yeah, with horrible jam, no doubt. Oh, well, never mind your poor old mum, as long as your customers get a bit of decent grub.'

Ginny placed Lucky back on the carpet. 'You'll have to give her back to Mary.'

'Mind your own business.'

'How old is she anyway? She looks too young to be away from her mum.'

'You still here?'

Ginny scrunched her tired eyes, then turned to leave.

'Where you going now?' bellowed Birdy, causing Lucky to scoot under the sofa.

'I'm just going to talk to Suzanne a minute, then I'm off to work.'

'Talk about me, no doubt. Horrible cow. Stab me in the back soon as I turn, wouldn't you? Where's my Lee? I want to ring him. Pass me the phone. At least he cares about me.'

Yeah, that's why he moved to Yorkshire and never calls you.

'It's too early to ring him, Mum. He works late so won't be awake yet, remember?'

Birdy lowered her head. 'He's a good boy,' she mumbled, seemingly talking to herself.

'I'll see you later, Mum.'

There came no reply.

Ginny rested her head on the doorframe as soon as she left the living room and took a calming breath.

Suzanne waved her towards the kitchen. 'What was that all about? I heard raised voices.'

'Oh, just Mum feeling irritated because she hasn't got her favourite jam for brekkie. She'll be okay in a bit.'

Suzanne didn't look convinced, and Ginny wasn't surprised, especially if the carer heard some of the names that were spat out. 'I like your head scarf choice today, Gin.'

Ginny absentmindedly touched the polka dot red-and-white material covering her dark bobbed hair.

'I always like your 1940s get-up. You always look great.' Suzanne glanced at her own black pumps. 'I only wear these for work. I might invest in one of those tea dresses you wear though. Next summer probably. A bit too nippy now. Do you think forty is too old for a tea dress?'

'No. Wear what you want at any age, chick. I'll point you in the direction of some online shops.'

'Lovely. Now, shouldn't you be getting a wriggle on?'

'I wanted to talk to you about what happens to this house once a place becomes available in a care home.'

Suzanne shook her head. 'Don't worry about that, lovely. The council will sort it. Did you want to move back in?'

I'd rather eat my eyeballs.

'No. I'm happy in my house.'

'Don't blame you. These are nice and that, but I'd much rather have one of those pastel harbour houses up Berry Hill. You're lucky to have one.'

Ginny had no memory of her dad, but she certainly had a lot to thank him for. Had he not left her his money seven years ago, she wouldn't have been able to buy her home or café, which came with a flat above that she rented out.

'I need to get off. I'll be back after work. Oh, and please give the cat back to Mary, will you?'

Suzanne saw her to the door and waved her off.

Ginny sat in her old army jeep and stared out the windscreen for a while before starting the engine. There were moments when she liked to pretend she was only alone in the world because her man was in the military during the Second

World War. He'd return soon, and they would live happily ever after just like in the old war films she would watch as a girl. But until then, she had to knuckle down and simply get on with things like the women in the 1940s, her heroes. All that hardship, and yet they carried on. They had always been such an inspiration.

She parked up outside her pastel-blue home and quickly nipped indoors to pick up a cardboard box.

Harbour Light Café was just along Harbour End Road, at the bottom of her street, so it didn't take long for her to walk to work.

Annie and some other staff were already serving customers, so Ginny set about opening her box to place the fake pumpkins it held along the windows.

There. At least now it looked ready for the season, even if the décor clashed a tad with the nautical theme of the place.

Flopping back in a chair, Ginny stared at the fishing net adorning the ceiling directly above her. It could do with a dusting. Perhaps after work.

Tears blurred her vision for a moment, as she allowed a few seconds of self-pity to take control. Sniffing, she straightened and pulled herself together. She wasn't alone, not really. She had the most wonderful group of friends she could call on anytime, but she needed to crack on, so there wasn't time to feel deflated or cry on anyone's shoulder.

Ginny sprinted to the toilet, coated her lips with dark-red lippy, adjusted her head scarf, blew the mirror a kiss, then headed back to the front door.

Robson jogged by, stopping to wave.

Ginny stepped onto the pavement, gulped down the salty air blowing over from the sea across the road, and gave her friend a hefty pat on the back; he looked too sweaty to hug.

Robson jolted forward and laughed. 'For someone so petite, you've sure got some whack.'

'Sorry. Lots of arm muscles used in running a café, you know.'

'If you took on my pub, you'd have arms like Popeye.'

Ginny poked his biceps. 'So where are yours then, chick?'

'Oi, cheek. I am of the athletic build.'

'Oh, is that what it's called?'

'Here I am, out enjoying the early morning, and I get insulted by my best mate.'

Ginny nudged him. 'You want a bacon sandwich?'

Robson's piercing blue eyes sparkled as he patted his toned stomach. 'Ooh, don't tempt me.'

Ginny glanced down the road. 'I don't know why you get up so early when the Jolly Pirate doesn't open till eleven.'

'I do have a whole day to fit in before that time. Anyway, I like to keep fit. You should try it.'

'I hardly sit down, thank you very much. I've got Hub duty today as well.'

'What time?'

'When I close at four.'

'You still thinking about letting Samuel use the café as a food bank after closing time?'

Ginny shrugged. 'The Happy to Help Hub has the food bank. He just wants to offer free dinners to those in need. But honestly, Rob, I've got too much on at the moment.'

'How is your mum?'

Never one to tell what her mother was really like, she simply smiled politely. 'Doing good. We should get word on a care home soon.'

'That'll be a weight off.'

Ginny nodded, then gestured towards the Jolly Pirate pub. 'I'll pop by later for dinner. Your chef makes the best fish pies.'

'I'll make sure he saves you one.'

She waved him off, then turned back to the calm sea to watch the boats bobbing gently. It would be nice to sail away and forget about life for a bit. She blew a kiss out to sea. She did it every morning so it would float off to her soulmate, whoever the poor sod was. Some of her regular customers were heading her way though, so dreams were pushed to the back burner.

Safe travels. Wherever you are.

'My wife used to do that for me,' said the old man passing her by.

Ginny grinned at her friend Sophie's grandfather. 'Morning, Jed. You off to catch some fish?'

He pointed to the Happy to Help Hub. 'No. I'm opening the Hub this morning. Sophie's got enough for the fishmonger's today, so I offered to take the early shift. Makes no difference to me, as I'm rostered on to open up for the next couple of weeks anyway.' His slate-blue eyes twinkled with mischief as he gazed her way. 'So, who you blowing kisses to, young lady?'

'Whoever needs them.'

'You know, if you ever have a fella at sea, light a candle in your window each night to help guide him home.' He scratched his wiry grey beard and walked off.

Ginny stared over at the dark water. She was definitely lighting a candle tonight. Even though her dream man had only been invented to help keep her heart from giving up the ghost altogether, it was a nice thought that she could somehow manifest him or, at the very least, throw him some positive vibes. If she felt so alone at times in the world, maybe her soulmate was out there feeling the same way.

CHAPTER 3

Will

Will had been busy all week clearing out his grandmother's cottage He was so glad Marie had agreed to help him. The cottage was sold and the money would be banked for ongoing care home fees.

'I feel terrible doing this,' he told Marie, holding up a glass vase.

Babs had gone off with just a few pictures for her wall, her favourite chair, some trinkets from her early years with her husband, and her clothes.

Marie packed books into a box, ready for the charity shop. 'This is making me realize I don't need half the stuff in my house. I'll have a good clear-out in the new year.'

'I've never had much. I was hardly home anyway.'

'You could have bought this place now you're sticking around, then you could have had all this.'

Will breathed out a small laugh as he perused his grand-mother's things. 'Not sure we have the same taste.'

'What's your place like in Wales?'

'Pretty plain. Basic needs. Small flat. That sort of thing.'

17

Marie laughed. 'Sounds homely.'

Will tossed some bubble wrap her way. 'Hey, it does the job.'

'I guess it does, but homes are more than a roof over your head. You make it your own by surrounding yourself with things that spark joy.'

'My kettle sparks joy. I do love a cuppa first thing.'

'I'm being serious.'

Will laughed. 'So am I. Anyway, what's the point of any of it when it all gets thrown away when you're gone or carted off to a home?'

Marie huffed her way up from the floor and onto the sofa. 'The point is, you get to enjoy it while you're here. Don't you ever have those moments where you glance around your home and just smile because you love the wallpaper or your fireplace or rug or something?'

'Nope. Can't say that's ever happened to me.'

'Oh, Willard, that seems so sad.'

'Please stop calling me Willard. No offence to my grandad, but I've always hated my name. Will suits me just fine, thank you.'

'Okay, Will, but my statement still stands. You need a happy home, not a basic-needs one.'

'You know I was in the navy, right? Wasn't exactly all scatter cushions and eyelet drapes.'

'I'm now visualizing your flat painted battleship grey.'

Will laughed. 'Close.'

'What kind of property are you looking for around here?'

'Not sure yet. I'll have a look around while I'm staying at the B&B. I sold my houses back home a while back, and I'm about to put my flat up for sale, but I—'

'Houses? Plural?'

Will unfolded another cardboard box. He'd lost count how many he'd already filled. 'Yeah, I bought a few properties years ago. I have a mate whose dad is a property developer, so he taught his son to invest in that area, and he passed that knowledge on to me. Something for the future.'

Marie wrinkled her nose. 'Wish I'd bought my house when I was young.'

'You still can.'

'I'm forty, and my other half had to stop work due to medical problems, so we can't afford to go down that road now.' She sighed as she gestured across the living room. 'Your gran has gone into a lovely home thanks to the money she has from this place. You don't think about those things when you're young.'

'I wouldn't have thought about buying property if it weren't for my friend.'

'You're staying in Seaview B&B, up by the Jolly Pirate, right?'

He nodded, tugging at parcel tape with his teeth.

'There's an estate agency just round the back. Check them out to see what's available . . . Ooh, and pop in to the Happy to Help Hub. It's just along Harbour End Road. They have a noticeboard up on their wall. All sorts of numbers on there. Never know, might be something about local work or homes to rent. It's a drop-in centre, so no appointment needed.'

'Thanks. I might check it out after I've taken this lot to the charity shop.'

A knock on the street door interrupted them.

'I'll go,' said Marie. 'It'll be the people from Use Again.'

Will followed her, ready to help with removals. He figured he'd get that sorted, head off to the charity shop, then grab some lunch before checking out the estate agency and Hub.

Most of the furniture went off to the second-hand centre, leaving the cottage looking as empty as he felt. He tried to imagine what it was like back when the family were happy, then hoped the new owner would have better luck.

Marie swung around the door frame. 'Right, I'm off. I can help again for a couple of hours tomorrow, but that's all the spare time I have, I'm afraid.'

'Thanks, Marie. You've gone above and beyond. The skip will be here first thing for the rest of the rubbish, and

I've only got a few trips left to the charity shop. Honestly, you don't need to come back.'

'I'd still like to. Gives me a chance to say goodbye to the old place. I've been your gran's carer for near on ten years I feel a bit attached to the cottage.'

'You're a good person, Marie.'

She flapped one hand while the other swiped away an escaped tear. 'Ah, just doing my job.'

He waved her off, thinking he wouldn't be able to do her job. But that indeed he was in need of a job himself. Money wasn't a problem — he didn't financially need to work — but he still liked to keep occupied. Plus, he wanted to mix with people, not being one for his own company.

He loaded his dark pickup truck with the charity bags and headed off. At least his grandmother was keeping him busy for now.

The volunteers at the charity shop thanked him for the items, told him not to bring any more, as their shop was full, gave him the addresses of others, then expressed their sadness about his gran's situation.

Will was taken aback. He hadn't expected anyone there to know Babs, but then his knowledge of Port Berry was limited, seeing how he'd only arrived a couple of weeks back. Surely they couldn't all know each other though.

He entered the Happy to Help Hub, simultaneously rubbing his nose as the scent of lavender irritated his nostrils. The small hub was empty of people, so he strolled to the noticeboard to browse the pinned cards.

A place called the Sunshine Centre caught his attention first. Rest, recuperation, catering for all disabilities, arts, baking, sensory room — volunteers always needed. That one was only next door in Penzance. He was definitely putting that on his to-do list.

'They'd appreciate ex-navy over there, son,' said a man's voice.

Will turned to the back room where a fella in his seventies stood in the doorway. There was no way the man knew he was once in the Royal Navy; the only two people Will knew in Port Berry were his gran and Marie.

Ah, wait, the owner of the B&B. Yep, that'll do it. She had gossip written all over her.

He chewed back his grin as he gestured at the notice-board. 'Know this place, sir?'

'Name's Jed Moore, and yes. The centre has a few ex-military as members. One lad lost his limbs when he was a soldier, and there's another over there who swears the place helped cure his PTSD. They have therapists and social workers that work closely with the centre, you see. So join in. Could help if you're lost on Civvy Street.'

Will laughed. 'Do I look lost?'

Jed shook the kettle his way. 'Everyone who steps foot in here looks lost.'

'I was just looking for some local work. Perhaps some property to buy as well.'

'Sticking around then?'

'My grandmother lives here, so I want to be close by.'

Jed nodded, placing some chocolate biscuits on the light-wood table. 'Heard about Babs. Shame when the mind goes.' He motioned towards the window. 'As long as I can remember my love for the sea, I'll be okay.'

Will followed his eyeline. 'Were you in the navy?'

'Nope. Fisherman, me. And speaking of jobs, I don't need any more help, but I might know of some other fishermen that do. You want me to ask around for you?'

Will shook his head. 'Thanks, but no. I've given up my sea legs.'

Slate-blue eyes sparkled his way. 'No such thing, son.'

'Perhaps I'll still have the odd paddle.'

'You can come sea swimming with me anytime you like. I often go out with Matt. He's my granddaughter's partner. First guest this here Hub saw, you know. We fixed him up good and proper. Your turn, I guess.'

Will had to laugh. He thought he was popping inside to check out the noticeboard, but he'd been offered choccy bickies, swimming mates, and the offer to perhaps become a fisherman. 'I'm sure there are more in need than me. I'm just looking to settle in around here.'

'I'm sure there are, but it doesn't mean you can't be helped as well. You're Babs's grandson. You're one of us, and by the end of the week, you'll be Port Berry through and through. Come on, sit. I'm making tea.'

Will did as he was asked, glancing around at the framed affirmations on the walls. 'So what is this place exactly?'

Jed turned. 'A few of us along here got together and opened it up to help folk. Saw a couple of homeless people one day down by the harbour, and it got us thinking. We're a food bank now as well.' He nodded at the back room. 'Not a lot of space here, but we deliver some food parcels as well as hand them out here. We've helped people get jobs, therapy, haircuts, all sorts.'

'Sounds like a lot of teamwork.'

Jed beamed, showing his pride. 'We're a close-knit community here.'

Will smiled. That's how he felt about the navy. A hot brew was passed his way, so he happily dunked a biscuit, seeing how they were right in front of him. He still hadn't had lunch yet, but figured one choccy bickie wouldn't quash his appetite.

Jed sat opposite. 'Hmm, so, what kind of job can we get for you? Have you done much since jumping ship?'

Laughing through his biscuit, Will nodded. 'I just did a year as a rescue worker in Wales.'

'Firefighter?'

'Snowdonia.'

Jed nodded. 'Interesting. Not much call for that sort of thing around here. Although, the Sunshine Centre have rock climbing as an activity. You could help out with that.'

'Yeah, I'm going to pop over there at some point.'

'You eaten in the café along here yet? Harbour Light Café. Bit of a landmark around these parts. Always good for lunch and breakfast.'

'You should be a salesman.'

Jed grinned as he raked one hand through his salt-and-pepper hair. 'Lived here all my life. I know all the best places.'

Will touched his own hair. 'You can definitely sort me out with a barber.'

'I'm going to give you a list, son.' Jed reached over to the sideboard and grabbed a notepad and pen. 'Everywhere you should go around here. You'll soon get your bearings.' He raised the pen to his ear. 'Artie's son-in-law, Shaun, has his own building company. Fixing up Lottie's house as we speak, only up the road. You up for a spot of labouring? I can get you in there.'

'Erm, I—'

'Tell you what we'll do. You go have your lunch, then come back here. My shift will be over, and I'll take you to meet Shaun. If he's not about, we'll fix another time to see him. There, that's another thing sorted.'

It wasn't a bad plan, if a little rushed and unexpected.

Will nodded. 'Sure, that'll be great, thanks.'

'No worries. Go on, get going. Time and tide wait for no man.'

Will managed to get in one more gulp of tea before being manhandled towards the door.

'You're in safe hands, Willard Pendleton,' said Jed, giving him a hefty shove in the direction of the café.

Will brushed some crumbs from his lapel as he turned to speak, but Jed had closed the door on him. He had to laugh.

I didn't even tell him my name.

He glanced over at the sea, inhaled the salty air, and smiled at the seagulls circling a fishing trawler. There was something about the place drawing him in already, and that was without the old fisherman in the Hub trying to organize his life.

The crisp air nipped his neck, so he turned up the collar on his navy-coloured coat and hurried towards the café.

Whoa!

The nautical theme made him smile immediately. He glanced up at the fishing nets and fake seagulls above, then at the framed pirate story to his side. Now, if only he owned such a place, he'd never bother looking for work again. It was an idea. Perhaps he could get himself something similar.

Will sat by the window, perusing the menu. Harbour Light Café was giving him all sorts of business ideas, and he started to wonder if Jed had method in his madness when he sent him there.

He glanced up at a storm lamp hanging high above him. Yep, he could do something with a nautical theme, but what? A café of his own? No, they already had this one. Some sort of gift shop for the tourists, perhaps, but he'd seen quite a few in the area. He needed to find a gap in the market. Something they didn't have that would be a good fit for a seaside village and would make money all year round, not just peak season . . .

A tearoom.

He racked his brains, pretty sure Harbour End Road didn't have one. He'd double-check after lunch, but so far so good. He used to love going in the one along by his flat in Wales, and it was always busy. All he needed was to secure some premises. What a lovely way to become part of the area. He was sure the locals would enjoy having a tea shop along the harbour. And he wouldn't be stepping on anyone's toes.

CHAPTER 4

Ginny

Ginny entered Cockle Cottage, groaning with delight at the aroma of beef stew wafting from the kitchen. It was nice to be invited out to dinner, even if it was round Sophie's house and because her friend was alone for the evening. The week before, she'd had a fish pie at the pub, joined by Robson for all of half hour. Still, it was better than eating all alone.

'Hope you're hungry,' declared Sophie, lifting a large wooden spoon.

Ginny glanced into the pot. 'Ooh, yum. Have we got to save any of this for Matt?'

Sophie giggled. 'Yep, and Grandad. I've told him to move in now, before the weather really turns, but you know what he's like. Reckons he'll be back mid-November.'

'I really have no idea how Jed sleeps on a boat, let alone live there. I think it would make me sick, all the swirling and bobbing about.'

'Yeah, well, he's used to it. But at least he'll be here for dinner later.'

'What they up to?'

'Grandad wanted to take Matt out for a bit of night fishing. I can't see Matt making it past ten.' She laughed and scooped some stew into bowls.

Ginny grabbed the cutlery and sat at the table. 'Ooh, I don't know, chick. He seems to have found his sea legs since he moved here. How is Matt getting on?'

Sophie placed the bowls on the table and sat down. 'He's doing great. He's always so happy, and there are splodges of colour in his cheeks.'

'He certainly looks heaps better than he did when he first arrived.'

'If I walked all the way from London to Cornwall, I reckon I would have looked worse.'

Ginny brought some beef to her lips and blew. 'I'm so glad Matt found us.'

Sophie smiled a smile that seemed to be just for her. 'Me too.'

'Aww, look at you all loved up.'

'Oh, hush. But I so am. It feels good to be in a relationship where it just works.'

If only Ginny knew what that felt like. She was sure she'd never find such happiness.

Sophie glanced up and, as though reading her mind, changed the subject. 'How's it going next door with all the noise?'

'I'm at work when all the crash, bang, wallop goes on, so all good for me, so far. Lottie did say the renovations should be finished in a few weeks, then it's just decorating and stuff.'

'She'll have the biggest harbour house up Berry Hill now she's joining two homes.'

'Yeah, I guess it might look odd for a while seeing a double front. Ooh, speaking of which, brainstorm with me.'

'About?'

Ginny quickly chewed a piece of potato. 'I have an idea for the café. It won't be anything I do straight away, as I want to wait till Mum is in a home, then I'll have more time to myself.'

'Sounds intriguing. Spit it out, Gin.'

'I was thinking of pinching a bit of the café to turn into a tearoom. You know how much I want one, and there's no way I can get rid of the café. The locals would make me walk the plank.'

Sophie laughed. 'True.'

'So, I was wondering, as you're a local, what would you think?'

'Erm, well, elaborate.'

Ginny put down her fork and rested her elbows on the table. 'The café has a lot of space, double front and all that, so what about if I shave a quarter off one side? Put up some sort of partition wall? The café would still be big, and it's only a small section I'd be changing, and . . .' Ginny groaned, slapping a hand to her face. 'Don't say it. I know. The pitchforks will come out, won't they?'

Sophie looked sympathetic. 'It's hard to say. Look, it's been your café for seven years now. You can do what you like with it, but it has been around since the dawn of time, so—'

'Yeah, I know, the locals would come in for a T-Rex burger, it's that old.'

Sophie smiled. 'I guess if you made the tearoom an extension of the place it might be okay. You know, keep the nautical theme, maybe call it something like Harbour Light Tearoom. I don't know, I'm just a fishmonger. Sea Shanty Shack was named by my grandparents. If it was left to me, not sure what name it would have.'

'I like Sea Shanty Shack.'

'But do you like Harbour Light?'

'The previous owners did get away with adding Café on the end, so there's hope for me yet.'

Sophie shrugged. 'It's something to mull over. Harbour Tearoom sounds nice. Not so much of a mouthful.'

'My cakes would be a mouthful. I wouldn't do those skimpy slices.' Ginny sighed as she scooped up some more food. 'I really want a tearoom, Soph, but I can't sell the café.

It's such a great business, and there's nothing else available along the front, and I don't want a shop somewhere else.'

'Then pop up to Lottie's during the day, ask Shaun to take a look at the café, and see what he says can be done. Get a quote at least. Like you said, there's no rush. You probably wouldn't want it open till spring anyway.'

'Yes, ready for tourist season. Although Christmas in the tearoom could be nice.'

'I noticed you put some pumpkins in the café's window. I need to decorate for Halloween as well.'

'Speaking of which, I'm going to ask Robson to have a Halloween party in the pub this weekend. We can tell people to dress up, give a prize for best costume, and charge for tickets to raise money for the Hub. We haven't got long, so best spread the word fast.' She pulled out her phone and sent Robson a quick text.

Sophie nodded. 'Great idea. It's been years since we had a Halloween party.'

Ginny tucked into her grub, cleaning the bowl within minutes. 'Mmm, I need to come here for dinner more often.'

'You can come every night if you like.'

If there was one area of Ginny's life where she was blessed, it was with her friends. They were such a close circle and always there for each other, no matter what. Her heart warmed from the love she always felt in Sophie's kitchen. Her own seemed to lack something. She couldn't quite put her finger on it, but there was definitely something missing.

'You know what, Soph, I will talk to Shaun about divvying up the café. It's worth an ask. I'll pull him to one side when he comes in for lunch. Ask on the quiet if he can come back at closing. The last thing I need is to wake the troublemakers before I've decided anything.'

'If you do decide to go ahead with it, do you think it'll cost a lot?'

Ginny couldn't be sure until she spoke to the builder. 'I'm going to sell the flat above the café. The tenants move out soon, and I told the estate agents I didn't want to renew. I plan to use that money to set up.'

'Ooh, you'll get a good price for that flat. I know the flats above the shops aren't that big, but the sea view is the selling point. Why don't you convert that into the tearoom?'

'I did think about it, but I want my tea shop to be wheelchair and pram accessible.'

Sophie waggled her fork. 'Hmm, good point. Lottie would get the right hump if she couldn't get her wheelchair in your new premises.'

'A lot of my customers are elderly as well. I don't want to exclude anyone. And if I convert the flat to use as part of the café so I have more room downstairs, it means the staff will be up and down stairs all day. No, best I sell the flat.'

Sophie raised her fork higher, almost catching it in her dark hair as glee flashed across her face. 'Ooh, Gin, I know something that might help. I recently read about a tearoom repair shop.'

'What the blimming heck is that?'

'It's supposed to help stop people wasting clothes. They repair them, see?'

'I don't see what that has to do with tea and cake.'

Sophie finally put her fork down. 'It's part of a help-out scheme. Anyone who can sew, for example, can sign up, come down the tea shop at certain times, and help repair clothes brought in by those who aren't very good at that sort of thing. Luna would help. She can make anything out of a piece of cloth.'

'Well, it's something to think about, I guess.'

'It could help get people onside if things start going belly up.'

'Yeah, but is it hygienic? All that material dust flying around.'

'You could choose days when the weather's nice so they can sit outside. Put a canopy up, perhaps. Look, just stick this one in your back pocket so you've got it there as your weapon if needed. Plus, it's a lovely idea. We could set something like that up at the Hub next spring. Might be something we can offer once a month. We'll bring it up at the next meeting. See what everyone says.'

Ginny yawned. 'Oh, sorry. I'm just feeling it lately.'

'Gets you like that when it gets dark early.'

It was more all the running around she was doing. Suzanne was struggling to lift Birdy, leaving Ginny to pick up the slack. The sooner a place in a care home came up the better. She knew her mum hated the idea, but what else could be done? No one was coping.

Sophie reached across the table and lightly patted Ginny's hand. 'Hey, you burning the candle at both ends?'

'Seems that way. Mum's getting worse, so I have to do more. When I leave here, I have to go put her to bed, as Suzanne has to leave early tonight. She's so good. I swear she works after her hours have ended. She's sent another email on Mum's behalf as well. Demanding more help soon.' Ginny tapped her collarbone. 'You know, I'm the one expected to be chief carer, but I can't do it, Soph. I work full-time.'

Sophie gave her hand a gentle squeeze. 'It's hard, isn't it? I wouldn't want to put my grandad in a home.' Her green eyes held nothing but sympathy. 'I'm so pleased he can still take care of himself.'

'And he's older than Mum.'

'Not by much, not that it makes a difference. These things can happen to any of us at any age. Look at Lottie. Only last year she was knocked off her bicycle by a car and put in a wheelchair for the rest of her life. You just don't know what's going to happen.'

'At least Lottie can do loads for herself. Mum's going downhill fast lately.'

'I'm sure a home will come up soon. They can't leave people like that.'

Ginny shook her head. 'They're full up, Soph. People are living longer nowadays, and there's hardly any room. We're expected to look after our elders now.'

'But we can't unless we give up work, then what?'

'We were told she might get a place further away. Even out of Cornwall.'

Sophie's eyes widened. 'They can do that?'

'Yeah, they moved Shaun's gran to a place in Hastings. Some home the council are in association with. Mum would flip if they tried to move her further than Penzance.'

'What about your brother? Can't he help?'

Fat chance!

Ginny didn't like to badmouth him, even though he deserved it. Lee had done bugger all to help their mum, and he was the one she doted on.

'Oh, he lives too far away, chick.'

And the last time she tried to involve him, he told her quite bluntly to use her own money to pay for their mum's care.

She glanced at her friend clearing the plates, wondering if anyone else thought she should use her money to pay for a private care home. The sale of the flat might buy her mum a few years somewhere nice, but then what? And could she really go against her dad's wishes? He was so adamant in the letter he wrote accompanying his will that not one penny of his money was to be spent on Birdy. The curse words that followed were embedded in her forever. Whatever happened between them, one thing was for sure, they hated each other.

Talk about rock and hard place.

'You want some afters, Gin?' asked Sophie, head in the fridge.

'Sure, whatever's good.' Something sweet was in order to help cheer her weary soul, especially as her next stop was her mum's. She already knew she would hit the pillow later and cry.

Sophie plonked some chocolate cheesecake on the table. 'Why don't I come with you to your mum's after this. I can help you put her to bed, have a tidy-up, put on a wash, whatever. I don't mind.'

31

Ginny's tears almost surfaced there and then. What a wonderful offer and so utterly and completely needed, but she had to refuse. There was no way she wanted Sophie to hear the way her mother spoke to her. No one could know. The shame was too much to bear.

Pretending the task was not a big deal, Ginny politely declined and cut herself a large slice of cheesecake and quickly shoved some into her mouth, making the most of the sweetness.

CHAPTER 5

Will

The weekend had arrived and the Jolly Pirate pub was packed for the Halloween party. The lively atmosphere and people dressed up in costumes filled Will with a sense of community as soon as he entered the beer garden out front. Everyone was on top form, singing karaoke inside, laughing and taking photographs, enjoying the food coming from the outdoor grill area.

One thing Will loved was belonging somewhere, and since leaving the navy he hadn't found connection, even when part of a mountain rescue team. It was strange to think he didn't fit anywhere.

Jed approached him before he'd even had a chance to check out the bar. 'Will, glad you came. And you dressed up. Look at you. Who are you supposed to be?'

Will looked over his attire. 'A zombie groom.' He laughed along with the old fella dressed like a rather sophisticated vampire. 'There wasn't much left in my size at the fancy dress shop, so I opted for make-up and a wedding suit.'

'This is what happens when you're all muscle.'

Will laughed, flexing his biceps. 'I'm not that big.'

Jed showed off his own firm arm. 'Not bad for seventy.'

'It's all that fish you eat,' Will joked.

'I keep telling folk that,' said Jed seriously, making Will's smile stretch.

They headed inside the pub, where the music pumped and the noise was deafening. Jed led Will to the bar, warning him to avoid the green concoction in the punch bowl. The toy eyeballs bobbing on the surface were enough to put Will off without the heads-up.

'I'll introduce you to my friends,' said Jed, gesturing to the beer garden. He handed Will a bottle of lager and nudged his arm towards a small stage at one end of the room. 'Unless you want to sing first.'

That was actually a maybe. Will liked a singalong, but normally with people he knew. He figured he'd wait to see how he felt later, as the night was young and his drink untouched. He waggled a hand side to side, then followed Jed outside to stand by a tall patio heater.

Jed waved a woman over. Her tied-back white hair almost matching her ghostly face. 'This is one of my oldest friends, Luna.'

Luna immediately took Will's hand in hers, her midnight-blue eyes scanning over his palm.

Not what Will was expecting. 'See anything interesting?' he asked playfully.

Her gaze was filled with interest as she raised her head, then she smiled and patted his knuckles. 'Welcome to Port Berry, love.'

Unsure what to make of that, Will simply nodded. He'd met some intriguing people in his time, but Luna held something about her bordering on magical. She really was quite endearing — and a tad scary.

Jed nudged his friend's shoulder. 'Got a feeling about this one, Luna.'

'Me too, Jeremiah.'

A younger lady approached. 'Stop reading palms, Nan. We're at a party.' She turned to Will. 'Hi, I'm Alice. Please excuse my grandmother. She can't help herself.'

Will smiled at the woman dressed as a clown complete with spongy red nose. 'It's okay. I'm making friends.'

Alice nodded, causing her red wig to slip forward. She pushed it back while giggling. 'I'm not sure this is the best way to make new friends. You won't recognize half of us tomorrow.'

'Ignore her,' said Luna. 'She always wears that red nose.'

Alice pinched it, making a honking sound, and everyone laughed. 'Hey, feel free to pop in to the Treasure Chest any time. That's our family's newsagent's shop. It's just along the road. Ooh, and come here for dinner one weekend with us, and we'll introduce you to our team of Hub volunteers.'

Jed pointed at the grill set up beneath a shelter made of brick pillars and a high ceiling. The large grill had a small kitchen behind it and an athletic man dressed as a skeleton, dancing with his barbeque fork aloft. 'That's Robson. Owns this place, and he's another volunteer at the Hub. Come on, let's grab a hotdog and say hello.'

The scent from the food made Will's mouth water. He was getting something more juicy than a hotdog. The steaks looked good, especially with hot sauce and a toasted bun. Yep, that was dinner sorted.

Robson was so friendly, and he told Will dinner would be on him if he decided to join them one weekend. Alice swiped some sliced cucumber from the foil platters on the counter and grinned, causing Robson to flick a piece of lettuce her way.

Will watched them mess around, then turned his attention to Jed and Luna, in a conversation with some others he didn't yet know. Everyone looked so relaxed in each other's company, and Will wanted to be part of their world already.

Robson sorted Will a steak, then pointed out a spare seat at a table quite close to the road that passed along the harbour front.

Will decided he'd pop over to the small pier across the road to sit and eat, giving his eardrums a rest for ten minutes.

He wandered down its length before plonking himself down at the end, dangling his legs over the side. The dark sea below was calm, and the sky held a thousand stars. Just how he liked it. He ate his steak burger and drank his lager, feeling content.

Wales and his old life seemed so far away. Could he really settle in this fishing village? He certainly could be at one with the pier. How tranquil his setting was.

'Hello,' said a female voice. 'Looks like you had the same idea as me.'

Will glanced up to see a petite zombie bride smiling his way.

'Do you mind if I sit?' she asked, before he had time to speak. She thumbed behind her. 'Or I can go over there if you want to be alone. It's just, seeing how we're dressed, I figured we should sit together.'

He glanced at his costume, then once more at hers. Patting the ground to his side, he said, 'Pull up a pew.'

She shuffled to his side, then bit into her hotdog. 'I'm Ginny,' she said, mouth full, cuffing her lips.

'I'm Will.'

She playfully nudged his arm. 'They do say you can find your soulmate anywhere.'

It took a moment to figure out what she meant, then it hit him. They were dressed as a zombie bride and groom. He breathed out a quiet laugh, then supped his drink.

'It's nice here, isn't it?' she said softly.

'Reminds me of a B-movie.'

Ginny laughed. 'Why do you say that?'

'It's Halloween, dark, we're alone, dressed as zombies, surrounded by water.' Will pointed at the sea. 'Round about now a great white shark should catapult out the waves and gobble us whole.'

'Well, that's cheerful.'

Will threw his head back and laughed.

'Anyway,' added Ginny. 'We're zombies. We're already dead.'

'That's debatable.'

'No, it's not. You have to be dead to be a zombie. It's like zombie law.'

'Yeah, but they're still around, attacking people. Are you really dead if you can do that?'

Ginny nodded. 'You might have a point.' Then she finished her hotdog, leaving Will wondering what kind of conversation he had got himself into.

The sea gently lapped against the pilings below, creating the only sound as the two strangers sat in silence for a while.

'You're not from around here,' said Ginny, waking Will from his trance with the biggest star in the sky.

'What gave it away, me being a zombie or the Welsh twang?'

Hazel eyes twinkled his way. 'You just don't have a Port Berry vibe.'

Will snorted a laugh. 'And what's that when it's at home?'

Ginny shrugged. 'People from around here have a look about them that says they're happy to be home.'

'What's my zombie face telling you?'

'Not sure. Are you on holiday?'

Will stared at her for a moment before turning his gaze back to the sea. 'I came here to find my family.'

And I told her that why?

He mentally shook his head and glugged some booze. What started out as a nice enough night had turned into something quite odd and unexpected, and he wasn't at all sure why he hadn't headed back to the pub yet.

'Did you find what you were looking for?' Her voice was so soft, it almost sounded sad.

Turning her way, Will tipped his head from side to side. 'Sort of. I guess.'

'Sounds unfinished.'

No way was she reading into any corners of his mind. It was finished. It had to be. He'd felt sick to his stomach since finding out how he was conceived. The subject had been locked away before it had the chance to destroy him. He deeply inhaled the night air; he was feeling a bit queasy.

'It's finished,' he told her, hoping he sounded confident, because he wasn't exactly feeling that way.

'It's okay. Life can be strange.'

It wasn't her words that floored him, rather her cool hand gently resting over his for a few seconds. Something stirred, and it wasn't helping his unsettled tummy. She was staring out to sea, and he was looking directly at her. Had they met before? Could be déjà vu. He wasn't certain. All he knew was something felt familiar.

Ginny sighed, raised her legs straight out in front of her, then dangled them back over the edge of the pier. 'I've been coming down here since I was a kid. I've always liked staring out to sea. Are you a fan of the waves?'

His Royal Navy uniform flashed through his mind as a twitch hit the corner of his mouth. 'It's okay.'

'Some people think it's creepy of a night, but I think it's peaceful. Not that I could live on a boat or anything. Can you imagine? All that motion of the ocean keeping you awake.'

Will smiled to himself.

Ginny raised her index finger at the sky. 'Love it when the stars are out though. They can guide you home.' She faced him and smiled. 'Celestial navigation, it's called. Comes in handy if your GPS packs up.'

Will quietly laughed.

Ginny lowered her head, and Will saw her smile fade. 'It would be nice if something showed you the right way to go, wouldn't it?'

Maybe it was his turn to hold her hand. *Nope! I'm not going there.* But she did need cheering up for some reason.

'Some woman read my palm earlier. You could try her.' He smiled, hoping she would join in.

Ginny glanced back at the pub. 'That would be Luna. Resident psychic. Did she tell you anything?'

'No. Just looked intrigued.'

'She does that. Leaves people wondering. Take her with a pinch of salt.'

Will bobbed his head. 'So . . .' He left his word hanging, wondering what to add.

'Do you ever feel alone?' she asked. 'Not lonely or anything, just alone?'

It had always hit the hardest when on leave and with no one to go home to. Being alone was part of who he was. The question made him wonder if he was used to his way of life or if it still niggled him. If he was honest, then he would tell her he wished so hard to have had a family. To *have* a family. Someone who wanted him more than anything.

Will's gaze dropped to her lips for a second, then moved to her cheek. He felt he could sit and talk to her all night, but words failed him.

'It's okay,' she said, barely a whisper. 'I understand.'

Do you?

He wasn't sure she would. He was only starting to get to grips with his backstory. How was he supposed to share or explain that to anyone?

'Being alone isn't so bad.' The words seem to slip out by themselves.

'I don't like it,' she said softly.

Neither do I.

'Haven't you got family?' he asked, clenching his hands so he didn't reach out for hers.

'No one that loves me.'

Maybe she would know how he felt after all. She sounded as sad as him.

'Sorry,' she added quietly. 'Ignore me. I'm not normally like this. Blame it on the night air.' She laughed but it was weak. 'Okay, let's cheer up. How about a game of I spy?'

Will laughed. 'Go on then. You start.'

'I spy with my little eye, something beginning with . . . S.'

Will glanced up, then down. 'Sea.'

Ginny chuckled. 'Wait, I can do better than that.'

'Oh no, you had your turn.' He looked around them. 'Hmm, something beginning with G.'

'You have to say the whole thing otherwise it doesn't count.'

'Seriously?'

She gave a curt nod.

Will grinned. 'Okay. I spy with my little eye, something beginning with G.'

Ginny pointed along the pier. 'The grill over at the pub.'

'Nope.'

'Great big sparkly things.'

Will burst out laughing. 'And where's that?'

She pointed at the sky. 'The stars.'

'Nice try.'

'Oh, come on, there isn't anything around here beginning with G.'

'Look closer.'

'I give up.'

He nudged her arm with his own. 'Ginny.'

Ginny smiled. 'I'm not sure I count.'

'Oh, you count.'

She raised her chin a touch. 'Yes, you're right, I do.'

They gazed at each other, sharing a warm smile, and without any thought whatsoever, Will asked, 'Do you want some company tonight?'

Ginny stared at him for a moment, then thumbed over the road. 'I live just up Berry Hill. Do you want to come back to mine right now?'

He noticed her swallow hard. This was unusual for her. It wasn't exactly everyday for him, but he wanted to be with her. 'Yeah,' he replied, feeling his body tense.

Ginny stood first, offering a hand his way, which he took. Her head tilted backwards. 'You're twice the size of me.'

Will grinned. 'Try three times.'

'Are you sure you want to come home with me?' she asked, revealing a look of concern.

'Are you sure?'

She nodded and led him off the pier.

'You can change your mind at any point,' he told her, bringing her to a halt along the harbour. 'Any point.'

'I know.' She gestured to a steep hill. 'Just up here.'

Will took in the view before he entered the blue-washed harbour house. Maybe what they were about to do was reckless, but as she gently tugged him into her home and closed the door, he no longer cared.

CHAPTER 6

Ginny

Waking up with a spring in her step on a Monday was never on Ginny's to-do list, but ever since taking home a gorgeous, muscular man Saturday night she was smiling before she'd even opened her eyes. Goodness, had she really done that? What would her friends say? She knew perfectly well what they would say, and it would come with a few wagging fingers.

Ginny sat at her kitchen table, sipping tea, wondering if she felt liberated or just plain old stupid. Was thirty-four too young to have a midlife crisis? What possessed her? She hadn't had that much to drink. She really needed to stop going over it. All day Sunday had been bad enough. There was no point carrying it over into a new week.

A slow smile crept over her face as the memory of the stranger loving her for a couple of hours warmed her. How had she felt so safe with him? And why did it feel like she'd kissed him before? Everything about her encounter with him was odd, even the moment they'd stood side by side at the sink to wash their faces so they could see each other without the zombie make-up before heading to bed.

She glanced out the window to check the weather. A coat was needed. The memory of him wasn't about to keep her warm during a cold day.

Was it possible he was drinking his morning cuppa thinking about her? Probably not. She was sure that was the last she'd seen of him.

It didn't matter. Ginny wasn't about to cry over a one-night stand, especially as she'd helped orchestrate the thing. She had to laugh at her madness. At least she hadn't done the walk of shame, and neither had he, seeing how she'd waved him off while still dark out, neither of them swapping numbers or agreeing to see each other again, both seeming happy to have just had their shared moment.

Ginny whistled a merry tune as she sorted her bag. There was no way her mum was going to get her down. None of Birdy's negativity worked yesterday. Maybe it was banished forever. Perhaps now Ginny Dean was invincible.

Her grin stayed with her on the drive along the country lanes leading to her mother's house. The sun was rising, the birds waking, and all was bright and cheery in the world, or at least in her own little one.

It was quiet along her mum's street, and part of her wanted to turn around and drive off. If there was one person who had the ability to drain her of all energy in two seconds flat, it was her mother. Did she want to risk being taken down? Could her mum destroy her good mood today?

Lucky was mooching around by the wheelie bin. Skinny little thing looked hungry and tired.

'Oh, you're back again. Did Mary give you back?' Ginny sighed, getting out the jeep. 'Come on. Let's get you fed.' Scooping up the scruffy kitten, she whipped out her key and unlocked the door.

Suzanne wasn't about, so she quietly made her way into the kitchen to put the kettle on and see what was available for Lucky.

'You'll have to make do with some cooked chicken for now.' Ginny shook her head in disbelief at the lack of cat food as she got on with shredding chicken into a bowl. If her mum had made arrangements with Mary to keep the cat, she could have at least bought some food.

It was decided. Little Lucky would have to be returned again. That was a conversation she dreaded.

A thumping sound came from the ceiling, and Ginny visualized her mum's walking stick slamming into the beige carpet of the bedroom directly above her.

She fed Lucky, then quickly made the tea and headed upstairs. 'Coming, Mum,' she called, wanting her mum to know it was her and not some burglar helping themselves to the antique brass lamp.

'Where's Suzanne?' asked Birdy.

'Running late, I guess.' Ginny placed a mug of tea on the oak bedside cabinet. 'Drink that, then I'll help you into the bathroom.'

'Too late. I needed the loo ages ago and couldn't hold myself any longer.'

'Oh, Mum. Don't worry, I'll get you cleaned up.'

Birdy scoffed. 'Like you care.'

'Of course I care.' Ginny went to grab the top end of the quilt, but her mum slapped her hand away. 'Don't touch me.'

'You can't stay like that.'

'I'll wait for Suzanne.'

Ginny knew to pick her battles, so she nodded and slipped out the room to call her mum's carer to see how long she would be.

'I can't reach my tea, Gin,' called Birdy.

There was no answer on the phone, so Ginny went back into the bedroom to help her mum.

'I'm going to send another email today about getting you into a home. You need round-the-clock care now, Mum.'

'Why do you always want to send me away, Ginny? What have I ever done to you?'

How long have you got?

'It's not about me, Mum. You need professional help.'

44

Birdy tried to toss her mug at Ginny, but her hand was too weak, causing the mug to tumble straight onto Ginny's wrist.

'Ow!' Ginny jolted backwards, then rushed to the bathroom to run her skin under the cold tap.

She will not ruin my day. She will not ruin my day.

Ginny repeated the mantra until her wrist felt a bit better, then she headed back to her mum to pick up the mug and mop up what hadn't landed on her.

'You always were clumsy,' said Birdy, huffing. 'Where's Lee?'

It wasn't unusual for Ginny to hear her mum talk about Lee, but lately she was asking for him every day, and it was starting to become concerning. She would have to ring him later. See if he could pop down for a weekend or something. She wasn't holding out much hope, knowing what a selfish git he was, but still, if she explained how poorly their mother was, maybe he might have a change of heart.

Ginny attempted to help her mum out of bed again.

'Are you deaf as well as stupid?' Birdy yelled at the top of her lungs. 'Leave me alone.'

The scream vibrated through Ginny's body, removing anything warm and fuzzy immediately. She needed a timeout so went back downstairs to see how the cat was getting on.

'Ugly cow, you are, Ginny. You hear me?' Birdy bellowed.

There wasn't one name known to man that Ginny hadn't been called by her mother at some point in her life.

Ginny sat by the kitchen window, staring lifelessly out at the overgrown back garden. She knew how to shut down, avoid emotion, and pretend she was somewhere else far, far away.

Holding her own hand, she did what she often did. Pretended her soulmate was with her, holding her hand and making everything perfect. She stroked over her knuckles, but no smile followed, just more insults echoing in the hallway.

Time after time, Ginny made excuses for her mother's behaviour, and she was doing it again.

It's not her fault. She's sitting in urine. Embarrassed, I know.

Ginny tried calling Suzanne again. Straight to voicemail. Oh, where was she?

'Right, that's it!'

Lucky meowed, then padded off to the living room as Ginny marched up the stairs. One way or another, her mum was getting cleaned.

'Mum, I'm going to run a small bath for you.' Before a response came, Ginny got on with the task.

There was silence in the bedroom, and Ginny hoped her mother wasn't plotting something.

With the bath ready Ginny returned to her mum's side, bracing herself for whatever was to come.

Birdy moaned and groaned, trying to get her legs out of bed, and Ginny was starting to admire just how strong Suzanne must be to lift such a deadweight whenever alone.

The journey to the bathroom seemed to take forever, and Ginny was quite certain they wouldn't make it at one point.

'Almost there, Mum.'

The hardest part was getting her mother into the bath, as Birdy struggled to raise a leg.

Ginny flopped to the floor by the tub, drawing gulps of steam. Her mum was twice her size, but somehow she found the strength to get her into the warm water.

'Ooh, this is nice, thanks, love.'

Unclenching her jaw, Ginny stood. 'Just sit there while I change the sheets.'

Birdy grinned. 'It's not like I can move.'

Ginny took a calming breath as she entered the bedroom. She'd never felt so unfit. 'I need to start jogging with Robson.'

The sweetest song wafted out the bathroom. At least her mum was in a better mood. Ginny got on with the bed while mentally planning a spa day with friends. Perhaps a facial would lift the weary look her face always seemed to have. Shame it couldn't raise her spirits.

The stranger with the rather nice hands popped into her head. He definitely raised her spirits.

The front door slammed, making Ginny jump.

'Only me,' called out Suzanne. 'Sorry I'm late. Car trouble. Phone trouble. All sorts of trouble this morning.'

Ginny leaned over the banisters as Suzanne headed for the kitchen. 'Mum's in the bath. I'm just changing sheets.'

Suzanne said something about the skip next door being taken away, but Ginny couldn't hear her properly.

Birdy started singing something about sunshine just as light rain began to splatter against the bedroom window.

Ginny looked down at the garden, wondering what her one-night stand was up to. Was he looking at the rain thinking about her? She shook her head slightly, steaming the pane with her small laugh, then mouthed his name. 'Will.'

Will who?

She shrugged, gathered the sheets, checked on her mum, still happily singing, then headed off to the washing machine.

'You'll be late for work, Gin,' said Suzanne, putting milk in the fridge. 'Speaking of which, these extra hours you pay me for. Any chance I could get a raise? Only, things are a bit tight at the moment.'

What could Ginny say? She needed Suzanne until a care home became available. The private arrangement she had with the woman had worked out quite nicely, but could she afford to pay out more? Lee wasn't chipping in, and every penny of the benefits she got to help her mum was going straight to Suzanne, and there was no one else to help. The support plan she had in place sucked big time. Something had to change and soon.

'Sure,' she replied. 'We'll sort something. Oh, and we need to return the cat again.'

Suzanne pulled out some cat food from her shopping bag. 'Birdy's determined to keep her, and I bought the food today.'

Ginny sighed.

Suzanne smiled, then went upstairs.

After saying goodbye, Ginny stepped outside, pleased to see the sky had cleared a touch. She was about to walk to her jeep when she noticed a hooded man tampering with her neighbour's street door.

Babs had been taken into a care home, Ginny knew. Goodness, someone was trying to break in. Without thinking, she leapt over the bush dividing the houses.

'Oi!' she yelled.

The large man spun around.

Ginny went to approach but stumbled on a rock along the pathway, causing her leg to dip, and in one quick move, she hit the ground. Her spine bruised on impact.

The man rushed to her aid. 'Are you okay?'

She met kind dark eyes gazing her way as she gathered her bearings.

The man looked closer at her face. 'Zombie bride, is that you?'

It took a moment . . . Ginny was still slightly stunned from her fall. 'Will?'

His features softened as his smile grew. 'We meet again.'

Ginny was mortified. 'Are you a burglar?'

'What? No. This is my grandmother's place. Well, it was. I'm just locking up for the last time.'

Something else dawned on her. 'Have you been in there long?'

The fact he hesitated gave her the answer. The walls in her mother's house were paper thin. There was every chance he'd heard her mum shouting.

'Not long,' he replied. 'Just one last check round before handing the keys over to the estate agents.'

Ginny glanced at his chest, trying hard not to smile at her memory of it bare. They locked eyes for a moment, and she was sure he might kiss her. She hoped. But something else took priority. 'My back hurts,' she mumbled, unable to remain on the cold, hard pathway any longer, even though she liked looking up at him.

'Oh yes, let's get you up.' Will held out a hand, carefully peeling her from the ground. 'Are you okay?'

She tilted her body from side to side, groaning.

'How bad is it? Should I take you to get checked out?'

Ginny raised her palm. 'Stop fussing. It's just a bruised back, that's all.'

Will met her eyes. 'Where on your back does it hurt?'

After practically carrying her mother to the bath, then falling to the ground, Ginny had only one answer. 'Everywhere.'

'Let me take you home. You can put your feet up for the day.'

Ginny burst out laughing, then regretted it immediately, as the jolt hit her back. 'Fat chance. I'm already late for work.'

'Rest today.'

'I can't. I'm the owner.'

'Owner of what?'

'Harbour Light Café.'

Will smiled, and she so wanted to kiss him. 'I've eaten in there. Didn't see you.'

'I was probably in the kitchen.'

'You sure you can't take the day off?'

'Positive. I can't call anyone else in to help. It's short notice.'

Will's smile widened. 'Then it's settled. I'll drop these keys off, then head to the café and be your hands for the day. You can sit in the corner and give me orders.'

Ginny warmed from the inside out, hoping her cheeks didn't flush. 'You want to help me?'

Will shrugged. 'Least I can do. It's my fault you fell.'

'It's not, and you don't have to help me. I'm okay.'

'I want to.' His tone lowered, causing Ginny's butterflies to stir.

'Looks like we've got ourselves a date then.' Her neck heated as she realized what she had said.

Will pulled in his lips, then met her eyes. 'By the way, thanks for the other night.'

Thanks for the other night?

Not knowing how to respond, Ginny headed for her vehicle. 'I'll meet you at the café.'

'See you in a bit,' he called.

She climbed into her jeep, feeling like a spoonful of cough syrup. 'Guess I was just what the doctor ordered,' she mumbled to the steering wheel. Not that she could complain. After all, she did invite him home because it was exactly what she needed as well. So why was she feeling as though she'd just been dumped? 'Oh, get a grip, you silly mare.' She took a deep breath, started the engine, and set off, wondering if Will really would show up to work in her café.

CHAPTER 7

Will

As soon as Will entered Ginny's café, he marched directly over to where she sat, visibly uncomfortable, on a hard wooden chair by the back wall. 'Here, I bought you these to read.' He handed over two magazines. One was filled with crosswords and short stories, and the other was homestyle and gardens; he wasn't sure what she would enjoy. 'Give me two secs.' He dashed off to the door he figured led out back to the kitchen.

'Erm, who are you?' asked a woman in her fifties, adjusting her black apron strings and now looking at him aghast.

He went to hold out a hand but realized he was still holding the soft rectangular cushion he needed to sort. 'Sorry, I'm Will. I'm helping Ginny today. Did she mention me? Erm, can I just pop this in the microwave to heat up? It's like a hot water bottle, just safer.' He glanced around.

'Oh yeah, she did mention something. Hurt her back this morning. Over here.' She pointed to the large silver microwave. 'Let me.'

Will handed her the cushion and waited for it to warm. 'I'm Annie. You're new around here, aren't you?'

51

He must be sticking out like a sore thumb. The fishing village was small, but not that small. Surely not everyone he laid eyes on would know he was the new kid.

'How long have you worked here?' He figured small talk might stop the woman from sizing him up.

'I was here before Ginny took over. Been working here since I left school. Does me all right.'

The microwave pinged, so retrieving the now warm cushion from Annie, Will quickly headed back to Ginny.

'Ooh, that's nice,' she said, wriggling the heated cushion behind her back.

Will grinned, mightily chuffed with himself for helping her. 'Thought it might do the trick.' He waited for her to meet his eyes, then smiled. 'Tell me what else I can do?'

Ginny gestured at the wooden counter. 'Best just do whatever Annie says. She could run this place with her eyes closed and one hand tied behind her back.'

'I was going to do your job.'

'Yeah, well, you'll need more experience for that and a few certificates. Don't worry, she'll probably have you clearing tables and making sure the floor is obstacle free. Oh, and check the loo every so often. You need to make sure there's toilet roll, hand soap, and no blockages or mess. Oh, and that no one has stolen the air freshener off the windowsill, because, yeah, that happens sometimes.'

Will was taking mental notes — along with noting that Annie, working the coffee machine, had one beady eye on him.

Giving Ginny a reassuring smile, Will headed over to Annie to report for duty. He was handed an apron, cloth, and spray bottle.

Will swiped a pen from a glass jar by the till which he handed to Ginny with a warm smile. He liked smiling at Ginny, and he especially liked the shy smiles she was giving him in return. He got on with tidying tables, never having put too much thought into plate-stacking techniques before, but at least it helped keep his mind off the one-night stand he'd had with her, not that he wanted to forget how good it was. Normally, he wouldn't allow such an attachment, for fear of heartache, but for some reason he hadn't been able to put Ginny out of his mind.

'Will, right?' said a man, in hefty yellow boots. 'Jed pointed you out to me. I'm Shaun. Foreman at S&C Builders. Sorry I wasn't around the other week. Jed said you were looking for some work.'

Will lowered his spray bottle as Shaun closed the door behind him, keeping out the wind that had picked up. 'Oh yeah. I was planning on popping over to see you sometime today.' He raised his grey cloth. 'Didn't know I'd be helping out here.'

Shaun smiled. 'This is Port Berry. There's always someone helping out.' He sank into a nearby chair and picked up the menu. 'Jed filled me in. I can have you onsite helping out a couple of days a week, but that's all I've got for someone inexperienced.'

'That'll do me just fine, cheers, mate. I plan to settle in around here, so doing some odd jobs while I find my feet is all I need. I like to keep busy.'

Shaun laughed as he eyed the fake seagull hanging above him. 'You might get paid more here.'

'Nah, this is free.' Will noticed Ginny studying him, so he left Shaun browsing the menu and got back to work.

The café was busier than he'd anticipated, but at least it kept his mind occupied, because each time it wandered off, it went straight to the petite woman in the corner who looked like she'd just time-travelled from the 1940s.

Will had felt bad all morning, and not just because Ginny had hurt her back. When he was doing a final check around his grandmother's cottage, he'd heard all the shouting and cursing from next door, and since finding out it was the Ginny he knew being abused, part of him was crushed on her behalf, but he couldn't say anything. It was best he pretended he didn't hear a thing. Something told him she would prefer that.

Maybe Sweet Cherry Lane wasn't as sweet as it sounded. Will made a mental note not to live there. His family hadn't had the best time there, and by the sound of what happened next door, Ginny hadn't either. Nope, there was no way he was living on a cursed street. Civvy Street was hard enough to navigate.

Will stepped outside to clear away a table and chase after a chair blown into the road. As he straightened, he took a moment to look out over at the choppy waves. Life sure was easier in the navy.

Ginny opened the door. 'We should get these tables and chairs inside.'

He instantly warmed in her presence. 'You should be sitting down.'

She rubbed her lower back as she stretched. 'I needed to move. I was seizing up.'

'Well, you're not carrying anything.'

'They're only foldaway.'

He wished he could kiss away that purse in her lips, and almost dared himself to at least peck her cheek, but instead, he pointed at the door. 'Go rest your back. I've got this.'

After a salute, she went back inside, and Will folded some chairs while planning the rest of his day, thinking it best to clear his head of making moves on Ginny. It was hard enough not smiling each time their eyes met.

Before he knew it, he was sweeping the floor for the final time, a touch sad his working day had come to an end. The only thing stopping him from hanging out with Ginny longer was the fact he wanted to see Shaun, then he'd planned to go over to the Sunshine Centre to volunteer.

He motioned towards Berry Hill as Ginny locked up the café. 'Do you want me to carry you home?' He could easily swoop her up into his arms and hold her close.

She laughed, shaking her head while putting her keys away in her bag. 'Rather not have everyone gossip about me, thanks.'

'I'll tell them you're injured.'

Ginny headed off. 'I'm fine.'

Will watched her for a moment, then jogged to catch up with her. 'At least you can put your feet up for the rest of the day now you're done.'

She glanced his way for a second, and it looked as though she was about to say something, but then she turned away.

'In case you think I'm following you, I'm not. I'm off to speak with the foreman working in the house next to yours. Said he's got a few shifts for me.'

'Oh, I should pay you for today. I completely forgot.'

Will laughed. 'It's my fault you nearly broke your back. I think that's worth at least two weeks of free labour.'

'Two weeks! There's no need for that. You go find yourself a proper job.'

'Don't worry about me. I've got my plans.'

Ginny glanced his way and smiled. 'Sounds intriguing.'

Will tapped the side of his nose. He saw her to her door, held himself back from kissing her cheek, then dipped below the scaffolding next door to see Shaun.

The chat didn't take long, and as much as Will wanted to admire the view of the sea opposite the harbour houses, he needed to shoot off. He jogged all the way to his pickup truck parked outside Seaview B&B, battling the wind and spits of seawater blowing his way, all the while grinning from ear to ear, still warmed from his day spent with Ginny.

Even when driving over to Penzance, Will couldn't stop thinking about her. He was so glad her back had eased by the end of his shift.

The Sunshine Centre was way more than Will thought it would be. He was thoroughly impressed by its kerb appeal alone as soon as he pulled up in the car park.

An array of raised flowerbeds and large metal ornaments in the shape of ladybirds, hedgehogs, and hummingbirds filled the front garden, and the large whitewashed building had big colourful flowers painted on the walls. It was so cheery, Will's smile widened.

He entered through a wide lilac door and headed to the reception area, where he was immediately greeted by a middle-aged woman with bright eyes and a wide warm smile.

'Hiya, I'm Debra. You must be Will. Jed told me to expect you.'

Will was starting to wonder if the old fisherman had the same magical powers as Luna. It was funny, but he held back his laughter and opted for politeness instead.

'Will Pendleton. Pleased to meet you. I've got to say, this place looks way artier than I thought. I did hear you do arts and crafts here, but I wasn't expecting the building to actually have artwork on it.'

Debra chuckled. 'We want to spark joy for our guests as soon as they arrive. Let them know this is a safe space where they'll find peace and happiness.'

'I hear you work with ex-military as well.'

Debra nodded. 'Yes, everyone's welcome here. Jed said you were in the navy. Which areas were you thinking of volunteering for here, Will?'

'Tell me everything you have on offer. Jed mentioned rock climbing. I worked in mountain rescue for a year before I came here, so you can use me for those kind of activities. All activities actually. I love a bit of adventure.'

Debra laughed. 'And what about as a member? Would you like to come here sometimes for your own health?'

Will raised his eyebrows. 'My health?'

'Just letting you know people find their peace here, so if you do need respite anytime, feel free to bake a cake, paint a picture, or plant some seeds in the allotment. Whatever you need. We also have therapists here and social workers.'

'Oh, thanks. But I'm okay.' It was a complete and utter lie, but as she had blindsided him with her statement, he didn't know what else to say.

Debra walked around the reception desk to stand at his side. 'Come on, I'll show you around. We can walk and talk.'

As long as she doesn't try and delve into my feelings . . .

* * *

Will had a real spring in his step by the time he headed back to his truck. His estate agent in Wales had sent him a text, scheduling a date to take photos of the flat, so a short trip back there tomorrow would sort that. Life seemed to be coming together. He felt he might just be able to fit in at Port Berry and make friends — so very important for someone with no family.

All he had to do was forget how he was conceived, the fact his mother didn't want him, and that he couldn't run away with the navy again.

Piece of cake.

CHAPTER 8

Ginny

'You stand with your hands against that wall, young lady, and if you dare move, you'll feel the flat end of my slipper.'

Ginny quivered at her mother's sharp tone. Her palms were pressed against the flock wallpaper, her head dipped, and eyes filled to the brim with water.

It wasn't her fault the kettle was broken. Lee dropped it, not her, but when asked, he blamed her and that was that. He could've said aliens landed on the roof and stole the aerial and their mum would've believed him, because her precious son never lied.

Ginny gulped down some silent deep breaths, steadying her nerves. The slipper was coming at some point. Once mentioned, it was used. The punishment of standing against the wall was simply torture added into the mix. Mind games were nothing new in the Dean household.

A small dinghy gently bobbing on the calm sea looked so tranquil as the sun woke the sky. The name **Blue Man** *was scribbled on the side in dark blue, and a tall mast held a white flag with a silhouette of an anchor.*

Ginny visualized her getaway vessel in bright, bold colours. Someday she'd sail away to a place where no one could hurt her again.

She wished she could hold her own hand. It always comforted her.
Raising her gaze to the wall, she wondered why she bothered with endurance.
She was going to take six of the best to the backside no matter how long she
stood for. But survival mode kicked in, as always, telling her not to move.

She closed her eyes, seeing only the boat once more, but it was sailing
away. Leaving port without her.

'No, come back, Blue Man,*' she yelled, too afraid to move her hands.*
'Don't leave me here. Please, please. Come back, come back. Save me.'

* * *

Ginny jumped, inhaled deeply, and sat up to stare down at
the pool lounger she was sprawled on. She must have drifted
off. The deep tissue massage she'd not long received at the spa
certainly hit the spot if it had made her that relaxed.

'You okay, Gin?' asked Sophie, sitting cross-legged on the
sunbed next to her. 'You woke with a start.'

Ginny shook her head and faked a laugh. 'Think I had
a mad dream.'

Sophie rubbed a white towel over her damp legs. 'What
was it about?'

'Can't remember,' she lied, glancing up at the glass roof.

There were two recurring nightmares Ginny had, and
neither of them were up for discussion.

'I bet you watched something scary last night. That'll do
it.' Sophie glanced over the other side of Ginny to where Lottie
was resting, reading a paperback. 'You should give her some of
your romance reads, Lott. Might help her sleep better.'

Lottie lowered her book and smiled. 'You not sleeping,
Gin?'

Ginny rolled her eyes at Sophie. 'Ignore her, chick. I'm
fine.' She indicated at Alice doing lengths in the pool. 'I might
take a dip in a minute,' she added, wanting a subject change.

'Ooh, sounds heavenly,' said Lottie.

Sophie leaned over. 'We can all hold you up, Lott, if you
like.'

Ginny nodded, glancing at her friend's electric wheel-chair to her side. She often wished she was as positive as Lottie Jordan. There wasn't a person in the world she knew with more spirit and drive. Ginny was sure had she been run over and lost the use of her legs, she would've fallen apart at the seams. 'With your upper-body strength, you could probably outswim us all without any help.'

Lottie beamed and flexed her biceps. 'You know it's true.'

They shared a laugh, and the last dregs of Ginny's nightmare dispersed.

'How's the house getting on, Lott?' asked Sophie. 'Almost there?'

Lottie nodded. 'Almost. The two houses are now one, and everything's a lot tidier, thank goodness. I really hated all that mess.' She looked at Ginny. 'What about you? Any news in your life?'

Ginny's tummy flipped as thoughts of Will flashed through her mind. Did Lottie know about him or suspect something was going on? 'Why did you ask that?'

Both women raised their eyebrows.

'What you hiding?' asked Sophie, grinning.

'Nothing.'

'You acted defensive,' said Lottie.

'Did not.'

Sophie laughed. 'Did too.'

'I was only asking to see if you had more news on your tearoom idea,' said Lottie. 'But Sophie's right. You're hiding something. Spill the beans.'

Ginny tutted, folding her arms. Should she mention the man with the muscles who helped out in her café on Monday? Was there any point? She'd not seen hide nor hair of him since, and it was Saturday now, not that she expected to see him again, after all, she had told him she didn't need any more of his help in the café.

'It's a man,' said Sophie, nodding over at Lottie. 'Has to be.'

Ginny frowned, annoyed her friend was inside her head. 'Why does it have to be?'

'Because you clammed up,' said Lottie, giggling while tying her strawberry-blonde hair into a messy bun.

The cat was well and truly out the bag and without one word being spoken. Ooh, how Ginny wished she could hide her crushes from her mates.

'Oh, come on, Gin,' said Sophie. 'Who is he?'

'I'm not sure there is anyone, exactly,' she replied. 'I mean, I did meet a man, but, well, I'm not sure yet.'

'You take your time, Ginny. Don't rush into anything,' said Lottie.

Sophie scoffed. 'That's rich coming from you. You've only been with Samuel since the summer, and he's moved in with you already.'

Lottie raised her arm. 'He was helping me when I broke my arm, thank you very much.'

'But he didn't go home once it was better.' Sophie waggled a finger her way.

Lottie bit her bottom lip and grinned. 'We love each other. We don't like being apart.'

Ginny's heart warmed for her friend.

'What's your new fella like, Gin?' asked Sophie.

'He's not my fella! I've only just met him.'

Sophie raised her palms. 'Well, you can still describe him.'

Ginny tried to control her smile. 'He's taller than me.'

Lottie laughed, then slapped a hand to her mouth. 'Sorry.'

Ginny shook her head. 'Yeah, I know, everyone's taller than me. Anyway, he's new here, looking to settle so he can be close to his grandmother, who, by the way, is Babs from next door to Mum's, would you believe?'

'I didn't even know she had kids, let alone grandkids,' said Sophie.

'I think her daughter died young. I don't have any memory of her being around, and Babs didn't talk about family.' Ginny thought back. 'Mum might have mentioned it once.'

Lottie sighed. 'Aww, at least she's got someone to visit her in the care home. Any word on a home for your mum yet, Gin? It's taking ages, isn't it?'

It felt longer than ages. It felt like forever, and Ginny was slowly losing hope a place would ever become available. She had visualizations of carrying her mum to the bathroom while needing carrying herself.

'I sent more emails again. I was told there was a vacancy at one care home but it was private, and I can't afford that. Mum didn't buy her house, so it can't pay for private care.' Ginny didn't want to add that what she pays Suzanne had eaten away into her savings.

Sophie looked at Ginny. 'It would be easier if you had a partner to help you.'

'I kind of like being on my own sometimes,' said Ginny, holding her own hand.

Sophie leaned back on her lounger and sighed. 'Yeah, but it's also nice when you've someone to cuddle when needed.'

'Someone you can trust,' said Lottie. 'Who loves and respects you so much.'

Ginny wondered what Will was up to while she was enjoying her spa day with friends. They hadn't made any plans to hang out, and they certainly hadn't spoken about their steamy Halloween night.

Will, the new kid, was starting to take over her days. Perhaps it was time she accidently on purpose strolled by Seaview B&B to see if she could spot him standing on one the balconies. Her nose wrinkled at the thought. Maybe it was best to see if he popped into the café again.

Sophie stretched. 'Ooh, I'm so looking forward to dinner tonight at the pub.'

'Me too,' said Lottie. 'I told Sam to meet me down there.'

Just in case she bumped into Will at the pub, Ginny decided she'd have a facial and get her hair sorted after a quick swim. She so hoped she'd bump into him again at some point.

'Ooh,' said Sophie, 'we need to talk Christmas already.'

Lottie scoffed. 'Really? It's November.'

'The food bank is going to get extra busy this time of year, Lott.' Sophie nodded at Ginny. 'Samuel told me to expect more donations closer to the time. It's when people are at their most generous.'

Ginny raised a finger. 'Ooh, we should do something so we can raise money to buy a few chickens to add to the food parcels. Store them in your shop, Soph. Maybe we can make them look like Christmas hampers. That'll be cheerful. Can we use some ribbons and cellophane from Berry Blooms, Lott?'

'Sure. I'll put some red and green ones to one side. Ooh, maybe silver. I can make some bows.'

'Are you busy making Christmas wreaths in your shop already?' asked Sophie.

Lottie shook her head. 'No. I've just been making some poppy wreaths for Remembrance Sunday. Councillor Seabridge is holding a short service down by the memorial column, then Father Stephen will be continuing the service at church. We've still got some poppies for sale in the flower shop. Make sure you buy some.'

Ginny nodded. 'I bought a knitted one from Luna, but I'll pop in and buy a pin from you too, chick.'

Lottie thanked her, then went back to reading her book. Sophie had her eyes closed, so Ginny made her way over to the slanted wide steps of the pool.

The tepid water made her smile, taking her back to the days she'd slip off after school to the small beach by the harbour and paddle away her troubles. Life was a lot easier now, she reminded herself, even if she felt sandwiched between her job and mother. At least she had choices now.

Floating on her back, Ginny closed her eyes and smiled. It was a cold November day outside the spa, but in the pool, it was as though springtime had come early, easing her bruised back and soothing her weary soul.

CHAPTER 9

Will

Will had just got back from Wales. He thought he'd be back before Saturday, but things had dragged with the estate agents. At least his flat was now on the market. All he had to do was clear out the last few bits and pieces before any handover, then he could kiss goodbye to the area he grew up in and start afresh in Port Berry.

He was pleased to be back. Pleased he would get to see Ginny again soon. He'd grown accustomed to her face already, and each time she entered his mind, he smiled.

The elderly lady who owned Seaview B&B was watering some leafy plants by the arched main door. She lowered her watering can, then attempted to swipe an orange feather duster over the stained-glass window at the top of the door. As she was short, her cleaning aid barely made it to the hull of the boat in the glass.

Will crossed the small foyer to help.

'Cheers, lovey. I was going to get the stepladder.'

'No need. Anything else I can help you with, Mabel?'

She pointed a bony finger to the top right of the window. 'Missed a bit.'

Will grinned as he covered the pane with the duster. 'Better?'

'Brilliant. Go grab yourself a bickie.'

'I'm good, thanks.'

Mabel's splodges of pink blusher gave the impression she was rather hot and flustered, not that she ever gave off that vibe.

'Do you want me to make you a cuppa?' he asked.

Mabel nudged his arm. 'Get away with you, young Will. You're a guest.'

Will followed her over to the light-wood reception counter, where a large guestbook sat open. 'I don't mind.'

'You're a good egg. I can tell. So, did you get everything sorted in Wales?'

'Pretty much. Erm, not sure how much longer I'll be here, Mabel. I need to start looking for somewhere permanent. Speaking of which, I've been meaning to ask you something. You wouldn't happen to know if any of the shops along here would be available soon? I did speak to an estate agent, but he wasn't aware of anything. Thought you might know if anyone's mentioned moving on soon.'

'Goodness, Will. Must be some fairy dust floating around your head, son.'

He had no idea what that meant but judging by the sparkle in her pale-blue eyes, it was good.

Mabel squealed quietly as she clasped her wrinkly hands. 'Come with me.'

'Where we going?' he asked, following her outside.

An icy breeze whipped up the salt from the sea as a seagull cried overhead before swooping down to swipe something from the top of a litter bin.

Mabel waved over at the perfume shop two doors down. 'Not been here long. Never did too well. Takings are low, low, low. Sheila wants shot. Told me so yesterday. Who wants a perfume shop along here? No one, that's for sure.' She placed a palm out, stopping him from entering. 'What you got in mind?'

'Tearoom. Noticed there wasn't one along the front. Thought it might make a good business for me.'

'Ooh, I'd say, lovey.' She winked, then tugged him towards the door. 'Leave it with me.'

Will tried not to laugh as he entered the premises. He sneezed straight away as a sickly-sweet overpowering scent invaded his nostrils. 'Oh, excuse me,' he said, wiping his nose with a tissue he pulled from the pocket of his dark cardigan.

'Hello, what can I do for you two?' asked the woman behind the glass counter.

'You want to take early retirement, don't you, Sheila?' Mabel said, seemingly doing a double take of the woman's long floaty blouse sleeves.

Sheila looked about as confused as Will felt. 'Erm, yeah, so?'

'Got a buyer for you.' Mabel tipped her head at Will. 'My friend here is looking to open his own shop along here.'

As Sheila lacked interest, Will threw in his two-word pitch. 'Cash buyer.' That perked her up.

Mabel grinned. 'Can't beat that, eh, Sheila? Well, don't keep the man waiting. You in or what?'

It wasn't exactly what Will had in mind when talking business deals, but the two women seemed to have their own way, and after observing their back and forth for ten minutes, and totally admiring Mabel's haggling skills, an agreement was in place, and Will hadn't said a word more. All he had to do was hook himself a solicitor and the shop was his.

'Told you I'd sort it,' said Mabel, slapping his back as they went outside.

'Did that just happen?' He was mostly asking himself.

Mabel smiled. 'Ooh, let's grab that cuppa now, and once you're up and running, I'll be expecting the odd slice of cake for free.'

'You sure you don't want to come into business with me?' He laughed as she beamed his way. 'I think I like having you on my side.'

'I've got enough on my plate running this place.' She pointed up at the large chalky white B&B. 'I wouldn't mind retiring myself, but what else would I do? Don't know any other life. I was born here, you know. Although I do have a little dream about moving to Jersey.'

Will followed her back into the warmth of the foyer. 'Did this belong to your parents?'

'Goes further back than them. Been in my family forever. Used to a tavern back in the day. There were four of them along here. The Jolly Pirate kept its name and is the only one still a pub. Then there was the Black Ship — that's a chippy restaurant nowadays. The Old Inn is one of those mini supermarkets. And my place was the Bell of Blood. You can see why that name wasn't kept. Hardly screams cosy B&B by the sea.'

Will burst out laughing. 'It's got a nice ring to it.'

Mabel took him through to the kitchen. 'Got a name for your tea shop?'

He hadn't got that far. The fact he had some form of spit-shake securing him premises was still sinking in.

Mabel chuckled as she grabbed the kettle. 'The Sailor's Slice.'

Will laughed. 'A work in progress.'

'Now we just need to find you a nice home.'

'You're as bad as Jed. He likes to organize me as well.'

Mabel chuckled. 'Ah, it's what we're like around here, lovey. We're a small community with a big heart. You'll see, and once word gets out we're getting a tearoom along the front, you'll be well and truly loved.'

'I wouldn't mind keeping it under wraps for now. Just till I get sorted.' Will wasn't entirely sure she had the ability to keep a secret, as she hadn't stopped gossiping about the locals since he met her.

Mabel tapped the side of her nose. 'Don't you worry, son. I won't say a word. It'll be a nice surprise for everyone.'

He liked to think so. What better way to fit in than to have something that would add charm to the setting.

I'll need a really sweet name.

Will sat at the table, waiting for his tea. He scanned the practical kitchen, thinking he'd have to see about getting some sort of hygiene certificate. He noticed there were some framed documents in the café.

'I wonder what will become of this place once I'm gone,' said Mabel, jolting him out of his thoughts.

'Haven't you got any family to pass it on to?'

Mabel crinkled her nose. 'Got two grandkids. Twins. Boy and girl, well, grown adults now. But still, fat lot of good they are. He's in prison because he's an idiot, and she's a right greedy mare who would sell this place before the ink was even dry on my will. Not that I've put either of them in it.' She sighed deeply as she sat opposite him. 'Not all families are happy, Will. Mine's pretty crap.'

He knew how that felt. Although Babs seemed nice enough. 'Do you visit your grandson much?'

'Not seen him since he went away.' She paused, looking deep in thought. 'Do you think I should write to him?'

Will shrugged. Who was he to give advice on estranged families?

'He'll be thirty-one next year,' she added quietly. 'Went inside when he was twenty-three. Guess he could have grown up by now.'

'As long as you would feel safe contacting him. I wouldn't want any danger coming your way.'

Mabel smiled softly, lightly tapping his hand. 'It's okay, lovey. My Jamie was a good lad. Had a big heart, but then he got in with a bad lot, and, well, I don't know, he started getting into all sorts of trouble. He never hurt anyone, Will. Just robbed a few places. This is his second time in prison. He got a short sentence first time. The judge wasn't so lenient the next time round.'

'Let's hope he's learned his lesson this time. Like you said, maybe he's a changed man now.'

Mabel nodded. 'You know what, lovey. I'm going to take a leaf out of your book. New beginnings and all that. I'll write to him. See if we can make amends. After all, when he's released, he won't have anywhere to go but here. Perhaps I can help him one last time.'

'I can always help mentor him when he gets out. Don't worry, I won't put him through basic training or anything, but I could befriend him, take him along to the Sunshine Centre, where I'm going to be volunteering. Who knows, might spark something for him.'

'Ooh, you're a good lad, Will. That would be brilliant. See, you're one of us already.'

The thought of belonging warmed Will no end.

'Let's get that tea down us, then we can both get on with the rest of our day.'

Mabel was right, he still had so much on his to-do list, and Alice had invited him for dinner at the pub. He'd better get a wriggle on. Knocking back his cuppa, he thanked Mabel once more for her help with the shop.

* * *

Will approached the Jolly Pirate, trying hard to imagine what the area used to look like back when the Bell of Blood was in place. The pub was so busy, he couldn't see any familiar faces until Alice bounced over, all smiles and flailing arms.

'This way, Will. We have a table.'

He followed her through the crowd, bumping shoulders and making apologies along the way. It was a lot more settled in the restaurant side, but still vibrant and full.

'Meet the team,' said Alice, rolling out one hand. 'Not sure who you've met already, but we're the Happy to Help Hub volunteers.' She went on to introduce those he'd met and those he hadn't. 'Jed, Sophie, Matt, Lottie, Samuel, Spencer, and—' she pointed over at the bar — 'Robson.'

Will smiled at the group. 'Yes, I met some of you at the Halloween party.'

'There's one more of us, but she's just in the bathroom. Sit down, Will. Get involved.'

Will's shoulder was lightly patted by Matt as Alice plonked him down next to the dark-haired man.

'I hear you're Jed's new catch of the day,' said Matt, grinning.

'Matt's his old catch,' said Sophie, nudging her partner.

Will watched them share a loving smile before examining him again. 'He seems to have adopted me.'

Jed raised a glass of water. 'Newcomers always need guidance. Just doing my Port Berry duty. Ooh, speaking of which, how do you fancy joining our choir? It's not what you think.'

Spencer laughed, rubbing over his copper hair. 'Nothing's ever what it seems with Jed.'

Will grinned. 'Now I'm intrigued.'

Jed put his drink down and leaned closer. 'We're taking the buckets out in a couple of weeks to raise money for chickens for Christmas. Make someone's day seeing one of those in with their food bank parcel.'

'Unless they're vegetarian,' said Lottie, giggling.

'We'll have some vegetarian treats too,' said Samuel, her partner, smiling her way.

Will was a little lost. 'What does taking the buckets out mean?'

Jed bounced a hand up and down. 'Collection buckets. We sing, folk donate.'

That seemed simple enough. Will had one more question. 'What does your choir sing?'

'Sea shanties.' Jed looked rather proud about that fact. 'We're the Berry Buoys. Been in competitions, so we have. On the news once.' He turned to his granddaughter. 'Remember that, Soph?'

She nodded. 'Of course. We have the footage to prove it.' She smiled at Will.

'And you've got room for me?' he asked the old man, trying for casual.

'Yep,' said Jed. 'So you come to rehearsals at the church hall Tuesday and Thursday evenings, and we can get cracking. Christmas will be on us before we know it.'

'Do you even know if he can sing yet?' asked Sophie.

Jed tipped his head Will's way. 'Of course he can sing. He's a sailor.'

'You are?' asked Lottie, eyes wide.

'Retired,' replied Will.

Alice shuffled forward. 'That's why he's here. Settling down and ready for a new life.'

'Which I'll help sort for the fella,' said Jed, making Will's smile grow.

'If Jed's on your side, you've got no worries, mate,' said Spencer.

'He's one of us,' said Jed. 'Born here, see. I know his gran, Babs.'

Sophie choked on her orange juice. 'You're Babs's grandson?'

Will noticed her exchange glances with the woman in the electric wheelchair. Did they know something about his family he didn't?

Two waitresses came out of nowhere, placing down plates full to the brim with roast beef and lamb, giant Yorkies, and veg. The smell of the food was making Will's mouth water, so he ate a roast potato straight away.

Robson joined them, bringing over more food. 'Glad to sit down for five minutes,' he said, nodding a hello to Will. 'So, what did I miss?'

'Grandad signed Will up to the Berry Buoys,' said Sophie, pouring hot gravy onto the meat on her plate.

'I'm surprised he hasn't put your name down for a shift at the Hub,' said Robson, eyeing the old man.

Jed cut into his beef. 'I was about to.' He glanced up at Will. 'When's good for you, son?'

Taken aback, Will didn't know what to say. 'Erm, I'm not sure I'll know what to do there. I haven't been briefed.'

'Oh, it's simple enough. You just have to care, that's all there is to it, right, everyone?'

A few of them nodded while the others started eating.

'You can do your first shift with me,' said Matt. 'I'll show you the ropes.'

Sophie nudged his elbow, causing him to drop his fork. 'Would Monday between four and six suit, Will? I know it's short notice, being Saturday today.'

He mentally flicked through his diary. 'I've got some labouring work in the week with Shaun, but I can do Monday at the Hub.'

Matt frowned. 'I won't be on that—'

Sophie nudged him again. 'That's great, Will. You come over then.'

Will smiled her way. 'I'm already signed up to volunteer over at the Sunshine Centre in Penzance. Just seeing where I might be able to fit at the moment.'

'You fully retired then?' asked Spencer.

Will shook his head. 'No. I'm going to sort myself a business, so I'll have some money coming in, but I'll get other people to run it so I can put myself into volunteering roles. Well, that's my plan. Have to see how it goes.' He knew he was keeping his cards close to his chest, but he didn't want to talk about the tearoom until it was finalized. He could just see them being pleased for him.

It was a nice feeling being in a group again. Loneliness had taken a back seat, leaving room for friendship and hope.

He glanced over at the empty chair opposite him, thinking whoever was in the bathroom was going to end up with a cold dinner.

'Oh, there you are,' said Alice, looking up. 'I was about to send out a search party.'

Ginny pulled out the empty seat. 'All right, chick, I got chatting to—'

'Hey,' said Will, offering a small wave.

'This is Will,' said Sophie quickly. 'He's Babs's grandson.' She went back to slicing a roasted parsnip. 'Yep, her grandson. Will,' she added slowly, without looking up from her plate.

The corner of Will's mouth twitched as Ginny's face held a blush.

'Jed's reeled him in to the Berry Buoys,' said Matt.

'And he's doing his first shift at the Hub on Monday between four and six,' said Lottie, looking directly at Ginny.

'That's Ginny's shift,' said Jed. 'She'll see you right.'

Will placed a baby carrot in his mouth as he stared over at Ginny. It was amusing to see her at a loss for words. Perhaps he should lighten the load. 'Ginny and I have already met.'

Her eyes shot up, alarmed.

'I helped her out in the café the other day,' he added, and watched her shoulders relax. He went back to his dinner as the others happily chatted away about the Hub, café, and the sea shanty choir, not gazing up until a pea landed by his plate.

'Ooh, sorry,' said Ginny. 'Accidents happen.'

Will looked at the pea. Was that her way of telling him the night they shared was an accident? He couldn't be sure. He chanced a look her way to see the smallest of grins on her face, but that could be because she was talking to Robson. In fact, they looked quite comfortable together. Had he got it wrong about the chemistry he thought he had with her?

Ginny met his eyes, and her slight blush was back.

Maybe there was something. Perhaps he'd test the waters at the Hub during their joint shift. See if he could figure her out once and for all, because one thing he was sure of, he liked her, very much, which was a tad nerve-wracking, as he didn't allow himself to get attached to women in case they left him.

'We'll be having this grub again for dinner tomorrow, Will,' said Matt. 'Join us if you like.'

Will motioned towards the main doors. 'I heard there's a service taking place for Remembrance Sunday by the memorial column along the harbour. I'll be attending that.'

'Oh, we're all going,' said Jed.

'Councillor Seabridge lays a wreath, then we head over to the church, where Father Stephen continues the service,' said Sophie.

Spencer nodded. 'Then we come here for lunch.'

'Okay, but I'll have to miss dinner, as I'm going to see my gran,' said Will. 'I'll meet you all down at the harbour in the morning though.'

Jed nodded. 'There'll be a few ex-servicemen like yourself there.'

Ginny's eyes widened as her head shot up. 'You were in the military?'

It just dawned on him he hadn't mentioned much about himself to her. 'Royal Navy,' he replied. The chatter continued, so it was hard to hear what Ginny said next, but he was sure he heard her mumble something to herself about a *Blue Man* boat.

CHAPTER 10

Ginny

Ginny paced in the back room of the Hub, nervously squeezing her fingers. Will was due any minute, and she was supposed to show him the ropes. Why Sophie had placed him on her shift was so obvious, it had caused her to blush at the time. Ooh, how her friends could be so irritating, interfering like that.

She glanced at her watch, but only a few seconds had passed since she'd last looked. This was getting ridiculous. She needed to get a grip. Why was she so bothered all of a sudden? She was fine when he worked a shift in her café.

It was her recurring nightmare about her escape vessel leaving port without her that played on her mind. Ever since Will mentioned he was ex-navy it niggled away, causing a sleepless night.

Was it a sign? Had she manifested him somehow? The *Blue Man* boat, her way out of the misery. It seemed so real now — and stupid. She chastised herself for trying to dissect such nonsense. Seriously, what was the point? It couldn't mean anything. She was just being daft.

Ginny left the back room to make a cup of tea. There were no visitors to the Hub, so she needed something to occupy her mind.

It didn't matter what she did, hope followed her around. The thought of the dinghy in her dream representing Will was beyond bizarre. So what, he was a sailor, no big deal. Oh, but it was, and it was determined to torment her.

It meant something. It just had to. All those years she'd spent gazing out to sea, blowing kisses that way, pretending her soulmate was alive and well and would find her one day. Maybe the universe was paying attention. Maybe Will picked up on her energy. Maybe she was just nuts.

Ginny started laughing, bringing a tear to her eye in the process. Holding her aching stomach, she plopped down into a big blue comfy chair. 'Oh, goodness, get a grip, woman.'

The door swung open, and in walked Will with a wide smile and a bunch of flowers.

The memory of him laying a poppy wreath at the memorial column the day before washed over her. He looked super smart in his dark blazer. Ginny had stared at the woven RN badge attached to the left breast pocket below his medals, wondering how it made him feel to wear such an honour. It was a surreal sight. He'd stood to attention for a couple of beats, causing Ginny to straighten her shoulders, not that she bothered placing her thumbs in line with the seam of her trousers, like he had. His stand was definitely on point. Heels together, feet at forty-five degrees, chest out, looking straight ahead. Yep, he was back in service, and Ginny felt a tad proud.

'Hello,' she said politely. 'I was just about to have a cuppa. Here, sit down and join me. We can chat about this place while we dip into the Jammie Dodgers.' She moved some magazines from a chair and waved him forward.

Will sat, twiddling with the packet of biscuits on the table. 'So, you helped set this place up, did you?'

Ginny glanced over her shoulder at the smiley face sticker glued to the front door, remembering placing it there. 'Yeah, it was a bit of a challenge to begin with, as some of the locals weren't too keen.' She grinned, then turned back to make the tea. 'They were worried it would lower the tone around here. Dug their heels in good and proper at one point, but then we got Councillor Seabridge on side and went from there.'

'And Matt was the first through the door, is that right?'

Ginny brought the tea over to the table and sat back down. 'Yeah, bless him. He was homeless and so lost when he arrived, and the first person he met was Jed.'

Will laughed. 'I can only imagine.'

'Jed took him for a pedicure, spa treatment, haircut. Spruced him right up. Even took him to the dentist. Oh, Jed went all out.' She snuggled back in the comfy chair and smiled. 'I'm glad he did. Matt only needed someone to care about him. Jed made such a difference to his life.' She raised one finger. 'Don't get me wrong, Matt was making his own life better by giving up the booze, but it still helps when you have a circle of support around you.'

'And that's what you do here, is it? Support the homeless?'

Ginny waggled a hand from side to side. 'That's one thing, but we offer whatever's needed. We've helped get people jobs, therapy, advice. Now we have a food bank as well. It's quite new, and small, but you'd be surprised how many walk through that door hungry.'

'So what sort of thing will you want me to do?'

'Listen to people mostly. Some only come in for a chat. Just let them tell you what they need, and if you can't sort it yourself, ask one of us. We have a large team here, not just us main volunteers that you see working. There's the dentist I just mentioned and the spa girls. We got all sorts signed up to the scheme when we started.'

'Sounds good.'

Ginny cupped her tea and smiled. 'It is. We're so pleased with how things are going. Obviously not the fact that people need help, but you know.'

'Yeah, I know.'

'So, what's with you volunteering all over the place?'

Will shrugged. 'I like to be of service, that's all.'

Ginny examined him, sensing more to the sentence. 'Hmm. Is that why you joined the navy?'

It took a beat before he answered, giving the impression he was searching for the right words. 'I grew up in care,' he said quietly.

'Oh.' She didn't know what else to say and immediately felt sad for him.

Will's dark eyes slowly met hers. 'I never felt I belonged anywhere.'

She knew how that felt. 'I understand.'

His expression held sympathy and confusion. 'I guess I've spent most of my life wishing I had a family — I never stopped to think that if I had one it might not be all rainbows and moonbeams.'

Ginny breathed out a soft laugh. 'No, not all families have that.' Her smile faded. 'Mine didn't.'

'That bad, huh?'

She lowered her gaze. 'I don't really talk about it.' Shrugging, she added, 'Don't see the point.'

'A therapist would probably tell you it helps to get crap off your chest.'

'Did joining the navy help you lose all the crap?'

Will raised his palms, then dropped them back to the table. 'I don't know. It gave me a family, but each time I was on leave, I was reminded I had no one.'

Ginny shuffled so she was leaning closer to him. 'You'll feel a sense of family here. I do.'

'But you do have a family here.'

'Just my mum. My dad left when I was a nipper, and he's dead now. I do have a brother, but he lives in Yorkshire, and he rarely comes back.' She swallowed the lump in her throat, then met his curious eyes. 'In all honesty, I wish I'd run away with the navy years ago.'

Will's hand was suddenly covering hers. 'You're tougher than that, Ginny.'

She didn't agree. 'I'm tired, Will,' she said so softly, her voice cracked.

'Hey, whatever you need, I'm here.'

The words, the tone, the look in his gentle eyes all caused Ginny's breath to catch. There was no way she was crying. Nope. Wasn't happening. She managed a weak smile as she thanked him.

'I mean it, Gin. I'll help.' The corner of his mouth twitched. 'I'm beating the Scouts with all this volunteering malarkey, so don't stop me now.'

'Yes, you are a busy bee.'

'It helps me as well as them. I won't lie, I do feel the loneliness when left to my own company for too long, and one day is too long.'

Ginny gave his hand a light squeeze. 'We sound like a right pair.'

Will's thumb lightly stroked across her finger. 'At least we can keep each other occupied.'

'Oh, is that right?'

His eyes widened in horror. 'Oh no, that's not what I meant. Please, excuse me while I go stick my head in a bucket.' He burst out laughing, sliding back into his chair, taking his warm hand with him.

Ginny wished she had the guts to shoot forward and snatch it back. His hand on hers felt so right.

'Sorry about that,' he added, shaking his head. 'I sounded like some sort of sleaze.'

'No, you didn't. It's okay.'

He smiled as he reached out for his tea. 'Glad we got that sorted. It's good we're friends.'

Friends?

'Uh-huh.' Ginny sniffed, then chewed the inside of her mouth while thinking what to say. She thought they had chemistry, but it must have been something else, seeing how he just tossed her straight in the friend zone. Maybe it was for the best.

While Will started eating biscuits, Ginny visualized him in uniform aboard a ship. She kind of liked the look. She kind of liked how he looked now, snug and happy dunking bickies.

'I'll show you how to make up food parcels after this,' was all she could think to say.

He nodded. 'Sure.'

Ginny swallowed hard. 'And just so you know, if you ever need anything, I'm here for you too.'

They locked eyes, and Ginny was sure her heart skipped a beat.

She looked away first. 'I just know how it can all get a bit much sometimes.'

'Yeah, I guess we all need some respite every so often.'

Ginny felt she needed a lifetime's worth. 'I normally sit down by the harbour for five minutes. That's my break from life.'

Will glanced up as he cuffed his bottom lip. 'Hey, how do you fancy a road trip at the weekend?'

That floored her. 'What?'

'I'm putting down roots here, so need to fetch the last of my things from my flat in Wales. It's on the market now, and the estate agent reckons it will get snapped up. So the sooner I get on with the job the better. You ever been to Wales?'

Ginny had hardly been anywhere. 'Nope. Have you found somewhere here then?'

'Not yet. But I'm looking.'

Should she mention the tenants living in her flat were moving out in a few days? The plan wasn't to rent it out again, not that she had much of a plan. Her tearoom was still on the back burner until her mum was sorted with new accommodation. Should she sell now and help her mum? Her dad would turn in his grave. Her dream was the tearoom. She must stick to that. At least that idea didn't drive her round the bend.

'Would we drive there?' she asked, thinking a change of scenery would be good.

Will nodded. 'Yep, got my truck. The only thing is, we'd stay over at mine, then head back the next day. Would that be okay with you? I have two bedrooms.'

Ginny smiled. 'Sure. That's fine.' All she had to do was pay Suzanne more money for extra hours and double-check with Annie that the café would be fully staffed.

'We'll leave Saturday morning after breakfast. Sound good?'

'We can have breakfast together, chick,' she blurted, surprising herself.

His warm smile hit her straight in the heart. 'Yeah, okay. Yours or mine?'

Ginny laughed. 'On me, in the café.'

'Ooh, not sure I like a woman paying for me.'

'Don't be sexist.'

'It's not sexist. It's tradition.'

'That comes from what? Oppression? The gender pay gap?'

Will laughed. 'What?'

Ginny shook her head. 'I like to pay my own way.'

'Fair enough.'

She folded her arms, snuggling into the comfy chair. 'Good. So from now on, don't oppress me. If I want to treat my male friends, I will.'

Will laughed again. 'Good for you. However, I might kind of like buying things for you too. I've always been a giver, see.'

'I'm a giver too.'

'Well, that's us screwed.'

Ginny burst out laughing.

Will raised his palms in defence. 'But just so you know, I promise to never oppress you.'

'Good. So you'll eat the breakfast I serve you.'

'I'll always eat the breakfast you serve me, and I won't say a word about it.'

Ginny smiled. 'You are allowed to compliment the chef.'

'You look beautiful.'

He'd caught her off guard again, and she cursed the blush creeping up her neck.

'I meant the food,' she said quietly.

'Can I ask, why do you dress that way? I've never met anyone with that look.'

Ginny glanced at her vintage top and dark skirt. 'I feel comfortable.' There wasn't more she wanted to add. Not feeling as though she belonged anywhere in life made it easier for her to pretend she belonged somewhere else.

'You look as if you time travel.'

'Ooh, I'm sure there are women today who like deep-red lipstick.' She pouted to emphasize her lips.

'There are blokes that like it too. And I definitely like it on you.'

Ginny laughed.

Will pointed at her hair. 'I like the headscarves you wear as well.'

Ginny reached up, catching her finger between the plum material and her pin curls. 'What's your style called?'

'Comfy and cheap. But if you'd prefer, whenever I'm walking out with you, I can slip on a tank top or whatever it was the gentlemen of that time wore.'

'Walking out with me?'

'That's what they called it.'

Ginny held back a laugh. 'I think that meant going out with each other, you know, like dating.'

He stared at her for a while, and she couldn't figure out what he was thinking. 'What should we call it?' he said, finally.

Was that her cue to label whatever it was they had? There was no way she was holding that weight. What if she got it wrong and embarrassed herself? He was still quietly waiting, chewing on a biscuit and acting rather laid-back about the question hanging between them.

Ginny swallowed hard, hoping he didn't notice. She had to say something. 'Road trip buddies.'

His eyes dipped to his tea as he grinned. 'I'll take that.'

She went to add more but the door opened and an old lady entered in need of a food parcel.

'Hello, Mrs Banks. I'll put some extra tins of chicken soup in for you, shall I?' Ginny smiled at Will as she got up, then introduced him to the local resident while getting him to unfold a cardboard box.

'Ooh, is that biscuits I see?' said Mrs Banks.

Will waved her towards a chair. 'Yep, and how about a nice cuppa to go with them? There's a bit of a nip in the air out there, eh?'

Ginny got on with her task while keeping one eye on Will, not that she needed to. He had it all in hand, and Mrs Banks looked quite settled with him.

He turned Ginny's way for a split second and winked, and Ginny found she too was quite settled in his company.

CHAPTER 11

Will

Will perused Ginny's brown dungarees, forest-green jumper, and camouflage headscarf as she clambered into his truck. She certainly had the ability to make him smile, and the fact she'd agreed to go to Wales with him had made his whole year. 'You got everything you need?'

Ginny nodded, rummaging around in her cloth bag. 'Yep, think so.' She looked up as he started the engine. 'I'm sure there are shops in Pembrokeshire anyway.'

'Ooh, I reckon we can find the odd one.' He grinned as he pulled away from Harbour End Road.

It was early, and their stomachs were full, thanks to Ginny's full English in the café.

'How long does it take to get there?' asked Ginny, placing her bag on the floor.

'I normally average five and a half hours, which is why I like to set off early before the traffic starts to build.'

'Wow, it doesn't look that far away on the map.'

'Nothing does in this country, but we have speed limits so . . .'

Ginny settled into the comfortable seat, and Will was pleased to see her looking so relaxed.

'How's your mum getting on?' he asked, opting for some small talk to pass the time.

All night he had mentally compiled a list of subjects for their journey so they wouldn't have any awkward silent moments. He questioned that decision immediately when he saw her hands clench into fists.

Ginny cleared her throat, then smiled weakly. He was starting to recognize her fake smiles. 'She's okay. We're still waiting to get her into a care home. How's Babs getting on in hers?'

Seeing his grandmother was on his to-do list as soon as he got back, as he didn't like to leave it too long in between visits, trying his hardest to see her most days. 'She seems okay, you know, considering.'

'Dementia is terrible for everyone involved, isn't it? It's just so cruel.'

Will nodded. He wished he'd found Babs sooner and built a relationship. She hadn't had a lucid moment with him since she went into the home, so it was tricky for him to form any kind of bond. 'She's well taken care of though. It's a lovely place she's in.'

'Oh, what's it like?'

'It's a big place. Newish building. There are about eighty residents, and they each have their own room with an en suite.'

'Ooh, that sounds nice. Hopefully my mum's one will be similar.'

'I'm pretty pleased with the set-up they have. They have security cameras and a lot of staff working at all times, so that's good. I know it's a tough gig being a care worker, so it's helpful when there are more hands on deck.'

'I don't feel so bad now about putting my mum in one.'

Will glanced her way for a second before turning back to the road. 'Have you been stressing?'

Ginny scoffed. 'I'm always stressing.'

'It's a difficult decision. With Babs, it was already happening before I arrived, so I didn't have to do anything. Marie, that's her carer, arranged the lot. She's worth her weight in gold, that one.'

'They didn't move Babs far, did they?'

Will shook his head. 'No. It's just on the border of Port Berry and Penzance.'

Ginny sighed. 'There was talk of a place for my mum over in Dorset. I'm not sure how much choice we have when it comes to the council paying. I'd like to keep her in Cornwall.'

'There are loads of residential homes here. I'm sure they won't move her far.'

'They need to get a wriggle on. She's getting worse every day.'

'Try getting your GP involved.'

'Oh, everyone's involved. We have a social worker linked to the Hub, Henley, and even he's on the case. It's just, with more and more people living longer, the care homes are filling up. Years ago, families would care for their elders, but now everyone's working and can't fit it all in.' She bobbed her head. 'Trust me, it's a lot.'

'You're a good daughter, Ginny.'

She gazed out the side window, not adding to the conversation, so Will switched the radio on low to listen to the news.

'Good grief,' he mumbled to himself. 'Snow. That's all we need.' He glanced at Ginny, who looked to be in a world of her own. 'Did you hear that, love? They reckon snow is on its way.' He looked at the clear sky, not seeing signs of much. It wasn't lost on him that he'd just called her love, but as her only reply was a light groan, he ignored it as well.

After two and a half hours of chit-chat, music, and companionable silence, they pulled into a service station to grab a bite to eat and use the bathroom.

Will was glad to stretch his legs, and Ginny already looked tired. He hoped her mum was placed into residential care soon, as even he could see how much of a break Ginny needed, and he hardly knew her.

The queue for coffee and sandwiches was long, so Will waited in line while Ginny went to freshen up. He'd just reached the front when he heard a faint scream. Everyone in the vicinity turned to see where the commotion was coming from.

'What's going on over there?' the young man serving asked Will.

Will shifted around the small crowd behind him, then noticed people had started gathering outside the women's toilets.

Ginny!

He darted across the forecourt, pushing through the crowd until he reached the entrance to the loo. 'Ginny?' he called.

Her strained voice cried back, 'Will, help!'

With little thought to where he was heading, he dashed inside to see a few ladies gathered outside a closed cubicle.

'The door's jammed,' said one woman.

'Someone's gone to get the janitor,' said another.

But Will was only half listening. He thumped on the door. 'Ginny, you in there?' He heard a whimper.

'Will, please . . .'

Straight away he could hear her breathing was off. 'Stand on the loo,' he told her. 'I'm going to kick the door. Stay as far back as possible, okay?'

'Okay,' came the faintest of replies.

Two kicks to the cheap wood had the door hanging off its hinges, and Will tugged the obstruction out the way to a few cheers from the surrounding women.

'Well done, mate,' said one.

He felt someone's hand slide from his shoulder as he rushed inside the cubicle to find Ginny curled up in a ball on the closed toilet seat. 'Hey, hey,' he said softly, wrapping her in his arms. 'It's okay.'

Ginny was sobbing silently, burying her head into his chest as he lifted her.

'You're okay now, babe,' said a woman, as Will carried Ginny out the bathroom.

'No one likes getting stuck,' said another. 'Terrible time I had in a lift once.'

Will ignored the people staring and the women from the toilets telling everyone what had happened and how the trapped lady is just a bit shaken but okay.

Ginny was shaking and not looking away from his chest.

He carried her all the way to the truck, his place in the food and drink queue now the last thing on his mind, then settled her inside, fetching a soft blanket from the back to drape around her, hoping she'd stop shivering. 'You're safe now, love. I promise.'

'I'm sorry,' she whispered, gathering the blanket up to her neck.

'Hey, you have nothing to be sorry about. You got stuck, that's all. Loads of people have claustrophobia. It's really common. Even if they can do things like trains, they still don't appreciate being stuck in one if it breaks down or something.' He leaned in the opened door and stroked back a piece of hair, fallen loose from her scarf. 'You're okay.'

Ginny sniffed, raising watery eyes. 'It's triggering for me,' she whispered.

Will got the immediate impression there was a backstory that didn't involve being stuck in a lift one time. 'What is it?' he asked gently, placing a hand on her shoulder.

There was a lost little girl somewhere deep within those hazel eyes that blinked his way.

'My mum sometimes locked me in the cupboard under the stairs if I was naughty.' Her voice broke, along with Will's heart. 'I wasn't naughty,' she added quietly, shaking her head a touch. 'I was the good one.'

Will reached in, huddling her into his body as much as he could. He had no idea how she could care so much for a mother who'd been so cruel. It made no sense, but it wasn't the time nor his business to discuss the matter, so he just held her until she stopped shaking.

The large car park of the service station wasn't the best place for a walk, but he felt she needed some air, even if infused with fumes.

'You okay for a minute?' he finally asked, stretching his back. 'I'll just go fetch us some lunch, then we can sit over by those bushes and take five.' He made sure the window was down and that she was okay with him closing the door before he shut it softly.

He got a few stares as he quickly grabbed some food and ordered drinks, and the man behind the counter asked after Ginny. No one accosted him about the broken door, not that he cared. All that mattered was seeing to Ginny.

She was sitting up and breathing normally when he returned, which was a relief. Her face was still pale, but at least she wasn't shaking anymore.

'Come on,' he said, holding up the food. 'Let's go hang out with nature for a bit.'

Ginny got out the truck, keeping her eyes on the greenery over the way.

Will couldn't be sure if she felt embarrassed to look at him or if she was still in a bit of shock, so he offered an elbow, which she took, and guided her to the side of the car park.

Two empty crisp packets, a bottle of lager, and scattered cigarette butts were tangled into the thick brambles lining its edge, not exactly giving off a calm feeling, and what with the hum of nearby motorway traffic, it wasn't the best place to have a picnic, but needs must.

Will plopped down onto the cold, hard ground, encouraging Ginny to join him, which she did. 'Here, eat something. We've still got a long way to go.' He glanced at her sorrowful face as she reached into the bag for a chicken sandwich. 'Or would you like me to take you home?'

'No, I'm okay.' She raised her sandwich. 'Thanks.'

Will couldn't help himself; he leaned over and kissed the side of her head.

'I'm sorry about before,' she said, then bit into the wholegrain bread.

'You've got nothing to be sorry about. And just so you know, you certainly don't ever have to be sorry around me. It's okay, Ginny. Everything's fine. I don't want you worrying about this.' It was clear she already was.

'I don't freak out often,' she said, offering a small smile.

'Well, whenever you do, we'll sort it.' He gestured at her crossed legs. 'I reckon you've got it in you to boot down doors to help me if needed.'

Ginny's laugh was quiet, but the fact she had one cheered Will no end. 'You got doors keeping you in?'

'Ah, we all have.' He shook his head, more so at himself. 'Everyone's got something going on, and I've got too much crap in my head for me to manage right now.'

Ginny gently nudged his elbow. 'Maybe I can help.'

'That's kind, but no one can do anything about my past. It's done, isn't it? All you can do is live with it now.'

'I guess it depends on what's haunting you. Today has made me think I might need some therapy. I'll talk to my friend Jan when we get back. See what she says. I know a few people that have therapy sessions with her.'

'Sounds like a good idea to me. Perhaps I'll join you.'

'Was being raised in care that bad?'

Will shrugged, swallowing some food. 'Lonely more than anything, but it's more the part of how I was conceived that's bothering me.'

'Nothing any of us can do about that, chick.'

'No, I know, but finding out your biological mum was a sex worker and your old man was a punter doesn't exactly warm the cockles of your heart.'

Ginny lightly touched his knee. 'Bloody hell, Will. That's a lot for anyone to process.'

'Yep.'

'I'm not sure what I can do to help. Do you want to talk about it?'

'Not much else to say.'

'I meant how you're feeling. You can yell out to the brambles if you want. I'll hold your hand, yell with you, whatever works.'

He smiled at her kindness. 'Thanks, but I'm okay right now.'

She touched his arm. 'Here if you need me.'

'Same.' Will gestured behind them. 'Shall we take this back to the truck? I'm getting a numb bum.'

Ginny motioned at the shrubbery. 'And it's not the best view.'

'No, but there's something healing about nature, and right now, that's all we've got. When we get back to mine, I'll take you down to the sea. That'll see us right.'

Ginny stood, picking up their rubbish. 'I can't tell you the amount of times I stood staring out to sea when I was a kid. I used to wish I could sail away.'

Will breathed out a small laugh through his nose. 'Me too.'

They shared a look, then headed back to the vehicle. He made sure she was comfy before starting the engine and setting off.

Traffic had picked up, so it took a little longer to get to his flat than expected, but Ginny was peacefully reading a magazine he'd bought for her, so he wasn't too bothered about timing.

'We're here,' he announced quietly, pulling into his designated parking spot.

'Ooh, I wasn't expecting to be on the seafront,' she said, stepping out the truck on arrival. 'You kept that quiet. Nice surprise though.'

Will glanced up at the blue coastal home divided into six apartments, noticing the *For Sale* sign. 'I've had this place a few years. Come on, let's get inside and have a cuppa, then we can have a stroll along the beach.'

Ginny smiled as she stared out to sea. 'Ooh, Tenby has grown on me already.'

'Yeah, it's a beautiful place.'

'And you grew up here?'

He led her into the building. 'All over Wales. Got moved about a bit, but I always liked this place so made it headquarters.'

Ginny went straight to the front window to peer at the view as soon as he opened the door. 'I can see why Port Berry might suit you.'

'It's closer to Babs.' *And now you.*

He turned to the bedrooms, pointing out which one she could use. 'I've not got much, as this is my last time here. I've arranged for the beds to go tomorrow and that sofa, then I'll put the keys through the letterbox at the estate agents. We'll have to make do and eat out or grab a takeaway.'

'That's fine.' She mooched around the small open-plan kitchen. 'At least you have a kettle.'

'Yeah, that's coming with us.' He nodded towards some stacked boxes. 'And that lot.'

'Will you miss this place?'

He shrugged, unsure. 'I wasn't here much. I used this place during leave and when I retired from the navy, then I was lodging at a mate's holiday centre for a year while working in search and rescue over in Snowdonia.'

'And you're sure you're ready to settle down?' Ginny laughed. 'Doesn't sound like you can keep still for too long.'

Will stared at the back of her head as she turned to put the kettle on. 'Yeah, I'm ready,' he said quietly, slightly worried by how attached he felt to her.

CHAPTER 12

Ginny

It was the next morning, and with the exception of the bathroom episode she'd had at the pit stop on the way over yesterday, Ginny was having the best time in Wales. She wished she had more time to visit places; she wanted a longer break than one night and only just realized how much she needed a change of scenery.

She opened the window and leaned out on the ledge, inhaling the bitterly cold air. It didn't matter how crisp it was, it was fresh and filled with salt and warmed her heart.

Will was in the bathroom, and it felt so nice to pretend she lived with a man for a while. They seemed to have a lot in common. Both fighting off misery, that was for sure.

A cloud of air blew out of her parted lips as she laughed at the madness of her life. What if she asked Will to do a house swap with her? Could she really up sticks and move to Wales? Anywhere away from her life seemed good, but she knew she wouldn't take any leaps away from her mum. Birdy needed her. There was no one else who cared.

Ginny watched a man walking his dog along the front, wondering if he had any worries. Oh, why did she have to go and spill her guts to Will about her mother's form of discipline? She hadn't told anyone that before. Only her brother knew about her getting locked in the cupboard. He used to bang on the door and laugh. At least Will comforted her.

Wiping the past from her mind, she gazed out to sea, then turned when Will made an appearance.

'Hey,' she said. 'I nipped down to the shop and got some lunch bits.' She sat on the sofa and sighed. 'I don't want to go home yet.'

'We can come back another time. Make more solid arrangements. Book a hotel or something. Perhaps in the summer. Even invite some of the others. Hire a coach or something. Jed might like to fish here.'

Summer was the busiest season in Port Berry, but she still nodded. Dreams made her smile more than reality, and it was nice to think of having a holiday with friends, or just Will.

Will unwrapped a cheese baguette and opened a small bottle of orange juice. 'I see it's started snowing already. Let's hope it stays light.'

Ginny whipped around to face the window. 'Where did that come from? It wasn't there a minute ago.' She jumped up to take a better look. 'Ooh, I love the snow.' The warmth from his body met hers as he leaned over to peek outside.

'It's all well and good while you're indoors.'

Ginny smiled. 'It's Christmassy.'

'Yeah, it'll be December soon enough.'

She turned, not realizing she'd be so close to his face. Goodness it felt nice. If only they were a happy couple living their best life, she could reach out and toss her arms around him. It wasn't as though they hadn't been wrapped around him before.

Will turned back to the food and grabbed a packet of crisps. 'The men for the beds will be here any minute, then we'll head off.'

'If you're worried about driving in the snow, we could stay here another night.' Ginny knew it was hope and dreams controlling her words, but still, she wanted to make the most of her time pretending she had a different life.

'It's in for the week, apparently, so best get back, else we might be stuck here without heating, as that gets shut off today.'

Trying not to take it personally, as what he was saying made sense, Ginny ate a ham sandwich.

The intercom buzzed, and Will let the collection men in to remove the beds. He went downstairs with them, loading his truck with the boxes.

Ginny went back to the window to have a nosey. She liked watching Will from afar. Quite often she'd remember him without his clothes on, and it always made her smile.

The light snowflakes filled the air, making everything look dreamy and magical. Will blended in perfectly. There was something so enchanting about her one-night stand. For one, he hadn't tried to get in her bed since, which raised a thousand questions. Not that she'd made any offers. The fact he spoke to her through the bedroom wall all night proved he was staying well and truly in his own bed, but it was okay. She felt comfortable enough in the other room and had a good night's sleep.

Looking down at him, she figured she'd better help pack the few bits left, so she poured away the warm dregs in the kettle, then held it out the window to cool down some more.

Will was frowning up at her. 'You catching snowflakes for our tea, Gin?'

It did look that way. 'I didn't want to put it in the box while it's still a bit hot.'

He gave her the thumbs up, then went back to sorting his truck.

Ginny smiled once more at the snow, then got on with her task, and before long, Will was saying goodbye to his old home.

'Do you want to visit anyone before we head off?' Ginny asked. 'I don't mind if you want to pop in and see your old foster mum or someone?'

'Nah, it's okay. The only one that gave me a touch of stability died a few years after I joined the navy.'

'Oh, that's a shame.'

Will shrugged. 'Story of my life. Anyway, time to move on again.'

'I feel sad on your behalf,' she told him, climbing into the truck.

'Don't be. It's all good. I've had a lot of homes. Not found one I've missed yet.'

'I hope you find a home in Port Berry,' she said softly. 'And I don't mean a place to live. I mean somewhere that feels homely that you would miss when you're gone.'

'You didn't want to leave here a minute a go.'

Ginny laughed. 'True. But I do love my home.'

'Well, I have plans to put down roots, so—'

'You do?' There was way too much excitement in her tone. She told herself to reel it in as he jumped out the truck to stick the envelope containing his door keys through the letterbox at the estate agents.

'I'll tell you my secret if you promise to keep it to yourself.'

Ginny almost squealed at him sharing private matters. They really did need something uplifting to bond over. It couldn't all be doom and gloom that brought them closer.

Will pulled out of Tenby, hitting a main road and thicker snow. 'I'm starting a business in Port Berry. A shop.'

'Ooh, what are you going to sell?'

'Tea and cakes, I guess. I'm opening a tearoom.'

Ginny frowned. 'Where?'

'Along the front. Harbour End Road. I noticed there wasn't one, and I think it would be a good fit, don't you?'

Yes, she knew that. She'd known way before he came to town with his cute smile and sexy man hands, which were now annoying the life out of her.

He glanced her way. 'What do you think? A tearoom will do well along the front, eh?'

'Well, yes, but—'

'That's what I thought.'

Ginny told herself to calm down. It wasn't as though any premises were available along there anyway.

'Mabel hooked me up with the woman from the perfume shop,' added Will. 'Sheila wanted out and fast, so we got a solicitor on the case straight away. She wanted the money as soon as possible. Don't know her story, but I think she got lumbered with the place after her husband died. I didn't get into it with her. Anyway, she signed on the dotted line as soon as someone handed her a pen. I think she said she was moving to Florida. There were a few swear words involved about her husband, but I shut off halfway through the conversation.'

He was the only one smiling and hadn't noticed the scowl on her face.

Ginny unclenched her fists and took a calming breath. The news was all a bit too much.

'I won't make a start until the new year,' he added. 'But I'll probably have a clear-out once Sheila's packed up her stock. Perhaps get the shopfitters in. Feel free to give me some pointers.'

It was too late. The rage was burning the back of her eyes, and the fire in her gut was ready to erupt. How bloody dare he muscle in on her idea and take over! Of all the cheek. That was her dream not his.

'You can't open a tearoom,' she snapped.

Will glanced her way for a second, frowning. 'Why, what's wrong? I think it's a great location, and it'll give me a steady income. I've been doing some research, and it's definitely a great investment.'

'Investment, yes, but do you even bake cakes? Is it your dream?' she snapped again.

'Erm, no, I don't bake, and I wouldn't use the word dream exactly. This is business, and I want something staff can run while I focus on my voluntary jobs. It's perfect for me, and for the community. I thought you'd be pleased. Mabel reckons everyone will love having a tea shop along the front.'

'Well, Mabel's right, but you don't understand.'

'Understand what?'

Ginny tapped her chest. 'That was my idea.'

'Oh, sorry. I didn't know. When were you opening?'

'I'm not. Well, I plan to. I just don't have anything set in stone yet.'

'So what are you saying here? You just had the idea and that's it?'

Ginny shrugged. He had her there. How could her idea compete with his actions? 'I was in prep mode.'

'Is that right? And now what? You've got the hump with me for getting on with it?'

'Yes!'

'You're being ridiculous.'

Ginny huffed. 'I'm being ridiculous?'

'Yeah, you are. You can't have a go at someone for opening a shop that you just dreamed about. If you told me you already had the wheels in motion, then I would sell something else in my shop, but all you've got is an idea that no doubt a lot of others in Port Berry have.'

'Oh, well, just stomp all over me why don't you.'

'I'm not stomping on you, Ginny. You have a café. If I were opening one of those I'd see your point, but as it stands, your point is stupid.'

'Got any more names you want to call me?'

Will sighed. 'I'm sorry. I'm not calling you any names. I wouldn't. I'm merely pointing out how unfair you're being.'

'Unfair? I'll tell you what's unfair. Some stranger buying your dream, then no doubt buggering off in a couple of years to see if he can find another home.'

'I told you I'm settling in Port Berry.'

'Way to make friends, Will.' She folded her arms, staring out at the thickening snow falling harder and faster.

'Oh, that's just great!'

At first she thought he was talking to her, but then the truck slowed, and Will peered closer to the front window.

'What's wrong?' she asked, wondering what her chances of survival were if she jumped out and scarpered down the motorway.

'Accident up ahead. We're being directed to the slip road.'

The snow was getting worse by the minute, and Ginny wished they had stayed in Tenby another night. The windscreen wipers were on full, and the vehicle mooched along at a snail's pace. Visibility was poor, and neither of their bad moods helped.

'They call this karma,' she said, leaning forward as though her eyes would help with the driving.

Will scoffed. 'Karma for what?'

'Stealing people's dreams.'

'Oh, really? Well, in case it slipped your mind, you're in this with me.'

'But you started it.'

'I didn't start anything. All I did was share my plans with you. I actually thought you'd be pleased for me.'

'Why would I be pleased? That's my tearoom, not yours.'

'I . . . Bloody hell, I've missed the turning now.'

'Just turn around.'

'I can hardly see a thing.'

Ginny scanned the area, not seeing much but snow and greenery. 'Ooh, look, what's that? There's a sign.'

'What sign? Where?'

'There. Right there. Can't you see?'

'I see a blizzard.'

'Oh, you missed it. Look, take that road. It must lead somewhere.'

Will blew out a puff of aggravated air. 'Yeah, they all lead somewhere.'

Ginny flopped back, crossing her arms once more in a huff. 'I'm just trying to be helpful.'

'You know what would have been helpful? If you had just been supportive when I told you my happy news.'

They may be crawling along a country lane, but Ginny's mind was going full steam ahead.

'Why on earth would I support someone stealing my idea?'

'Because it's an idea you're not doing anything about. Anyway, the way I heard it, the café was your dream.'

'It was. Once. But now I have new dreams.'

Will sighed loudly. 'Look, I'm sure we can—'

'Don't talk to me. I don't wish to be your friend.' She saw him glance her way.

'You don't wish to be my friend?'

Ginny turned to face the side window.

After a few minutes of silence, Will pulled up.

'Why are you stopping?' she asked, looking out at the blizzard hitting them from all angles.

'I can't see a thing. I don't even know if we're still on a road or in a field. We'll have to wait it out.'

'We will not!'

He shuffled in his seat to face her. 'Got a better plan? An idea that perhaps you might actually work towards?'

Ginny pursed her lips. 'Yes, put the satnav on. At least we can get an idea where we are.'

'It's broken, and I haven't got around to getting it fixed yet. Didn't think I needed it for this trip, seeing how I know the way.'

Ginny reached into her bag and pulled out her phone. 'I've got no service. You?'

Will checked his own phone. 'There's a bit. Let me open the map. Oh!'

'Oh, what?'

'Battery died.'

'Are you kidding me?'

He turned it her way as proof.

Ginny tutted. 'We can't stay here, Will. Who knows how long this blizzard will last. You said it was due to snow all week.'

'There's a blanket in the back.'

100

Ginny poked a finger towards the windscreen. 'Can we just drive? For all we know there might be a town up the road, or somewhere we can shelter.'

'It's dangerous to drive in these conditions.'

'Do you want me to drive?'

Will shook his head. 'I can manage, thank you. It's not about me or you. It's about that.' He gestured to the large clumps of snow bashing the vehicle.

'Can we at least try, please?'

'Fine, just keep your eye out for any signs of life.'

Ginny shuffled forward, leaning her arms on the wide dash. 'There are lots of little villages just off motorways. We're bound to find one.' She sighed heavily. 'Not sure I'd want to live close to a motorway.'

'I don't suppose they did either, but seeing how the roads were built through the countryside, I'm guessing they didn't get much say in it.'

They drove along, scanning the area in silence, seeing nothing but snow, snow, trees, and snow.

'Ooh, what's that?' Ginny snapped to attention. 'See? A sign. Yes, we're saved.'

Will pulled up, unwinding the window for a better look, causing Ginny to laugh when his face was covered in snow within one second. 'You can get out and look if you want.'

Ginny giggled. 'No, thanks. I'm good.'

'Hmm.'

'Well, what did it say?'

'Happy Honeymoon something.'

Ginny frowned. 'We're lost in a blizzard. This isn't the time for jokes.'

'I'm not joking.' He pulled the truck forward. 'I think it's a hotel.'

'I'm not staying in a honeymoon hotel.'

'Fine. You can stay in the truck.'

She wasn't about to do that either so quickly chose the lesser of two evils, which was the warmth and comfort of a building, hopefully one that had a loo.

They both stared at the large farmhouse as they pulled up outside.

'What if they haven't got any rooms available?' Ginny felt like crying. Not only had she just had a row with Will, she was stuck in a blizzard in the middle of nowhere, and the only thing she could see was a huge pink love heart flapping in the wind beneath porch lights welcoming her to the Happy Honeymoon Hotel.

Great!

'We don't need a room. This snow will probably ease in a few hours. Wait here. I'll see if it's open.'

That was a decision she was happy with. The heating in the truck was set to cosy, so she wasn't ready to leave it behind until she knew for sure it would be replaced with four walls and perhaps a crackling fireplace.

If I had a honeymoon hotel, I'd definitely have a big Father Christmas fireplace.

The door to the truck opened. 'They said come in. Hurry, it's freezing.'

Ginny clambered out into the cold, surprised when Will tucked her arm in his. Did he think she was incapable of running through a blizzard?

'We could always pretend we're married.'

She was sure that's what he said, but what with icy snow whipping into her ears, she couldn't be entirely sure.

'Oh, goodness. Look at you two,' said the elderly woman in the doorway. 'Come in. Come in. Quickly now.'

Ginny took a breath as she swiped her hands down her soaked jumper. 'Thank you so . . .' The whole of the hallway was bright pink. 'Much.'

'I'm Mrs Henshaw, and Mr Henshaw will be down in a minute. Haemorrhoids keeps him in the bathroom for a bit longer these days.'

'Ginny and Will,' said Will.

Mrs Henshaw's eyes peered at Ginny's wedding finger. 'Aren't you married?'

'Erm,' muttered Will.

Mrs Henshaw twiddled with her buttoned cardigan. 'It doesn't matter if you haven't reached that stage in your relationship yet. We'll not shoo you back into the storm. You've landed on our doorstep, and you need shelter.'

Will and Ginny smiled.

Mrs Henshaw waved them over to a small dark desk. 'Let me settle you into a room. This storm won't pass until the morning. Just said on the news. Best to get snug and warm.' She glanced up from her opened guestbook. 'We've only got one room available, as the other two are being decorated. Thought it best to get on with that task this time of year, as we don't get many guests. I'm glad we didn't strip them all now. Lucky for you, eh?'

Ginny gazed around at the numerous foil love hearts hanging from the ceiling while Will pulled out his wallet and paid with his card.

'I'll just fetch our bags,' said Will, heading for the door. 'Won't be a sec.'

'Who is that down there, Mrs Henshaw?' asked the smiley old man taking one step at a time as he descended the stairs.

Ginny offered a small wave. 'Your wife's rescuing us from the blizzard.'

'Ooh, it's got bad,' he said, gaining traction as he reached the bottom step. He glanced at her bare ring finger. 'Aren't you married, young lady? We normally have couples blessed under the eyes of the Lord here.'

Ginny followed his eyes up to the ceiling.

Mrs Henshaw turned to her husband. 'They're not on their honeymoon. They're sheltering from the storm.'

Will came bustling through the front door, bringing half the blizzard with him. 'Hiya. You must be Mr Henshaw. I'm Will,' he said, shaking hands with the old man. 'Thanks for taking us in.'

'Let me show you to your room,' said Mrs Henshaw. 'Then you can come down to the dining room and have some dinner with us later. Food is included in your bill, as is bedding and towels, but you will have to pay extra if you want to watch the television in the parlour without us. We don't have it on all hours. There isn't one in the rooms, you know, what with this being a honeymoon hotel. Folk don't stay here to watch TV.'

They followed her up the stairs and along the landing to room number one.

'Oh, good Lord!' Ginny gasped at the sight of the ruby-red bedding, sickly-pink walls, and heart-shaped cushions scattered on the maroon chaise longue over by the window.

Mrs Henshaw frowned.

'Thank you for blessing us with the Happy Honeymoon Hotel and Mr and Mrs Henshaw,' Ginny quickly added, looking at the pink ceiling.

Mrs Henshaw smiled, then left them alone.

Ginny immediately turned to Will. 'It's good of them to help us out.'

Will shrugged. 'Yep. For a moment there I thought we were going to have to pretend to be married.'

Ginny stared at the double bed. 'Hmm, well, husband or not, you can take the couch.'

Will tipped his head. 'Fine by me, wifey.'

CHAPTER 13

Will

While Ginny was out of the bedroom, doing who knew what, Will decided to make good use of the freestanding bath along the side wall. Its brass base and taps helped warm the look, as the lack of heating in the hotel left a chill in the air.

He picked up a pink ball resting on the top pink towel and read the wrapping. 'Ooh, bath bomb.' He plopped it into the running water, smiling as it dissolved on impact, creating red and pink swirls. 'Fancy.' He laughed, stripped, then sank below the magical-looking liquid.

The warm bath relaxed his cold bones immediately, making him groan with delight. What a strange day he was having, but none of it mattered while the sweet scent of strawberries and roses wafted up his nose.

Lovely.

The door opened, and he heard Ginny quietly gasp before stomping to the end of the bed to glare at him.

'What you got there?' he asked, peering over at the mass of pink fluff she'd tossed on the quilt.

'It's cold, so I went to find Mrs Henshaw to ask if she wouldn't mind turning up the heating.' Ginny tipped her head to the bed. 'She gave me these instead.' She raised her index finger. 'My mistake. She sold me these.'

Will chuckled. 'Ooh, got to love a bit of supply and demand. Is that a blanket?'

'No. They're dressing gowns. The only heating they have in this old house is the fireplace in the living room.'

'Oh, well, we don't have to wear them.'

Ginny breathed out a quiet laugh. 'We're expected to wear them. For dinner. Yep, dinner. I was specifically told to come down for some food in an hour, and as there are no other guests, we can wear our pyjamas.' She motioned towards the dressing gowns. 'Apparently, we'll feel snuggly when we watch the film afterwards.'

'What film?'

'The romance one Mrs Henshaw has planned. Yep, we're having a slumber party it would appear.'

Will pulled in his bottom lip as he laughed. 'I hope they have pizza.'

'Nope, chicken. It's roasting as we speak.' She took a step closer and frowned. 'Why is your water pink? Is that glitter?'

'Bath bomb. Strawberry and rose.'

'Ooh, it smells nice.'

Will waved a hand. 'Come on in.'

'I'm not getting in there with you.' Ginny lifted her chin as she turned her back on him. 'I'll have one when you're done.'

'There was only one bath bomb. Made for sharing, see.'

She turned, scowling down at him. 'As long as there's hot water for me. I need to defrost. I'm starting to lose feeling in my toes.'

'Not sure about the water. Best not to take the chance, I say. Come on, get in.'

Ginny folded her arms in a huff. 'I will not.' She went over to the window to stare outside.

Will rolled his eyes at the ceiling, then stood and grabbed his towel. 'Okay, your turn.'

Ginny turned, perusing the pink water.

'Come on, Ginny, get in before it gets cold.' He raised his eyebrows at her suddenly gawping at his bare chest. 'Can I help you with something?'

Ginny blinked hard, then turned to the bath. 'I was just seeing if you had turned pink.'

He glanced down at his body. 'No, but I'll turn blue in a minute if I don't hurry and dry off and get dressed.'

'Don't mind me.'

Will grinned. 'No peeking then.' He set about sorting himself, sitting on the edge of the bed, spending more time ridding his skin from pink fluff from the towel than anything else.

'Stay facing that way. I'm getting undressed.'

Will concentrated on the moisturizer on the bedside cabinet. It smelled like sweet lilies and helped make his skin feel fresh and cared for.

'I'm in now,' said Ginny.

Will didn't reply. He slipped his PJs on, then stood to shake out the dressing gowns to see which one was bigger.

'They're one size,' said Ginny.

'Not sure it'll fit me. I'm still surprised you bought me one.'

'It's cold, we both need them, and unlike some people, I'm not selfish.'

'How much do I owe you? Oh no, wait. I wouldn't want to oppress you. Thanks for the gift.'

'You can be sarcastic all you like. I'm just going to enjoy my nice hot bath.'

'May I remind you that it was my nice hot bath a moment ago. Thank me anytime.' He paused as he looked directly at her immersed in glittery pink liquid, make-up free, with eyes closed. A slight twitch hit the corner of his mouth, then he quickly turned back to the dressing gowns as she peeped his way.

'Try it on. It might fit.'

Will shrugged into the garment, surprised at how warm it actually was. 'A bit snug, but does the trick.'

Ginny giggled. 'You look like a marshmallow.'

'Everyone loves marshmallows.'

'Not vegetarians.'

Will grinned. 'You can buy vegan ones. Seen them in the shops. See, I'm still a lovable marshmallow to everyone.'

She muttered something, but he didn't quite hear.

'I'll just go and see if I can help the old couple with anything.' He slid into his slippers and headed for the door.

'Oh, don't mind me, alone in the bath.'

'And what exactly might happen to you if I leave?'

'We're in a strange hotel, who knows where. You've seen the films. I could get murdered.'

Will chuckled. 'Mr Henshaw, in the brass tub, with a walking stick. At least the blood will blend in with the water.'

'Not funny.'

Shaking his head, he left the bedroom.

Some old music was playing quietly in the kitchen as Will approached, and Mr and Mrs Henshaw were inside, slow dancing.

He stopped in the doorway to watch with a smile. What a wonderful sight, seeing two people hopelessly in love. He couldn't help but think of the woman he'd just left in the bath.

Not wanting to disturb them, Will turned, bumping straight into a donkey. 'Argh!' His short, sharp yelp had Mrs Henshaw by his side in a second.

'Oh, that's our Lily. She's not too keen on the snow.'

Will smiled warily at the creature staring his way, then reached out to tentatively pat Lily's head. 'Hello.'

Mrs Henshaw nudged his arm. 'Ooh, I see you like your robe. Sell a lot of those here.'

He had no comment about that. 'Erm, I came to see if you need any help with dinner.'

She smiled and waved him into the kitchen. 'You're a good lad. Come and chop some carrots with Mr Henshaw.'

Will glanced over his shoulder as he entered, watching the donkey slowly follow.

Mr Henshaw handed him a chopping knife. 'Dinner won't be long.'

The smell of the roasting chicken was making Will's stomach rumble. He made a start on his task, already knowing he would enjoy his grub, but then a fluffy chicken jumped up on the countertop, startling him.

'You get down, Hettie,' said Mr Henshaw, flapping the bird away.

Will glanced down to see another one clucking around his feet.

Mrs Henshaw chuckled. 'You might see a few of them around. Had to get them in, see. The snowstorm was scaring them.'

Will looked over at the oven, wondering if he was about to eat a family pet. Suddenly his appetite was gone.

'No, that's not one of ours,' said Mrs Henshaw, pointing at the food cooking. 'We wouldn't eat our own.'

Will jumped as Hettie pecked his slipper. 'Do you have many animals?'

'Chickens, donkey, and there's a cat around here somewhere,' replied Mrs Henshaw. 'Sometimes the squirrels come inside.'

Lily nudged Will's back as he continued to peel carrots, so he turned to offer her some shavings, mindful of the big stained teeth approaching his outstretched hand.

'All our animals are rescues,' said Mrs Henshaw. 'Isn't that right, dear?'

Mr Henshaw plopped some broccoli into a pan of water. 'What? Oh, yes, yes.'

She turned back to Will. 'He doesn't always hear too well.'

Will nodded, wiping his hand on a tea towel, and Mrs Henshaw directed him over to a Welsh dresser.

'You lay the table for me, Will.'

Gathering some vintage-looking plates, he headed for the dining room, with Lily not far behind. 'Don't worry, I'm not going to steal the silverware,' he told the donkey, who seemed to hold a suspicious glint in her eye.

She nudged his back as he leaned over the large dark table.

Will frowned. 'Do you mind?'

Mrs Henshaw brought in some glasses for the table, shooing Lily out the way.

'So, how long have you been married?' asked Will.

'Fifty-five years.'

'Wow! That's some marriage.'

Mrs Henshaw smiled a smile that seemed to be just for her, and it warmed Will's heart to see how in love she still was with her husband.

A scream ripped through the air, gaining attention.

'It's okay,' shouted Ginny, leaning over the banister. 'I'm okay.'

Will grinned up at her. 'Did you meet a chicken by any chance?'

Ginny looked none too pleased as she rolled her oversized sleeves up on her pink robe. She marched down the stairs, looking set to trip over the dressing gown swamping her petite frame. 'Just for the record, I am not afraid of chickens. I just didn't expect to see one when I opened my door. It made me jump, that's all.'

'Come and sit up at the table, Ginny,' said Mrs Henshaw. 'We're just waiting on the veg to boil. Not long now. I'll pour you both a drink.'

Will bit his lip as Ginny came to an abrupt halt in the dining room doorway.

She looked back at him while pointing the other way. She whispered, 'There's a donkey in here.'

'Name's Lily.' He followed her in and sat in one of the farmhouse chairs.

Ginny shuffled to his side, gathering her robe up to her lap. 'Why are there animals in here?'

110

Will raised his palm towards the window. 'Scared of the snowstorm.'

Ginny's mouth opened to speak, but then she squealed instead and pulled her feet up. 'I've been pecked.'

'That's Hettie. Got a thing for feet, I guess. Where are your slippers?'

'I didn't bring any, and I didn't have any clean socks.'

He watched her scanning the carpet for any approaching beaks. 'You can't sit with your feet up through dinner.'

She flashed her toes through a gap in the robe. 'I can if it saves my feet.'

Will sighed. 'Here. Put my slippers on.' He expected a short argument so was surprised when she quickly agreed and swiped them straight off his feet.

Dinner was soon served, and it was funny to see Ginny avoid the cooked chicken on her plate while Hettie was watching her.

'Tell me how you two met,' said Mrs Henshaw.

Will figured he'd cut a long story short. 'Ginny grew up in the house next door to my grandmother's.'

'It's nice to grow up together,' said Mr Henshaw, cutting into a roast potato.

Will gave Ginny a warm smile, pleased she smiled back. At least she looked more relaxed around him since their argument. He really needed to sort that.

The chatter turned to the weather, the Henshaws wedding day, and how Mr Henshaw had made a lot of the furniture in the room.

Ginny was happily joining in with the conversation, showing off her small-talk skills.

All in all, it turned out to be a nice dinner with a friendly couple, and just for a moment, Will felt he was in a relationship with the woman at his side. It was easy to get carried away, touching her hand on occasion on the table and swapping happy glances.

Oh, if only his life could be that simple. He needed to get his head back in the game, remain focused on his goals, and get stuck in to his plans as soon as they were back in Port Berry.

'Let's take our drinks through to the parlour,' said Mrs Henshaw, helping her husband to a stand.

Will picked up his glass of white wine, then waited for Ginny to untangle herself. He held back a laugh while she wasn't looking, smiling widely to himself.

The living room was cosy and a little quaint, with two loveseats facing a large television above a brown-brick fireplace. The small flames flickered and crackled, warming the lavender-scented air.

Mrs Henshaw gestured at the pink seat. 'You two sit there, and I'll put the film on.'

Will eyed the plump sofa, thinking it fit for two smaller people than him. He glanced at Ginny, then back at the loveseat, figuring they might fit, seeing how she was small.

As though having the same thought, Ginny said, 'You sit first.'

He did, sinking low into its squishy material, then waited until Ginny sank into his side. He had to admit, it was comfy.

She flicked the slippers off, tucking her feet up into her robe on the seat, then sipped her wine, seeming happy with their snuggly situation.

'Hope you like old movies,' said Mr Henshaw. 'It's all we watch.'

Will wasn't much of a TV man, but he wasn't fussed. Ginny was snuggled to his side, his stomach was full, his body relaxed, and not even Lily coming in to stand behind him could spoil his good mood.

Mrs Henshaw started the romance story, and everyone settled down for the night, including Hettie and some of her friends.

The next thing Will knew, Mrs Henshaw was tapping his shoulder.

'Wake up, Will. It's time for bed.'

He blinked hard, stretching his eyelids while gathering his bearings.

'I've already put my other half to bed,' she whispered. 'Looks like you need to do the same.'

Will turned his head to see Ginny fast asleep on him. She looked so serene, he didn't want to disturb her.

'I've locked up for the night,' added Mrs Henshaw. 'I'll see you in the morning.'

He waited until she left, then turned back to Ginny. Carefully, he slipped off the sofa while keeping her head in place, then scooped her up like a bride and headed for the stairs.

Ginny stirred but remained glued to his chest, causing all sorts of emotions to build in him.

After struggling with the door, Ginny's robe, and the bedding, he gently tucked her in bed, then silently sighed at the chaise longue, knowing he was in for an uncomfortable night.

There was a red blanket folded on the seat, so he grabbed that and used only one cushion for his bunk.

It was no good. No matter which direction he turned, he couldn't make himself fit. The blanket was getting tangled with his dressing gown, the cushion had fallen somewhere he couldn't see, and then he somehow rolled sideways and hit the floor.

'Ow!' he mumbled, groaning to a stand.

'Get in the bed, Will,' said a croaky voice.

He squinted his weary eyes down at her face, hidden in the darkness of the room. She looked to be still asleep, so maybe he imagined hearing her voice. He was just about to sit down when Ginny spoke again.

'Get in bed.'

Not needing any more confirmation, Will trotted around to the other side of the bed, whipped off his robe, and scrambled under the covers, glad of the warmth Ginny had already placed there.

He stared at the back of her head, smiled to himself, closed his eyes, then fell fast asleep.

CHAPTER 14

Ginny

Ginny woke to find herself attached to Will's chest. His breathing was steady, giving her the impression he was still asleep. She wanted to take a peek at his face but didn't want to move in case he woke and found her wrapped around him, even though he was doing the wrapping too.

It felt nice lying there, so she gave herself a couple more minutes while issuing her fingers strict instructions not to stroke over his arm. It was so tempting, but she couldn't allow herself to get carried away with the situation. They weren't on their honeymoon, she wasn't even his girlfriend, just one moment lost in time.

There were many times when Ginny daydreamed about waking in the arms of a man who loved her. It was stupid to attach a dream to the man in bed with her, especially as he cared little for her, proven by his tea shop theft.

Giving herself a mental shake, she lifted slightly, glanced at his peaceful face, dropped her gaze to his lips, told her heart off for giving her feelings, then slipped out of bed to look out the window to see the settled snow while shivering at the instant chill in the air.

'Morning,' he murmured.

Ginny turned.

'Did you sleep well?' he asked.

'Yes, it was okay.'

'Lot warmer in here, right?'

She twisted her mouth at his smug grin. Ooh, he wasn't winning her over anytime soon.

One idea was to get back in bed and pinch his warmth once more, but she went with plodding off to the bathroom instead, as their bedroom may have had a bath, but it certainly didn't have anything else she needed.

After freshening up, putting on some warm clothes, and not having much to say to Will, she went down to the kitchen to rustle up some breakfast.

Mrs Henshaw was pottering about, cleaning the handle on the back door. 'He always leaves a bit of dirt there.' She looked over her shoulder and smiled. 'There's some tea in the pot, dear.'

Ginny poured a cuppa, glad to have a morning brew. 'I can make you brekkie if you like. I'm used to it, as I run a café.'

'No, no. This is my domain. But you can help me put these chickens back in their pen. Mr Henshaw has cleared the path.'

'Where is he now?'

'Out front. Shovelling more snow, then salting the ground ready for the next lot.'

'Oh, when is that due?'

'Not until tonight, apparently. So you should be good to head off after you've eaten. But feel free to stay if you want.'

Ginny wanted very much to stay at the farmhouse love hotel despite her confused feelings around Will the dream stealer. Waking in his arms was so lovely, but she had a life waiting for her back home. And a mother, who would no doubt moan as soon as she saw her.

Mrs Henshaw gestured at a side room and told Ginny to grab a coat, wellies, and hat from in there. She opened the back door, letting in a blast of cold air, then waved Ginny over. 'Come on. The fresh air does you good.' She inhaled deeply, then coughed.

White sheets of snow covered the fields far and wide, making the area look pretty and clean.

'Oh, wow! It looks stunning.' Ginny took in her surroundings, still unsure of where she was. There were no other houses in sight, just land and a few trees dotted about all covered by the blizzard.

Mrs Henshaw grabbed a chicken pecking the ground close to her feet, then opened the large enclosure they'd reached. 'You grab Hettie, dear.'

Ginny widened her eyes at the ball of feathers mooching behind her, looking to prefer the kitchen. She'd never held a live chicken before. How hard could it be?

Hettie made it extremely hard, and it took Ginny all of ten minutes to capture the sprightly creature.

'Just plop her down in here,' said Mrs Henshaw, scooping out some feed. 'The others will soon follow.' She handed Ginny another scoop and gestured towards the feeding pots.

Ginny got on with her task, finding it quite therapeutic. 'Have you always wanted animals?'

'We rescued a chicken years back from a neighbouring farm. Found it wandering along the road. Terrible state it was in, poor thing. Had hardly any feathers about it. Looked as though it had just escaped someone's cooking pot. Anyway, we took it to the farm only to discover it had closed down. The little thing must have somehow been left home alone, so we took her home, fed her up, and Mr Henshaw built this here enclosure and henhouse.'

'It's very nice, and there's lots of space.'

'Yes, we knew straight away we were going to take on more.'

Ginny smiled. She liked the idea and wondered if it was something she could do. She liked her harbour house. It took a battering from storms, but it was snug inside, and she got to stare out to sea every day and dream about her soulmate. Perhaps it was time to move inland. Sell up and buy a farmhouse of sorts, then she could enjoy rescuing animals as well. It certainly brought a smile to Mrs Henshaw's face.

'What made you buy a hotel?' she asked, squatting to give some extra feed to Hettie.

'Oh, this was a working farm when we came here, dear. We were only young and had run away from home. The people here took us in, gave us jobs, and left this place to us when they passed on.'

That was intriguing. Ginny straightened, lowering her scoop. 'Run away from home? Sounds like you have some backstory there, Mrs Henshaw.'

She gave a little shrug as she closed the large metal dustbins containing pellets and mixed corn. 'Probably a bit different to most.'

'How different?' Ginny was being nosey, but she figured after running a café for years, she'd heard all the stories of the world. She now had the feeling she was about to hear a new one.

'We grew up in the same neighbourhood, but our families were at war with each other.' She shook her head slightly. 'Hated each other more than I could tell you. Had been that way for generations. Started with some dispute over a business deal. I honestly don't even know the half of it. Over the years, it just became normal for our families to fight.'

'But you and Mr Henshaw didn't fight.'

Mrs Henshaw linked her wrinkly fingers up high. 'No. We fell in love.'

'They do say love is stronger than hate.'

'It is, and we thought it might be the thing to bring our families together, but no. Just made things worse.'

'Oh, that's sad.'

'It was for me. I was devastated, as they tried to keep me from him.'

'So you ran away together.'

Mrs Henshaw nodded. 'We did, and it wasn't easy leaving my family. It took all the courage I had, but with my love by my side, I knew we'd be fine somehow.'

'Did you ever contact your family again?'

117

'No. It was for the best to leave that life behind. They weren't exactly the reasonable type.'

Ginny smiled warmly. 'I'm glad you found happiness.'

Mrs Henshaw sat on a wooden stool. 'The hard part for us was not having money. But faith is strong, dear.' She pointed at the sky. 'Some might say we stumbled across this place, but we were guided. Just like you.' Her smile was filled with wisdom.

'Maybe it's all mapped out for us before we even arrive.'

'Some say that.'

Ginny glanced around at the snow-covered fields rolling on forever. 'So this was a working farm?'

'Yep, but we changed that once it became ours, as we liked the idea of a honeymoon hotel. It stands for everything we are.'

Ginny walked over to the bins holding the feed to put the scoop away. 'It's good you both wanted the same thing.'

Mrs Henshaw chuckled. 'Oh, we're two peas in a pod, us. It's like we were made for each other.'

Ginny's thoughts turned to Will. 'Do you think all soulmates have to be the same?'

'No, dear. None of that matters. It's about love and respect. Being a team. You can do that with ease with the right one. They'll love you as much as you love them. Balance, see?'

Ginny nodded, leaning on the side of the enclosure. Had she ever had balance in her life? Her scale seemed to lean more to the side of misery.

Mrs Henshaw started to hum as she petted the chickens snuggling around her wellies.

She changed her life. What have I done . . .

Ginny pictured her home, then the café. She had taken huge leaps to find her happiness, but it didn't take a genius to figure it out. All the time she had her mother in her life, she would never be truly happy. But could she turn her back now? It seemed such a cold thought, but it was there. Her mother would never love her. Perhaps it was time to throw in the towel. At least then she wouldn't waste any more years looking for love in the wrong direction. She glanced at the sky.

Will called out from the back door. 'I've got some bacon sarnies on the go, and I've settled Mr Henshaw in front of the fire. I'll clear the front after I've eaten.' He waved them over. 'Come on. Food will get cold.'

Ginny's heart filled with fizz at seeing him standing there wearing an old coat and dark wellies, looking every part the farmer.

'It's a nice life,' said Mrs Henshaw, passing her by.

'Hmm?'

The old lady gestured at Will. 'When you get a good one.'

Ginny watched Will go back inside the house. Was he a good one? He didn't seem too bothered about stealing her tearoom dream, but there was still something so endearing about him. She went into the kitchen, washed her hands at the butler sink, then squished into the chair by his side, smiling to herself as she bit into a bacon sandwich.

'You okay there, love?' he asked, raising his brow.

'Yes, I'm fine. Hmm, this is good, thanks.'

He grinned as he ate his breakfast. 'Nice here, isn't it?' He nudged her arm, gesturing to Mrs Henshaw taking a plate of food out to her husband.

'I love it here.'

'We're leaving as soon as I've cleared the front for them. Time to go home.'

She stared at him for a moment.

He nudged her elbow again. 'Eat your food.'

'I'm thinking of selling my house.'

'Oh, where do you want to move to?'

'Inland I was thinking, then I can rescue some chickens as well.' She lowered the rest of her sandwich. 'Would you like to live somewhere like that or do you prefer a sea view, you know, what with you being a sailor?'

'I'm not a sailor anymore.' He sighed deeply, then turned to face her full on. 'I honestly don't know where to live.'

'I thought you wanted to stay in Port Berry.'

'I do.'

'But you've changed your mind?'

'Let's talk more when we get back.'

Ginny smiled softly. 'Or we could stay here.'

He met her gaze. 'This isn't our life.'

'I want to pretend it is. Just for a few minutes.'

Will went to speak as Mrs Henshaw entered the kitchen, then Ginny completely lost her mind.

Before she had time to think, she leaned forward and placed her lips on Will's.

'Aww, love is the best,' said Mrs Henshaw, heading to the fridge.

Ginny went to move away, but Will placed his hand around the back of her head and pulled her closer to his face for a deeper kiss, and just like that every part of her melted.

Will pulled away, keeping eye contact with her. 'Finish your breakfast. I've got work to do.' And with that he upped and left the room, taking Ginny's breath with him.

CHAPTER 15

Will

The atmosphere on the drive to Port Berry was light and cheery, with talk of chickens and donkeys and how much snow had hit the country. Most of the main roads were clear, but Will had to slow for the back streets as he got closer to the harbour.

Due to their happy chatter, he took a turning leading away from Ginny's house, driving on autopilot straight towards the B&B. He wasn't too bothered once he'd realized what he had done, as he only had to pull around the corner and head up Berry Hill, but the way he was going meant they would pass by the shop he'd bought, and within seconds of Ginny seeing the place, their tearoom conflict came flooding back, and the whole mood in the truck turned to ice.

'You can stop at the B&B,' she told him flatly. 'I'll walk the rest of the way.'

'No, it's fine. It's just up the road.'

'Yes, I know. That's why I can walk.'

'But it's cold.'

She turned in a strop. 'Are you seriously going to make me do a stunt roll-out of this vehicle?'

121

Will parked and shook his head. 'What is wrong with you?' Like he didn't know. 'Let me take you home. The pavement is covered in snow.' It made no difference what he said, Ginny was already halfway out the door.

'Hello, lovey,' called Mabel, sweeping snow from her doorstep.

Will raised a hand her way, then tried to help Ginny with her bags.

She tutted, snatched back a holdall, then marched off, crunching through slush and ice.

'Ginny, come on,' he called, but she turned the corner, leaving him alone.

Will was deflated on every level, so he headed off to his room, put his things away, then came back down to help Mabel clear the pathway and pavement out front.

Jed stopped to say hello. 'I saw your Babs this morning. Was up at the home visiting a friend.'

'I'll pop up later. How was she?'

'Doing as well as can be expected. Didn't remember me, but it is what it is. You come to choir practice tomorrow. It'll help cheer you up.'

'Who says I need cheering up?'

Jed pointed at him. 'Your face.'

Maybe he did look how he felt. He was too busy sweeping snow to care. 'I'm okay.'

Jed folded his arms. 'Talk to me.'

Will straightened, holding the broom in front. 'Life was a lot easier at sea.'

'Life's always easier out there.' Jed motioned across the road. 'But we have one right here too, and we just have to get on with it, no matter what.'

Will inhaled the salt in the cool air and relaxed his shoulders.

Jed thumbed up the road. 'I'm just popping in to see Luna, then I'll be on *Mrs Berry*. You come sit on my boat with me in a bit, okay?'

Will nodded. He put the broom back inside the foyer, then walked along the road to see if Ginny had popped into her café on the way home.

She wasn't there, and maybe that was a good thing because he honestly had no words for how immature she was being about the tea shop.

He walked to the Hub and had a nosey at the notice in the window advertising Christmas opening times. With or without Ginny's approval, he was going to help wherever he could for the festive season, but it did make him think about his priorities.

I'm taking on too much.

Babs needed more attention, and he could take his time with the tearoom, as he wasn't expecting to open until spring-time anyway. His focus needed to be on finding a permanent home.

Alice whipped the door open, waving him inside. 'What you standing out there for? It's blimming cold.'

'I was daydreaming.'

'I'm always daydreaming, even when I'm busy. I'm think-ing, when I finally reach my goal, I might just stop.'

Will laughed, heading for the kettle. 'You mind?'

Alice shook her head. 'No, go for it. Just make me one while you're at it.'

'So tell me, what's your dream, Alice?'

'I want my own B&B, preferably like Mabel's.'

Will plopped teabags into two mugs. 'Yeah, I've seen you over there. You eyeing up the competition?'

Alice laughed. 'No. I've been helping Mabel for years, doing bits and bobs in my spare time. I've always loved it over there. She knows I'm saving for my own B&B, so she's teach-ing me the ropes now, bookkeeping and that. Robson says I should just go to the bank and get a loan. With my savings, business plan, and knowhow, I should get the funds needed, but I don't know if I'm ready yet.'

'Basically, the only thing you're lacking is confidence, right?'

'Sums that up.'

'I didn't have much confidence until I joined the navy. That life definitely changed me.'

Alice slumped into a chair. 'I feel like I've had a few lives. Does that make sense?'

'If you're a cat.'

She chuckled as he brought the tea over. 'Sometimes I don't know who I am.'

A teenage lad opened the front door and leaned in. 'Alice, I'm going over to Anchorage Park. We're building a snowman.'

Alice frowned at the dark-haired boy. 'Isn't fourteen a bit old to make a snowman?'

'You're never too old to build a snowman. I'll be back for dinner. Stay warm.' He closed the door and sprinted off.

'Who was that?' asked Will.

'My nephew, Benny. I adopted him after my sister died. He doesn't have a dad.'

Will leaned closer to the table between them. 'I'm sorry, Alice. I didn't know.'

'Thanks, that's okay.'

'What happened to your sister?' He shook his head at himself. 'I just blurted that out without thinking. Never mind me being nosey. I'll—'

'It's fine. It's no secret. The long and short of it is, she had cervical cancer.' Alice's gaze drifted to the window. 'She'd be thirty-four now.' She met his eyes. 'She was only twenty-seven when she left us. Benny just seven. It never feels right.'

'Life can be pretty shit at times.'

'Do you have any siblings?'

Will shook his head. 'None that I know of.' What could he say? Maybe if he knew who his dad was, he might find a whole other family out there, not that he wanted anything to do with the man who used his mother. 'I was raised in care,' he added.

'Oh, I didn't know that about you.' Alice smiled softly. 'I guess we don't know much about each other, but that will all change now you're settling down here.'

'We could go outside and bond over building our own snowman,' he joked.

Alice laughed. 'Flipping heck, I think that would kill me.' She tapped her collarbone. 'I have a medical condition called fibromyalgia. I'm in some level of pain every day. I give it a score between one and ten. I'm at a four today.' She nodded at the window. 'This weather goes right through me, even when I'm indoors. That's why Benny told me to keep warm. It's not good for me to be out in the cold or rain for too long. It can give me a flare-up.'

'I've got to say, you'd never know you were in pain.'

Alice winked. 'I'm used to it now, and I know how to work with my body, but you should see me when I hit level eight. That's when I want to cry. I've got a neck brace, a walking stick, ice packs, and hot water bottles.' She shook her head as she breathed out a small laugh. 'My nan's healthier than me.'

'I think I need to up my health. I haven't been for a run in ages.'

'I sometimes jog with Robson in the summer. Oh yeah, I love those good days when I can take on the world. You'll have to come out with us. I'm not fast, mind. My legs aren't too clever. I have to just do what I can when I can. It helps relieve stress, which is always good, as stress triggers fibro flare-ups for me as well as the weather, so I like to stay calm.'

'How's that working out for you?'

Alice laughed. 'Calm and teenager don't exactly belong in the same sentence. Seriously though, I'm quite happy plodding along, doing my own thing, and Benny is a good lad. He doesn't bring trouble to our door. I have a nice family. I just need to get my own place with him so we've got more room. It's a little cramped in our flat above the newsagent's.'

'You're more confident than you give yourself credit for. You get down that bank and ask for that loan.'

Alice shrugged. 'Perhaps I'll start looking next year. See what's available.'

'And you can put my name down as a helper when you find one. I'm sure I can turn my hand to a bit of decorating or something.'

'Aww, thanks, Will. I'm going to hold you to that.'

Will supped his tea, wondering if it would be appropriate to ask questions about Ginny. Alice was her friend so might not take kindly to him poking his nose in her mate's business.

I could just tell her about the tea shop idea. See what she thinks.

He went to speak but a flyer pinned on the noticeboard caught his attention. 'The RNLI,' he said, talking to himself.

'Ooh, you're ex-navy,' said Alice, with a squeal. 'Should be your cup of tea. That's where you should volunteer. I did hear you've been looking around, signing up everywhere.'

Will had to laugh. 'I know. I just rushed in, trying to fit in everywhere, but you're right. That might just be the place for me.'

'Contact them and ask about training and stuff.' Alice stood looking out at the sea. 'I wish I could do something like that.' She turned his way. 'We do have a collection box in the shop. Sophie's got one in the fishmonger's as well.'

It certainly gave Will something else to focus on. He liked the idea. Bit by bit, his life in Port Berry seemed to be coming together. He just needed to smooth things over with Ginny somehow.

Jed opened the door to the Hub, banging his boots on the pavement, kicking off some snow. 'Come on, son. Let's go sailing.'

Alice's light-brown eyes widened. 'You're never going out now. It's freezing.'

'Ah, Alice. Don't feel the cold, me.' He laughed, coughed, then pounded his chest with his fist. 'Besides, I've got my thermals on.'

Will wished he had his. He wished he was still snuggled with Ginny in bed at the Happy Honeymoon Hotel. The thought of waking with her draped across his chest warmed him no end. It was a memory he would hold on to forever, he was sure.

126

'You two are nuts,' said Alice, seeing Will to the door.

He said goodbye, then headed over to the jetty with Jed to board *Mrs Berry*, Jed's summertime home. 'Do you really want to take her out?' He thought he would just sit on deck for ten minutes with the old-timer and chew the fat.

'Yep. You being a captain, it'll do you good.'

'I'm not a captain.'

'What was your navy title then, son?'

'Petty Officer Engineering Technician.'

'Ooh, fancy. Well, you hold on, and I'll start her up.'

Will stared over at Harbour Light Café, then up Berry Hill to the row of pastel houses. Ginny was around somewhere, and he missed her being around him already.

'You don't get seasick by any chance?' joked Jed.

Will laughed, inhaled the cold air, then settled down on a hard seat to admire the clean deck. 'You know, on the warship, we'd use the upper deck as a running track at certain times of the day. We'd run clockwise one day, and counter-clockwise the next.' Staring at the deck brought the memory back, making him smile to himself at his old life.

Jed laughed. 'Your story just made me think of Harold Lane. He used to drive the local bus. One day, he started driving round the one-way system the wrong way. Singing at the top of his head he was. Pissed as a newt. Funny old sight, obviously not for his one and only passenger, and I should know, as it was me.' He roared with laughter, then started singing a sea shanty.

Will gazed once more over at the harbour as they sailed further away, and as he was now an official member of the Berry Buoys, he happily joined in with the song.

CHAPTER 16

Ginny

'Ginny, Ginny,' squealed Suzanne, rushing into the hallway at Birdy's as soon as Ginny stepped foot inside. She clapped excitedly. 'We've only gone and got a blimming place, and it's in Cornwall. Come on, your mum's nearly ready. I said we'd take her over for a meet and greet. It's about an hour's drive away.'

'Why am I only hearing about this now?' asked Ginny, feeling a surge of mixed emotions.

'Henley sorted it this morning, that's why. Besides, you've only just got back from Wales.' Suzanne headed to the kitchen to zip up Birdy's bag on the table, then turned to lightly grab Ginny's elbows. 'This is going to be good for her, so don't you fret,' she said quietly. 'She needs round-the-clock care, and you need your life back.'

There was so much logic in Suzanne's statement, but it didn't stop Ginny from feeling like a terrible daughter. All her life her mother had told her so, and now she was proving the point. How on earth was she going to be able to live with herself knowing she'd stuck her mum in a home then buggered off to enjoy life?

128

As though reading her mind, Suzanne added, 'Hey, you're doing the right thing. Residential homes were created for this very reason. Some people just need more hands to look after them. She'll be with trained carers.'

Everything Suzanne said made perfect sense, and Ginny tried hard to raise her spirits, but as soon as she saw her mother's frightened face, her whole world came crashing down.

'I said I'd just look,' said Birdy, tightening her lips as Suzanne secured her into the stairlift at the top of the stairs.

Ginny figured it was a good start. Perhaps it would be best if she too looked at the visit that way. She told herself over and over that no decision had to be made on the spot, even though she knew she was bargaining with the inevitable.

The car ride over felt awkward and slightly nerve-wracking. Ginny was sure she would be ordered to abort mission at any given moment. Suzanne was the only upbeat person in the vehicle, babbling on about how good care homes were, and how she'd been on outings with residents in the past, and the fun Christmases she'd attended as a worker.

Ginny was only half listening, as her sickly tummy was gaining all her attention. She hoped she wouldn't have to pull over to vomit. How was this situation so hard? Her mum needed care, they were going to a place that offered just that, and loads of other families had just got on with it.

Her thoughts turned to what Will had said about his grandmother's home. It sounded lovely, and the last she heard, Babs was being well cared for. The same would happen for her mum, she was sure. She had to train her brain to be sure, else she was certain her digestive system would never be the same again.

Ginny's stomach was in knots as she parked along a narrow one-way street. Suzanne jumped out straight away to sort the wheelchair, and Birdy sat in silence, not even looking up from her lap.

The house looked in need of a fresh coat of external paint, and the small concrete area out front could have done with a few cheery plants or something.

Ginny didn't want to judge, but she couldn't help herself. There was something off, and it wasn't her guts this time.

A seagull cried overhead, reminding Ginny they were close to the coast, even if there were no other signs. The air wasn't exactly filled with the fresh salt of Port Berry, and the streets she'd driven down didn't look as clean. She knew she shouldn't compare, especially as Port Berry held awards for its cleanliness. She couldn't expect all coastal towns and villages to be the same.

Birdy groaned as she slumped in her wheelchair. 'I don't feel too good, Gin.'

You're not the only one.

'We won't stay long, Mum. Let's just have a bit of a nosey, yeah?'

'Suppose,' mumbled Birdy.

Ginny watched Suzanne greet a middle-aged man and woman at the door. She pushed her mother closer, not liking the look of the couple straight away. She told herself to stop being daft, then faked a smile as she approached.

Had Will exaggerated somewhat when talking about his grandmother's care home? What Ginny was witnessing on their tour didn't meet anything he had described. She figured all care homes would be different, but the one she was in wasn't anything like the one Babs was in. Maybe they were at the wrong place.

She locked eyes with the couple's thirty-something son, whose shifty eyes did little to soothe her pounding heart. Why couldn't she hold a real smile and feel some form of relief that her mum would be looked after?

The hard floors and hospital-blue painted walls lacked warmth, and Ginny expected a lift to take them to the upper levels, not a stairlift. She expected so much more. A games room for bingo night or arts and crafts, perhaps a beautiful garden with a duck pond and weeping willow. Large bedrooms decorated in light tones and views of rolling hills or the sea.

Her heart dropped as she came face to face with a small room containing a single bed, small basin, and the window view of a brick wall. She pointed at the marks by the bed. Off-white stains on the ghastly green paint. Surely someone could see that needed a makeover.

'What's that?' she asked, trying to remain impartial.

The woman who seemed to be in charge, waved a hand dismissively. 'Oh, it's where the last resident used to spit up the wall. It's been cleaned.'

Ginny had no words. She went to the window to stare out at the old brown bricks facing her. There wasn't much else going on down below. Certainly no green garden. Not a tree in sight. Oh, this would never do. How could she possibly sleep of a night knowing her mum was in this room?

'I don't feel very well,' said Birdy, and Ginny turned to see vulnerability, a rare sight on her mother.

'We can make you some dinner,' said the care worker.

Suzanne went to agree to the offer, but Ginny told them all they'd seen enough and would head home to think things over.

'We were going to take you down to the beach,' said the woman. 'Show you where we go some days. We're not stuck in here day in day out. There's lots to see, and we have a singer come over sometimes to entertain the troops.' She turned to Birdy, adding a huge smile. 'And if we settle you in before Christmas, you can join in with the festivities. You'll have such a good time. You'll see.'

Birdy simply stared at her, and Ginny noticed the water hit her mum's weary eyes.

'It's a bit overwhelming at the moment.' Ginny meant for herself as well. 'We'll speak to Henley when we get back. He'll let us know what the next steps are once we've decided.'

The woman nodded. 'Okay, but just so you know, this isn't house hunting, love. If your mum needs care through the council, then you don't get much in the way of choice.'

Yes, thank you, that was starting to dawn on her now. Jeez, Ginny needed some fresh air, preferably Port Berry air. She was glad to get back in the jeep.

'Dinner would have been nice, Ginny,' said Suzanne, a clear huff to her voice. 'I'm hungry, and Birdy needs some food too.'

'I'll treat us all to dinner at my café. It won't take long to get back.'

'I don't want to live there, Ginny,' blurted Birdy, bursting into tears. 'Please don't make me.'

Ginny had to slow the car, as water blurred her vision. She went to speak, but Birdy was in a terrible state, crying and gasping, begging over and over.

Suzanne tried to console her, but Birdy was getting worse, so Ginny put her foot down on the accelerator, hoping her mum would settle once she saw she was closer to home.

Birdy clutched her chest, and her sobs disappeared.

'Pull over,' yelled Suzanne.

Ginny glanced over her shoulder, seeing the state her mother was in. A lump hit the back of her throat as her legs turned to jelly. She quickly found a dip in the country lane and pulled in slowly. 'Mum, you need to calm down. It's going to be okay.'

'Call an ambulance,' said Suzanne, faffing about with the buttons on Birdy's blouse.

'What's happening?' Ginny started to cry as she fumbled with her bag to find her phone.

Suzanne threw open the door. 'Tell the operator she's having a heart attack.'

Ginny froze.

'Ginny!' Suzanne yelled. 'Ambulance. Now.'

Giving a destination was tricky when Ginny wasn't entirely sure what the stretch of road they were on was called. She did her best before helping Suzanne get Birdy out of the jeep.

Everything slowed.

The emergency operator's voice was slurred, the fields half-covered in snow were warped, and Suzanne was pressing on Birdy's chest while quietly singing some distorted song in time to her movements. It wasn't until sirens and lights filled the air that Ginny woke from the trance she had with her mother's lifeless face.

The paramedics took over from an exhausted Suzanne, and Ginny dropped to her knees by her side, feeling beyond useless.

'Mum. Mum.' Ginny nudged Birdy's shoulder after the medic packed the defibrillator away. 'Wake up, Mum. You can wake up now.'

'I'm sorry,' said a voice, but Ginny wasn't paying attention.

'Mum?' Ginny rested her head down upon her mother's forehead. 'Please wake up.'

Suzanne shuffled closer, resting a hand over Ginny's back. 'She's gone, love.'

'No. No.' Ginny sobbed. That couldn't be true. How could it? They just spoke in the car. Ginny had told her they were going home. They were going to have dinner in the café. How could she suddenly be dead? Nothing made sense. Not Suzanne, not the paramedics, and certainly not her tough-as-old-boots mother.

'Come on, Gin. Let the paramedics do their job,' whispered Suzanne.

'Job? Job? She's not a job. She's my mum!' Ginny burst into tears, unable to control the air restricting her lungs. Maybe she was having a heart attack too. Perhaps it would be for the best. After all, she had killed her mother.

Suzanne brought her to a stand, leaning her against the old army jeep. 'Just wait here. I'll sort everything.'

What was there to sort? Ginny knew she should be the one lying on the grassy verge, dead. How could she have put her mum through so much stress? She was a bad daughter. The worst. All those years, her mother had been right. Ginny Dean, you're worthless. Can't even look after your mum when she's poorly.

Ginny stared at the sky. More snow was due. Light, but snow all the same. Her thoughts drifted to the hotel with the chickens and donkey. She should have run away years ago like the Henshaws, then she wouldn't have been such a waste of space.

It was nice having a dream of a different life for a while. She was married, living in a farmhouse, she rescued animals during the day and snuggled with her husband every night. But that's all it was. A dream. She wasn't even speaking to Will. How could she have her happy farm life with him?

Her gaze went back to her mum being wheeled away to an ambulance. What life did she have? What life did she ever have? That stupid *Blue Man* boat only existed in her sleep, and the cold light of day was all that was left.

Ginny sat in her car, holding the steering wheel, not knowing what to do or where to go. Numbness took charge. That and the power of failure. Her mother's voice rang in her ears, haunting her. Nothing new. Birdy always haunted her. What difference would death make?

'I'll drive,' said Suzanne, her voice coming out of nowhere.

It didn't matter who did what. Nothing mattered anymore. Life had changed once again, but this time someone died because of her actions.

'I killed my mum,' she whispered, climbing out of the vehicle.

'No, you didn't. Don't say such a thing, Ginny. You listening?' Suzanne's voice faded into the icy breeze, and everything turned black.

CHAPTER 17

Will

Pulling up in the car park of Meadow House, Will was pleased to see the snow-cleared pathways. The large red-brick building was home to around eighty residents and had an excellent report for the past five years. He had no complaints about how well everything always looked.

Will passed by two large fake plants flanking the wide arched oak door. The scent of vanilla hit him as he entered the light and airy foyer. He approached the chunky desk, said hello to the lady sitting behind tapping away on a keyboard, signed in, then headed off to his grandmother's room.

A woman around his age waved and came out of a doorway along the corridor. She raised the small amount of knitting in her hand. 'Hey, Will. Nan's got me making a jumper. It's possible this is a cuff.' She laughed as she gestured to the room behind her. 'Bless her, she really misses being able to knit, and I don't know what I'm doing.'

Will glanced at the wool, then his hands, feeling blessed he didn't have arthritis. 'How's she getting on, Nat?'

'All right, mostly. It's a shame when your mind is fully there but your body lets you down.'

He wasn't sure what was worse, especially as he got to see his grandmother fading away. 'There's a blessing and a curse to getting old, isn't there? Anyway, best go see Gran,' he said, thumbing down the corridor. 'Good luck with your knitting.'

The woman went back to her grandmother, and Will heard them laughing.

It was heart-warming to witness families with so much love. He wished he had a backstory filled with weekend get-to-gethers and birthday celebrations.

The time spent with Ginny at the Happy Honeymoon Hotel was the most fun he'd had in ages. Acting like a couple, cuddling on the sofa, sharing a bed, even though just to sleep, it was so perfect in every way, and he missed her already. Missed that pretend life.

Will stopped to gaze out the window at the side garden. The winding pathway was clear, but the green patch that led to the pond was topped with snow. It looked so pretty untouched, and the water in the near distance finished off the tranquil scene nicely.

'Afternoon, Will,' said a male carer, passing by.

'Hi, Seth.' Will turned from the view, happy his grandmother was in such a beautiful home with such friendly staff. He glanced up at the security cameras, thinking he should get a wriggle on before someone watching might wonder why he was lurking.

A wide lift at the end of the corridor took him to the first floor, where he made his way three doors down to Babs's room.

Her door was open, showing off her favourite armchair and lamp from home.

'Hey, Babs. It's me, Willard.' He poked his head around the door to see his gran standing over by the window, shaking.

'Who are you?' she asked, backing away.

Will raised his palms. 'It's okay. It's just me, Willard.'

Babs furrowed her brow. 'You're not Willard. Leave me alone.' She huddled into the corner. 'Go away,' she yelled. 'Go away.'

Will panicked. He never knew what to do when she acted that way, and it was happening more often.

Babs continued to yell. Shaking and flapping a hand. She looked both angry and afraid.

Within moments, a carer rushed into the room. She smiled softly at Babs as she approached the other side of the bed. Holding out a hand, she said, 'Hello, Babs. Everything's okay. Let's go get a cup of tea, yeah?'

Will watched as Babs nodded and came out of the corner.

'Come on,' said the care worker softly, with her palm still on display. 'You come with me.' She glanced at Will as Babs walked around the bed. 'You okay?' she whispered.

'Yeah, thanks, Clare.'

Babs slipped her hand into Clare's and left the bedroom, not once glancing Will's way. All was calm, and he was scared about upsetting his gran again, so he told Clare he'd head off.

The walk back to his pickup truck felt lonely, and the spring he had in his step earlier had given up the ghost.

Will sat at the wheel and inhaled deeply. He truly had no one, and it hurt.

The Sunshine Centre came to mind. No matter what, everyone there always seemed to be in good spirits. Just what the doctor ordered. Maybe he should live in a respite centre. He certainly needed a break.

Will drove straight there, trying hard to wipe out the last hour from his mind. He hated seeing Babs in such a state, and he despised how seeing her made him feel even more unloved than he'd always felt.

Time and time again, he told himself not to return to the residential home. It wasn't doing either of them any favours. Babs would just freak out. And he would want to rip out his own heart.

Debra was in the doorway when Will parked outside the Sunshine Centre. She instantly waved, flashing a wide grin.

'Hi,' he said, approaching. 'I wanted to talk about me volunteering here.' He followed her into the warmth. 'I've decided to just help out with the adventure activities side of things in the summer months, if that would be okay.'

Debra laughed. 'You taking on too much, Will?'

'Feels that way. I tried to weigh everything up, see what would work best for me. I'm starting my own business in the new year. A tearoom in Port Berry, and I want to train for the RNLI. So, on that note, any other voluntary roles will have to be small, and I would like to stay helping at the Happy to Help Hub, seeing how it's on my doorstep.'

'Sounds like you've got it all figured out.'

Will nodded as he took a deep breath. 'We can only try and get our ducks in a row.'

'I have many ducks, definitely no row.' She narrowed her eyes. 'You okay? You look as though you lost your wallet.'

He pointed at his jaw. 'That bad, eh?'

Debra gestured towards the kitchen. 'I can fix that.'

'Fix what?'

She smiled and encouraged him to follow her. 'Some of the members are about to do some baking. You can join in, and it's not a suggestion.'

'Oh, I know I mentioned a tearoom, but, honestly, I don't know how to make a cake. I couldn't help with that task.'

Debra nudged him into the fun but sterile-looking room. 'You won't be teaching, Will. You're a member today.'

'But I haven't paid my way.'

'This one's on me. Come on, you certainly need a distraction.'

He always thought he could camouflage his emotions quite well. Maybe Debra was too much of a professional in the field of sadness.

'Hello, Deb,' said a young lad. 'I have laid out all the ingredients for the chocolate fudge cake. See?' His pale eyes scanned the items as his finger checked over each one.

'Ooh, well done, Alfie.' Debra approached the white countertop to take a closer look. 'I look forward to having a slice.'

'It's for my mum,' said Alfie, still bouncing a finger over the items. 'Wait. I can adjust my calculations.' He stopped moving his hand and silently stared at the round eight-inch cake tin. 'Yes, I can cut you a slice.' He looked up at Will. 'Are you having one too?'

Will wasn't sure what to say. The lad hardly looked impressed that he had to alter his slice sizes the first time. Did he really need to stress the youngster further?

Debra jumped in. 'I was wondering if Will could help you make your cake. He's new so might need some guidance.'

Will breathed out a small laugh. 'Might? Try, definitely.'

Alfie stepped closer, offering a hand. 'I can show you, Will.'

Will went to hold his hand, but Alfie quickly dropped his arm and headed back to the ingredients.

'We have to put the dry ingredients in one bowl and the wet in another, and we have to make a small cup of coffee.' Alfie gave the impression he was waiting for Will to approve.

Will simply nodded, even though the coffee had thrown him. 'Where should I start?'

Alfie walked over to the large metal basin. 'You have to wash your hands, as it's important to be hygienic.' He stood still, holding a green tea towel ready for Will to dry his hands.

Will complied as two more members entered the kitchen to make their own cakes. He said hello, then turned back to Alfie. 'Now what?'

Alfie handed him a white apron. 'It will keep your clothes clean. Cocoa powder likes to fly off. My mum says.'

Debra nodded, perching on a chair in the corner. 'Will is a newbie, Alfie, so we'd better make sure he doesn't use any icing sugar just yet either.'

The lad held nothing but seriousness in his face as he looked up at Will. 'Mum says, black icing takes no prisoners. You can spread the chocolate fudge frosting. You should be safe with that. But as you're new, the odds of you getting messy are still high.'

'You have been warned,' said Debra, chuckling.

Will got to mix the dry ingredients in a large cream bowl while Alfie supervised.

'Don't stir anti-clockwise,' said the lad, frowning at the wooden spoon.

Will changed direction, thinking it best to stick to orders, as Alfie seemed to have a routine.

'When I pour in the wet mixture, you mustn't over stir, but do get out any lumps.' Alfie went about lining a baking tin.

'This is a very wet cake,' said Will. 'I thought you had to fluff them up?'

Debra shrugged. 'The butter and chocolate are melted together with this one, then mixed with the coffee.'

Will laughed. 'I could do with a coffee.'

'You can't eat or drink while you are baking,' said Alfie. 'You have to concentrate.' He poured the mixture out evenly into the prepared baking tins.

'Yes, chef.' Will saluted with the spoon, then picked up what was left of the evaporated milk for a sniff. 'Erm, I don't think this has been used. Did we leave it out the mix?'

Alfie removed it from his hand and placed it back in its spot on the counter. 'That's for the frosting. Please don't move things.'

Will stepped back. 'Right.' He grinned at Debra before turning back to his boss. 'So, now what?'

Alfie carefully placed the baking tins in the oven. 'We wait until they are baked, then we wait until they cool, and then we can frost them.

'Meanwhile?' asked Will.

'I draw a dragon,' said Alfie, washing his hands and hanging up his apron on a hook by the door. 'By the time I've finished the tail, the cakes will be ready.' And with that, he left.

Will looked at Debra. 'He's very precise.'

'Yes, it helps keep him calm.' She climbed off her chair. 'Right, mister, let's go draw a dragon.'

'That I might be able to do without help.'

Debra's eyes widened. 'You can draw?'

'Doodle pretty well. Does that count?'

She laughed, then gestured at Alfie, who had already sat at the smallest table in the art room and lined up his pencils. 'Just don't touch his stuff.'

'Got it.' Will sat at the table next to the lad's and received an approving nod for his wise choice. He picked a sheet of plain paper from the pile in the middle, then set about sketching a friendly dragon.

He was really getting into his drawing groove when Alfie knocked on his table. Will glanced down at the knuckles still resting there. 'Am I done?'

'The cakes are. We must take them out of the oven to cool. Please stand.'

Will did as he was told and headed for the kitchen. 'Mmm, smells like heaven.'

'It smells like chocolate cake,' said Alfie, as though educating his new friend.

Will helped place the hot tins on a metal cooling rack. 'Should we remove these?'

'No. The cake layers are very soft. They cool in the tin.' Alfie took a step back, assessing where Will had placed one of the tins.

'I can move it if it's wrong,' said Will.

'It's where it should be.' Alfie glanced up at him. 'We can colour in our dragons now.'

Will was looking forward to the frosting part, hoping to lick the spoon once finished. He went back to the art room to finish his drawing, which he decided wasn't as bad as he first thought.

Debra joined his side, offering a hot mug of coffee. 'Here. Well deserved. You should come to the centre more often.'

'All I did was follow orders. Life's always simpler when someone else tells you what to do.'

'Is that your way of saying you miss the navy?'

Will tipped his head from side to side. 'Hmm, yes and no.'

'Well, feel free to come here whenever.'

'I told you, I'll help out in the summer months.'

Debra nudged his elbow. 'I meant as a member.' She smiled softly. 'Honestly, Will, I think this place is what you need right now.' She tapped her chest. 'Trust me, I know these things.'

He had to admit, ever since he walked through the door the weight dropped off his shoulders, and making a cake with Alfie had wiped his mind from all his problems. It was nice having somewhere to go where he could simply breathe and forget about the world for a while. He felt that at the hotel with Ginny. If only every day was as relaxing.

'Sure, I'll sign up.' He smiled at Debra. 'But does that mean I won't be able to become a helper?'

She shook her head. 'No. You can be both. We have lots of members here who help. Take Alfie, for example. He taught you how to bake a cake, didn't he?'

'I might offer him a job at the tearoom once it's open.'

Alfie looked up. 'I can do that. My shift would be between eight and twelve, and only on Thursdays, and you'll have to pay my mum on the day at zero eight hundred hours.' The slightest hint of a smile hit his mouth, making Will bite back a laugh.

'Yes, sir.' Will figured chocolate fudge cake would be the first item to hit the menu board. At least it was a start.

Debra started colouring in Will's dragon's tail while humming, and Alfie was back to being engrossed in his own drawing. Some people were pottering around, quietly chatting to each other, and an old lady sat comfortably in a wingback chair, crocheting a doily.

'That's Mrs Gibbons. She comes in most days just for the company, as she's got no family. We don't charge her.' Debra placed a finger to her lips and grinned. 'Shh! Else they'll all want freebies, then we won't be able to keep this place up and running.'

'It's a brilliant centre, Deb. Can't fault it at all.'

'Thanks. We rely on payments and charity. Any time we have fundraising events, make sure you join in, okay?'

'Definitely. Shame these aren't in every town.'

Debra glanced around the room. 'Yeah, we all need some peace from time to time.'

Will realized he'd been searching for inner peace his whole life. Hopefully, his new beginning would bring him happiness.

I'll take Ginny my slice of cake. Maybe it'll break the ice.

He smiled to himself, then reached for his phone vibrating in his pocket. 'I'll just take this outside,' he told Debra.

The reception area was empty, so Will answered the call there.

'Hello, Jed.' He was about to tell him he was at the Sunshine Centre, but Jed got in first.

'Thought you might like to know, son. Ginny's mum passed away today.'

Will's heart thumped. He didn't know what to say or what he should do. A thousand things whirled through his mind.

Jed's voice brought him back to base. 'She's home with her friends at the moment. Perhaps you could call on her later.'

Will wasn't sure if that was a good idea, but at the same time he wanted to run to her immediately. 'Erm, thanks for letting me know.' He hung up, then went back to let Debra know he was heading off.

Alfie shot up. 'You can't leave now. We haven't frosted the cake.'

That was the least of Will's worries, but after a stern look from Debra, and a worried one from the lad, he knew he had to complete his mission.

'Thanks for that,' said Debra, following him to the kitchen. 'Alfie doesn't do well if someone messes with his routine, especially if he let you into it in the beginning.'

Will nodded. 'Yeah, that's what I thought. I won't let him down. I'll stay until he doesn't need me anymore.'

'That'll be once the cake has been sliced. Let him do that, then you can go.'

Will got frosting, doing it just the way Alfie liked. 'Thanks for letting me help bake your cake, mate.'

Alfie's big eyes almost smiled. 'It's our cake, Will.'

'Yes, you're right. It is. And I can't wait to take a slice home.' There was no way he was giving it to Ginny now, as he was pretty sure she'd shove it in his face.

He still had no idea how to handle the situation as he pulled up at the bottom of Berry Hill. He'd already upset her with the tea shop idea and didn't want to risk upsetting her further.

Go home, Pendleton. Now's not the time.

After a swift shake of the head and a deep sigh, Will drove away. As much as he wanted to be there for Ginny, something told him it was best all round if he didn't show his face right now. She had her friends around her, so he knew she was being cared for.

CHAPTER 18

Ginny

A bitter wind whipped through Ginny as she tied multi-coloured Christmas lights above the door and windows of Harbour Light Café. It was about time she made the place look festive, as all the other shops along Harbour End Road had already decorated for the season.

'Oh, goodness, really!' she mumbled, as the wire slipped from her hand.

The ladder wobbled as a van sped by, splashing spits of slushy snow up from the gutter.

'Oi!' yelled Ginny. 'Slow down.'

'Need a hand?' asked Samuel, picking up the fallen lights.

'That's the third time I've dropped that.' She thanked him as he raised his arm her way.

Ginny secured the lights in place, then climbed down to stand back and take in her lopsided job.

Samuel pointed to her left. 'It just needs pulling up a touch that end. Here, let me.'

Before she could respond, he was sorting the matter, and to be fair, he was much better at the task. At least he had more patience.

Councillor Seabridge approached. 'About time, Ginny. For a minute there I thought you were going to let the street down.'

She narrowed her eyes at his greying bushy eyebrows, not one bit in the mood for his comments.

'We win awards, you know,' he added, the boom in his voice rattling her eardrums.

Ginny folded her arms. 'It's the first of December, Oliver. I wouldn't say I'm late to the party.'

His beady blue eyes sparkled as Samuel switched on the lights. 'Ooh, speaking of which. Don't forget we have the tree lighting ceremony on Saturday.'

'Yes, I know.' Seeing how it was on the first Saturday in December every year, it wasn't hard for her to forget, but she couldn't be bothered to say.

'Good, good. See you there.' He waved a hand to Samuel. 'You too, Mr Powell.'

Samuel gave him a quick salute, then grinned at Ginny.

Councillor Seabridge made his way towards the pub, and Ginny invited Samuel inside the café.

'I'll make you a cuppa.'

'Yes, then we can talk business.'

She watched him take a seat at the table nearest the large shiny coffee machine as she went about making the tea.

'I'm pleased you called me here for a meeting about the café. I know I've mentioned using it in the past, but I didn't think you'd ever agree,' he added.

'I'm not really sure how this food bank café thing is going to work.'

'Basically, anyone in need of food will be able to come in here between half four and half six and eat for free two evenings a week. I'm going to send one of my chefs over to assess your kitchen, as he'll like to see what's available for him.'

Ginny joined him at the table. 'Will I be expected to work?'

Samuel shook his head. 'No. But you can if you want. I normally have one paid member of staff, and the rest are volunteers. So feel free to fit in a shift if you can.'

146

'But won't I have to come back to lock up each evening?'

Samuel shook his head, and Ginny had no idea why she asked that question. After all, it wasn't as if she had anywhere else to go now that her mother's ashes were being prepared to be sent directly to Lee, as requested.

Peaceful Cremation Services had handled everything, from collecting Birdy's body to the unattended cremation, and even promised to deliver the ashes within two weeks. Ginny wanted to hold a small memorial, but Birdy had already made the arrangements for her own send-off, and it didn't include sausage rolls in the church hall.

Lee told Ginny he'd wait till springtime, then take a trip on the ferry to France, and they could secretly sprinkle her ashes into the English Channel, also Birdy's request, as that was where she'd met Lee's dad, the so-called love of her life.

Ginny had never felt so left out before. She wasn't even given the opportunity to say a proper goodbye. She swallowed hard, attempting to focus on her conversation with Samuel. It was quite annoying how her emotions were chopping and changing every five minutes since her mother's death. 'Erm, so . . .' She'd lost her train of thought.

'Hey, you okay?' Samuel reached across the table to hold her hand.

'Yeah, sorry, my mind just wandered.'

His soft smile was filled with sympathy. 'Your mum?'

Ginny shrugged. 'Feels weird, Sam.'

'I know. When I lost my parents, I was all over the place for ages. Grief doesn't have any rules. We just have to take it one day at a time.'

'I would have liked to have had some sort of memorial service for her. Just a gathering in my house or something. Nothing fancy. Just a goodbye, of sorts. Oh, I don't know.'

Samuel nodded. 'You can still do that. You don't need ashes or coffins. You just have your own moment where you say goodbye. Perhaps play a song, or put a small plaque on a bench, maybe you could plant a rose bush in your garden and say a prayer or something.'

He had a point, and it might make her feel better if she did say a few words, but it wasn't what her mum wanted. Birdy had been specific in her instructions, and none of it included Ginny.

'Maybe I can hang up a birdhouse in her memory.'

Samuel took a mouthful of tea, then smiled softly. 'Why was she called Birdy?'

'It was a nickname her mother had given her. No one knew why, but it stuck.'

'Well, I think a birdhouse in your garden is a great idea.'

'I'll wait until I move.'

Samuel's amber eyes flashed her way. 'I didn't know you were moving. Lottie's not said.'

'Oh, I've been mulling it over, but now I've made up my mind. I want to go inland. Buy a farmhouse. Have a bit of land out back for rescue chickens. Maybe a rescue donkey.'

Samuel laughed. 'A donkey?'

'Maybe.' She grinned, then sipped her tea.

'Hey, in all seriousness, it's nice you have this idea, but don't you think you should wait a while before making any moves? What I mean to say is, is it wise to change your life while you're grieving?'

Ginny knew where he was coming from, but she felt her life had changed regardless, so what difference would anything make now? 'I've already made my mind up, and I'm going to see the estate agents next week to put my house and flat on the market.' She pointed at the ceiling. 'I'd rather just get on with things.'

The thought of her new home, rescuing animals, and not staring out to sea each morning and night wondering where her soulmate was would do her the world of good. At least, she hoped it would.

'Well, if you're sure.' Samuel glanced around. 'I can help you move when the time comes, so make sure you let me know.' He tipped his head to peer at her. 'You're not alone, Ginny. We'll all help you, you know that, right?'

She looked up and smiled at the kindness coming her way. 'Yeah, I know, chick. And just so you know, I am definitely not alone, as I now have my mum's cat to look after.' She huffed while shaking her head. 'I tried to give her back to the lady Mum got her from, but she was having none of it. So, first rescue animal, tick.'

'I told Lottie I saw a black moggy in our garden yesterday. I bet that was her.'

'Probably. As soon as a door or window opens, she's out. I'll be glad once she's older and I don't have to worry so much.'

Samuel laughed. 'I felt that way about my little sister.'

'Ooh, how is Hannah getting on since you moved out?'

'Good. Felix and his brother moved in with her, and they seem happy enough.'

'Oh, yes, I forgot Felix helps care for Rupert. Aww, bless him. I don't know how I'd get on with three missing limbs.'

'It's quite surprising how we cope with the crap life throws our way.'

Ginny nodded, thinking of everything she'd been through. 'I guess we just get on with it, don't we?'

'Yeah, when it's not messing with our mind.'

She leaned forward and patted his hand. 'You did good, Sam.'

He breathed out a quiet laugh. 'Oh, I'm still fighting demons.'

Me too.

Ginny banged her palms together. 'Right, let's turn this café into an extension of the Happy to Help Hub. You get your people down as soon as possible, and perhaps we can open for the winter.'

'Great. One last thing. How would you feel about me buying your properties?'

The question floored her for a moment.

'You don't have to decide straight away,' he added.

'Sorry, no, it's not that. You just caught me off guard, that's all. Honestly, Sam, I wasn't expecting you to say that.'

'If you're selling, then I'm buying. I'd like to add your house into the renovations we're doing. It'll create way more floor space for Lottie's wheelchair to whizz around, and, yes, she often likes to whizz.'

Ginny laughed, knowing that to be true. She glanced at the fishing net hanging above her. 'Why do you want the flat?'

'I was thinking of having a headquarters for the Les Powell Trust. Most of my staff work from home, but it would be nice to have a place, rather than my house.'

'Makes sense.'

'So, will you consider my offer?'

Ginny beamed with delight at the opportunity to get things moving along faster than expected. 'Consider it a done deal.' She shoved out her hand. 'Do you want to spit shake?'

Samuel laughed. 'No. This is good enough. And thanks.'

'No, thank you. This makes life so much easier. We'll sort solicitors, and I'll sell at market value.'

'Sounds fair.' He sat back and laughed. 'Wait until I tell Lottie. Not sure what she'll make of another extension.'

'Oh, she'll love it. It'll give her more garden space for her allotment.'

'Yes, that's definitely coming along. Although she does miss George's help.'

Ginny had nothing but fond memories of the man who lived in the house between Lottie's and hers. 'He was a good egg.'

'He certainly was. I've hired a gardener to help out a bit. Lottie wasn't too keen at first, but now she appreciates his help, especially as I'm all brown thumbs.'

A fizz of excitement fluttered into Ginny's tummy, creating her first inside smile since her mum died. Was her farmhouse dream actually about to come true so quickly? Oh yes it was, and she really wanted to happy dance but thought it best to stay seated.

'Hey, Sam, by the time it takes everything to go through, and for me to find somewhere to live, it probably won't be until the new year, so if you want to surprise Lottie for Christmas, I can keep my mouth shut until then.'

'I like your thinking. Yes, let's do that. I'll wrap up a door key and pop it under the tree.'

'Aww, she'll love that, then no doubt tell me off for moving away.'

'Will you go far?'

Ginny shook her head. 'No way. I love Port Berry too much. No, I'll look inland, see what's available. Might have to buy a bit of land and build. See what happens.'

'Or you could buy Roger Lane's old place,' said Luna, coming out the toilet. 'Artie said he was putting his dad's home up for sale after Christmas. Have a word with him. That's a farmhouse with land.'

Ginny's mouth gaped for a moment. 'Luna, what are you doing in here?'

Luna thumbed behind her. 'Using the loo.'

'Yes, but I could've locked you in. If it weren't for me having a meeting here with Samuel, I'd have already gone home.'

Luna sat in the chair to her side. 'Don't you check the toilet before you go?'

'Well, yeah, but—'

'There you go then,' said Luna. 'I was perfectly safe.'

Ginny glanced over at the toilet door. 'What have you been doing in there all this time?'

'Listening to you two.'

Samuel bit his bottom lip as he laughed, and Ginny could do little else but chuckle too.

'So,' added Luna, fixing her eyes on Ginny, 'you going to talk to Artie Lane about his dad's place or what?'

'Erm, well, it does sound like a good idea.' Ginny looked at Samuel for confirmation, even though she wasn't sure why she was after a second opinion. She knew Roger Lane's house very well. Passed it enough times on her way to school.

Samuel nodded his agreement. 'I'll pop over there with you tomorrow if you like.'

'She likes,' said Luna, stealing his cup of tea. 'This is a good move for Ginny, I know.'

Ginny didn't want one of Luna's psychic readings, so she decided not to ask questions. 'I'll have to give Artie a call.'

'No need,' said Luna. 'I rang him when I was in the loo. He's expecting you at the farmhouse at eleven sharp. Morning, that is.'

Ginny and Samuel swapped a dumbfounded look.

'Why is Roger selling his home?' asked Ginny.

Luna's smile dropped. 'They're putting him in a home. Poor bugger. Can't fend for himself anymore.'

The small amount of happiness Ginny had just felt, dispersed. If she hadn't taken her mum to visit the care home, she was sure her mother would still be alive. It was too much stress, she was certain.

'Oh no, don't you go down that road, love,' said Luna, taking Ginny's hand.

'What road?' asked Samuel.

'She blames herself for her mother's death.'

Samuel shook his head at Ginny. 'No, don't do that. Your mum's heart attack would have happened anyway. Lottie told me that's what the doctor said.' He looked at Luna. 'I had this with Lottie when George died. Only, she blamed me until she found out heart disease had crept up on him.'

Ginny knew what they said made sense, and she had taken on board the autopsy report, but it still niggled at her, and she was sure her mum would blame her too. 'I can't help it,' she whispered, silently chastising herself for almost breaking down in front of her friends.

Samuel's voice was as quiet as hers as he said, 'I blamed myself for the death of my parents. If I hadn't needed the loo so badly, my dad wouldn't have pulled onto a verge along a dual carriageway, and that lorry wouldn't have crashed into them. See, Ginny, it's easily done. Life is one big domino effect. What we do in this moment affects the next and so on, but we're not to know what's around the next corner.'

'Well, some of us do,' said Luna, sitting back, hugging Samuel's tea.

'At least you can warn people,' said Ginny.

Luna shook her head. 'Doesn't always work that way. Especially when it comes to my own. I had a feeling something wasn't right with our Lisa, but I didn't know what, and look how that turned out.'

Ginny could see Samuel didn't know the story. 'Lisa was Alice's sister. Benny's mum. She died of cancer when he was little.'

'Sorry, Luna. I knew Alice had a sister, but I hadn't heard the details,' said Samuel.

Luna raised her mug in a cheers motion. 'Thanks. So you see, we have to muddle on through those tough times and carry on living our life without blame destroying us. You didn't kill Birdy, love, and you, Samuel Powell, didn't cause that accident, and I'm not to blame for our Lisa.'

A moment of silence filled the café.

'You're right, Luna,' said Ginny, knowing it to be true, but it was so easy for her to take the blame. She'd been trained to all her life.

A knock on the door interrupted them, and Ginny waved Jan inside.

'Ooh, got room for a little one?' said Jan, blowing into her hands. 'And a cuppa. Blimming freezing out there.'

Ginny got up to make her a cup of tea. 'So, why is our resident therapist walking about in the cold? You just done a shift at the Hub?'

Jan removed her coat and hat, releasing her mass of blonde curls. 'No, Lottie sent me to talk to you. She said you'd be in here with Samuel.'

'Who is just leaving,' he told them, standing. He tipped his head to Ginny. 'I'll pick you up in the morning.' He said goodbye and left, leaving Ginny looking over at January Riley.

'I can stay,' said Luna.

Jan's dark eyes smiled at Luna. 'I'd prefer to talk to Ginny alone.'

Luna tutted. 'Pfft! She doesn't need therapy, Jan. She just needs her friends. Anyway, we beat you to it. Ginny's sorted now. Right, love?'

Ginny plonked a cuppa in front of Jan. 'I'm not sure what Lottie's playing at sending you in here, but I'm fine. I don't need therapy.'

'She's getting chickens and a donkey,' said Luna, receiving a frown from Jan.

Ginny grinned. 'Honestly, Jan, I'm doing okay, but thanks. If I do need to talk, I will call you, I promise.' That was a lie. As much as she needed to clear away her past, the last thing she wanted was her friends knowing anything about it, no matter how professional they were.

Jan seemed to be assessing her every move, which only made it harder to keep her face neutral.

'The girl's fine,' said Luna. 'This place is transforming into one of Samuel's food bank cafés soon, so that'll keep her busy. And then there's the new fella.'

'What new fella?' asked Jan.

Ginny frowned. 'There is no new fella. Anyway, you two sup up, as I need to get home. I've got a cat to feed as well now.' The exchange of pointed looks between her friends didn't go unnoticed, but she ignored them by clearing away the cardboard box that held the café's Christmas decorations.

'Good luck tomorrow,' said Luna, heading for the door. 'Not that you need it. That farmhouse is yours already, love.' She tapped her nose, then left.

'Why is she wishing you luck?' asked Jan.

'I'm selling my house and flat and looking for a home with some land. I want to look after some rescue animals.'

'Hmm.'

'Don't hmm me, Jan. I don't need you scrambling about in my brain. I told you, I'm fine.'

'It's a lot of changes for you right now.'

Ginny hugged the cardboard box to her chest. 'Yeah, but change can be a good thing.'

Jan nodded. 'True, but only for the right reasons.'

The statement made Ginny think about her decisions for a minute. Yes, things had changed, and a lot of things recently, but being snowed-in at the hotel gave her a new dream that truly warmed her heart. She did know what she wanted, and she had the means to close the deal on her goal.

'You know what, Jan, it feels right.'

Jan smiled. 'Well, then, that's good enough for me.'

Ginny swirled one hand in the box and pulled out a silver star. Normally she would hang it in the window and wonder if she had someone out there who could be her North Star. She shoved it back inside, deciding that this year things would be different. Who needed North Stars and soulmates anyway? She had something new to focus on, and it didn't include her abusive mother, inconsiderate brother, or some new fella hell-bent on stealing her tearoom idea.

Nope! Ginny Dean was on a new mission, and nothing was going to get her down ever again.

She hoped.

Perhaps she could put the star in the window. It wouldn't hurt, and it did normally go there. It didn't symbolize anything. It was just a star for Christmas. It wasn't as if she thought about Will Pendleton anymore anyway. He didn't even bother to send his sympathies when her mum died. So, no, there was no connection between him and her star. None whatsoever.

'I'm hanging up my star,' she mumbled, defiantly marching towards the window.

Climbing the stepladder to place it high, her mouth gaped as she spotted Will over the road, staring out to sea.

Are you looking for your North Star?

He huddled his arms into his chest, then walked off in the direction of the B&B.

Something inside Ginny snapped. She took the star, ran outside, and yelled his name.

Will turned, surprise in his eyes.

155

Ginny shoved the star straight into his chest, forcing him to catch the shiny item. 'You do know my mum died, don't you?' she yelled into the gust of wind blowing around them.

He gave the most pathetic nod she'd ever seen.

'And you didn't think to pop by, see how I was doing?'

'I thought you hated my guts because of the tea shop thingy.'

Without saying another word, she marched back to her café, slamming the door for good measure.

Jan stepped away from the window, lowering the mug of tea from her lips. 'Good to see you're healing nicely, Gin. Now, sit down. We're going to talk some things through.'

Ginny glanced at the door. 'I do need therapy, Jan,' she said quietly, deflated on every level. 'Look what I just did to Will. That was so unfair.' She went to stand. 'I should go apologize.'

Jan waved her back to the seat. 'Take a breath, Ginny. Let's have a chat.'

CHAPTER 19

Will

The annual Christmas tree lighting at Old Market Square was supposed to be a happy event, but Will couldn't find his holly jolly anywhere.

All around were food stalls and smiling faces. The church choir was on top form, belting out merry songs while the bell ringers rang their instruments lined up on tables over by the entrance to Anchorage Park.

Will was due to perform with the Berry Buoys later to raise some money to buy chickens for the Christmas parcels. He was in no mood, and the reindeer antlers Jed stuck on his head didn't help matters.

The smell of hotdogs filled the air along with laughter and light snowflakes. Councillor Seabridge was gathering people closer to the tall Christmas tree while little children ran around his podium, waving tinsel hats and candy canes.

Will gazed at the steeple of the beautiful stone-built church peeping over a small hill, no more than a two-minute walk away, wondering if sitting inside might help clear his muggy head. He had a rotten cold, his throat was itchy, his eyes weary, and his heart torn in two by Ginny, who for some reason had practically stabbed him with a star a few days ago. He had thought about running after her, even contacting her the next day, but things seemed so messy between them. He really had no idea what to do for the best so ended up doing nothing at all.

Jed came bustling through the crowd, holding a disposable cup filled with mulled wine. 'Neck that, son. It'll sort your pipes.'

Will sniffed the drink, wishing he could simply snuggle in bed with some honey and lemon. Ginny would be another choice, but the idea of her becoming his partner had flown south for the winter. Probably forever, knowing his luck. Why did she get so far into his heart? He sipped the warm liquid and sighed. 'I'm not sure I'll be able to sing, mate.'

'Course you will.'

'I'll make us sound off.'

Jed flapped a hand, then used his other to wave at whoever it was dressed as Father Christmas. 'If it gets too bad, just mime. I swear that's what Artie does.' He slapped Will on the back, making him cough. 'Catch you later.'

Will sneezed, then blew his nose while glancing around to see who else was about.

Sophie and Matt were huddled in their white seafood truck, selling small pots of prawns among other snackable dishes, and they had drawn quite a few customers their way.

Will imagined his tearoom having its own market stall. Yep, cupcakes and Christmas-themed cookies would go down a treat on such a day. He mentally added it to his list, then wondered if Ginny would hate him even more.

Building a life in Port Berry wasn't as much fun any longer, and he was considering leaving. He could still live somewhere close to his grandmother, even though she no longer knew who he was, but the old fishing village had already got its hooks into him, or rather Ginny had. He really had to do something about their lack of relationship, but what?

'Hi, Will,' said Alice, passing with Benny. 'We're off to get a hot chocolate before the lights go on. You want one?'

He held up his drink. 'All good, thanks.' He sneezed again as they walked away.

Spencer and Robson were playing with the bells, laughing while trying to join in with the singers, and Will wished he could feel as carefree. He was waved over their way but declined, turning towards a winding road that led to a row of quaint cottage-style shops, hoping to find a chemist.

Nothing was open except a small slightly lopsided pub called The Crooked Hole.

Will tossed his drink into a nearby bin as he debated going home or grabbing a brandy, but then the noise around him grew louder, informing him of the tree lighting ceremony.

Following the moving crowd, Will made his way back to the square, finding a bit of space over at Sea Shanty Shack's trailer.

Councillor Seabridge addressed his audience. 'Hello, and welcome. I hope you've all had time to write down your wishes for the tree.' He gave a nod over to a table where people scribbled notes onto paper stars, sealing them in plastic baubles.

Will hadn't noticed that before. What could he wish for that he hadn't been wishing for his whole life?

'Make sure you do one,' said a small voice from behind him.

He turned to see Luna smiling his way. 'Not sure I believe in wishes anymore.'

Luna shoved a piece of her flyaway white hair under her woolly red hat. 'It's Christmas, Will. Time for miracles.'

He huffed out a laugh. Snuggling down into his navy scarf he turned back to the tree.

'On the count of three,' boomed Councillor Seabridge, even though he had a microphone wedged onto the lectern.

The crowd began the count. Will was quite possibly the only one there not to join in, and not because of his sore throat but because he felt deflated.

Suddenly multicoloured lights filled the square, causing lots of oohs and cooing.

'Now, children first,' said Councillor Seabridge, smiling widely as the little ones approached to hang their wishes.

Will thought about the star hanging in his bedroom at the B&B. Well, he had to do something with Ginny's *gift*.

'If you could make any of your dreams come true, what would it be?' asked Luna.

He went to respond by telling her he didn't have any, but she'd disappeared into the crowd, leaving behind her planted seed.

Had anyone asked him that before life in Port Berry, he would have told them all about his years wishing for a family. A home. But oddly enough none of that entered his mind when Luna asked. Ginny overshadowed the lot.

Blast that bloody honeymoon hotel. It had changed so much. All he wanted was the same life with her that Mr and Mrs Henshaw had, perhaps without the hotel part, and definitely minus the nauseating amount of pink.

Even though Will had his wants and wishes like any other human, he wasn't one for feeling sorry for himself, at least certainly not on the level he seemed to be at lately. Oh, it was all too much.

Sod it! I'm going home.

Just as he turned, Jed grabbed his elbow and marched him to the other Berry Buoys. 'We're up, son.'

Great!

Being one of the taller men in the choir, Will stood at the back, hoping he could blend into the Christmas wreath-making stall beside him, hosted by Lottie, with a fussing Samuel, faffing with a blanket on her lap.

No such luck. Two spotlights came on from somewhere, highlighting the singers, and Jed started the first song.

Will's throat caved immediately, so he did what Jed had suggested. He mimed. Swinging his storm lamp and trying for festive cheer, he made his way through two songs before spotting Ginny in the crowd, watching him.

Her gaze quickly diverted as soon as he locked eyes with her, so he lowered his head a touch, thinking the cobbles friendlier.

Lottie swayed some mistletoe along to the melody, which was the last thing Will wanted to see. The kiss he had shared with Ginny at the hotel was sure to stay with him forever, never mind anything else they shared.

It seemed like a million lifetimes ago.

Will chanced a look at the crowd. Ginny was gone, along with his spirit. He faked his way to the end of the performance, bowing and waving like the others while thanking folk for putting money in their collection buckets. At least he'd helped buy chickens.

Chickens and a donkey. Perhaps a cat. Worked for the Henshaws. Will groaned inwardly at the thought. Maybe that could be his Christmas tree wish.

He marched over to the table to scribble something on a star about wiping his memory of Ginny Dean, but as soon as the pen hit the paper, he wrote something entirely different.

I wish for all of Ginny's dreams to come true.

He sealed the bauble, then went over to the tree to find the highest available branch.

'Lovely,' said Luna, passing by.

Will frowned, then smiled when he saw Mabel struggling to reach the branch she wanted for her wish. 'Here, let me help.' He pulled it down for her, then gently put it back in place once she was done.

'Ooh, thanks, lovey. The kids touch all the ones down the bottom.'

'What do they do with the wishes after the tree comes down?'

Mabel pointed at the cobbles. 'Firepit. Not everyone bothers turning up for that part though, and Father Stephen reckons it's dangerous, but Councillor Seabridge won't back down. Stubborn as a mule, that one.'

Will wasn't too bothered what happened to his Christmas wish, as long as it came true. What a thought. And what if somehow Ginny read his wish? He didn't sign his name, so all should be good in wish world. He laughed to himself, then sneezed.

'You should be in bed,' said Mabel. 'I'll make you some chicken noodle soup tomorrow. That'll see you right.'

He thanked her, then watched her walk over to her friends sitting down to make Christmas wreaths with Lottie and Spencer.

A rumbling stomach told Will dinner was due, so he browsed the food stalls, deciding on burger and chips.

He took his food into the park and sat by the pond, away from the children's small funfair rides. The back of his eyes still twinkled from staring at the Christmas tree; he didn't need to add creepy tinkling music into his aching eardrums.

The ducks huddled on the other side of the water, showing no interest in burger bun crumbs or dropped crisps.

It was nice sitting alone in the dim light of a park lamp while gentle snowflakes continued to fall. The noise around him was muffled and the air not so stuffy from a hundred different scents.

Maybe it was staring at the water that calmed him, or perhaps it was feeding his weary body that relaxed him somewhat. All he knew was, for the first time that day, he felt settled.

'Mind if I join you?' asked someone behind him.

Yes, actually. I want to be alone.

He glanced over his shoulder to see Robson, holding a cardboard box filled with fish and chips. 'Sure.'

Robson sat down, offering a chip.

Will raised his biodegradable box. 'Got my own, thanks. You after a bit of peace as well?'

'Hmm,' replied Robson, snaffling a hot chip. 'Might as well put my feet up while I can. Gets busy at the pub this time of year.'

'Yeah, I can imagine. Let me know if you need an extra set of hands for anything.' Will lifted his half-eaten burger. 'I'm sure I can pull a few pints or something.'

Robson laughed. 'I might hold you to that.'

Will swallowed some more food, sitting in silence for a while. 'Do you get much family time when you have a pub?'

'I haven't got any family around here, Will. My aunt and uncle, who raised me, moved to Australia, so just me now. Well, and my Port Berry lot. Can't shake them off if I tried.' He nudged Will's elbow. 'Come to the pub for Crimbo dinner, won't you? We'll all be there.'

Mabel had offered to cook for him that day, but he knew she normally spent Christmas with her friends, as Alice had told him, so he pretended he had something planned. He was invited to his grandmother's care home but declined, afraid in case he scared Babs again.

'Yeah, I'll be there. Thanks, mate.'

'No worries,' said Robson, continuing to eat. 'You're one of us now.'

'People keep telling me that.' *Doubt Ginny feels the same.*

'Port Berry is an easy place to fit into, Will. There's always something going on and plenty of people to chat to.'

Will chuckled. 'You would say that. You own a pub.'

Robson nodded. 'You do hear some stories.'

'Yeah? What's yours?'

'All a bit doom and gloom for this time of year.'

'Not sure why we're supposed to be so happy just because it's Christmas. Loads of people get depressed in December.'

Robson slowly nodded as he ate more chips. 'Yeah, it can be lonely too. Well, I'm too busy to think about missing my wife, but it still slips in when I'm about to pull a cracker or something.'

Will had heard bits and pieces about everyone in Port Berry, thanks mostly to Mabel and Jed, so he knew Robson's wife had died of breast cancer at a young age. 'Sorry about your wife,' was all he could think to say.

'Ah, me too, mate. It just goes to show, you never know what's round the next corner.'

Will had seen how close Ginny was with Robson, and as much as he didn't want to ask, the thought of some history between them niggled at him. 'You ever thought about seeing someone again? I noticed you and Ginny . . .'

'Whoa!' Robson laughed, wiping his mouth from the vinegar-drenched chip he'd just shoved in. 'You don't have any worries about me with our Gin. She's like a sister.'

'I wasn't worried.' He totally lied and got the impression Robson knew.

'You were so worried.'

Will muffled his laugh, prompting a cough and sneeze. Apologizing, he laughed again. 'Am I that obvious?'

Robson offered an unopened bottle of water that Will gladly took. 'It's more Ginny who is that obvious. Look, mate, I've known her a long time, and I can see her major crush on you.'

'Major crush?'

'Yep.'

Will wasn't sure if that snippet of intel was helpful or not. 'I think she's changed her mind about how she feels about me. I pissed her off.'

'Ooh, tell all.'

Will shook his head, more so at himself. 'I bought that perfume shop round by Mabel's. My plan is to turn it into a tearoom.'

'Brilliant idea.'

'Seems Ginny thought that too. Just not for me.'

'She'll get over it. She's got one of the best businesses along Harbour End Road.'

Will didn't feel like eating any more of his food. He plopped his rubbish into the bin by the bench, then flopped back. 'Yeah, I know, but she had this dream, so she said.'

'I think she's focusing on her new dream now, so don't worry too much about it, Will.'

That was news to him. 'What new dream?' His gut churned, dreading Robson would say she was moving away.

'She's moving.'

Will's rotten cold seem to escalate, making him slightly light-headed. 'Leaving?' He cleared his throat, acting as if it was the soreness that caused his word to break, rather than his deflated heart.

'Only inland. She's in talks with Artie Lane about buying his dad's old farmhouse. Reckons she's going to have rescue chickens or something. I'm sure she mentioned a donkey, unless that was something to do with Christmas.'

Will laughed to himself.

Ah, Ginny, you go for it, love.

'If you like her, Will, don't hang about, eh, mate? If my life can teach you anything, it's life's too short.'

Right there and then, in among the muffled chimes of fairground music and the faint scent of Robson's fish and chip supper, Will decided it was time to rearrange his own plans. His friend was right. Life was short, and he needed to live out what time he had left as best he could.

'Achoo!'

But first he needed a good night's sleep.

CHAPTER 20

Ginny

Placing the last black bin bag in the wheelie bin at the end of the pathway, Ginny gazed back at her mum's house. There was no sentiment attached to the place where she grew up. She just hoped the next family to move in were happier than hers.

A magpie fluttered by the chimney, gaining Ginny's attention. Her gaze lowered to the window below and a wave of regret hit her. What a terrible life she'd had in that place, and for what? Because her mum hated her dad? How was that her fault?

'You have his eyes,' Birdy would say, her words filled with venom.

Ginny absentmindedly touched beneath her eye.

'Right, we're done,' said Suzanne, appearing on the door-step. 'The housing officer should be here any minute to check the place over, then you can give her the door keys, okay?'

Sighing deeply, Ginny nodded. 'Yep.' She gave Suzanne a hug, then handed her some money as an extra thank you.

There was no argument from the care worker. She quickly shoved the cash in her pocket, smiled, then headed off.

In a way, Ginny was glad Suzanne was gone. As great as she was as a carer, she cost a small fortune. At least now all savings could go towards the farmhouse she was buying from Artie Lane.

The street was pretty quiet, even the curtain twitchers were too busy engrossed in daytime telly to bother with the last day the Deans would be seen there.

Ginny went inside and slowly walked around the property, recalling the voices, scenes, and faces of yesteryear. It was quite surreal seeing the emptiness of the place.

She opened the cupboard door under the stairs and stared at the back wall for a moment before lowering to her knees to peer inside.

Along the other side of the doorframe, scratched into the wood, was her name.

'Stay there until you grow a brain,' spat Birdy, slamming the door shut.

Ginny lightly traced one finger over the etching.

'You ought to be ashamed of yourself, young lady, for ruining my life. Why can't you be like other kids?' sobbed Birdy.

Straightening, Ginny gently closed the door and looked down the hallway to the kitchen.

'I could put you in care, but I don't. The least you can do is cook the bloody dinner. Why is your homework more important than that?'

Ginny went upstairs to see her old bedroom one last time, unsure of why she was still in the house. Her breathing was steady, and her eyes dry. The ghosts weren't scaring her anymore.

Her attention dropped to between her feet. The carpet could tell a few tales if it could speak.

'You're just a waste of space, Ginny Dean. No one will ever want you,' whispered Birdy.

Ginny glanced over her shoulder. It was time to leave.

A young woman knocked on the front door as she called out, 'Hello. I'm Haley. Housing officer.'

Ginny greeted her, then handed over the keys.

'I only need a quick look round,' said the woman. 'Just need to make some notes if anything needs fixing.'

'I've already signed everything,' said Ginny. 'So is it all right if I leave you to it?'

'Yes, that's fine.' She rattled Birdy's keychain. 'Do you want this?'

Ginny glanced at the yellow circle that had the letter L embedded in its middle. Lee. 'No. You can just throw it later.'

'Okay.' The woman pointed at the stairs. 'Do you want a moment?'

Ginny shook her head. She had a lifetime of moments in that house. No more were needed.

The housing officer made her way upstairs, and Ginny turned to the front door.

'You're a horrible creature, just like your dad,' yelled Birdy.

Ginny stepped over the threshold. 'Bye, Mum,' she said.

The dustcart came bustling down the street, removing all peace and the last traces of Yvonne Dean.

Ginny sat in her jeep, waiting for them to pass, then turned and headed home.

The crisp winter air made the sea look deathly cold, and the flurry of light snow had Berry Hill looking picturesque, even with the scaffolding outside Lottie's harbour home.

Ginny went straight to the kitchen to have an early lunch, not that she had much of an appetite. It had been a weird day, and it wasn't even twelve.

Crash, bang, wallop came from next door, rattling the adjoining wall and startling poor Lucky.

'It's okay. Just the workmen.' Ginny pulled down some cat treats. 'Here, let that settle you.'

Lucky meowed, curled around her ankles, then snaffled some food.

Ginny made a cheese sandwich, then sat picking at it at the kitchen table, dreaming about everything she could do to her new home. 'You'll have lots of land to explore,' she told the kitten.

Mr Henshaw building the chicken coop came to mind. *I reckon I can give it a go.*

She envied the couple. Their happiness. Their love. At least she would have the home.

Lucky started clawing at the leg of a nearby chair.

'Hmm, we definitely need to get you a scratch post. Samuel won't be best pleased when he sees the state of the banisters, missy.' She looked out to the hallway. 'Mind you, he'll probably rip out the stairs.' She smiled at Lucky. 'Who knows! We won't care, will we? We'll be too busy loving our new home.'

Ginny's phone rang, revealing Sophie's name.

'Hey, Soph. Shouldn't you be working?'

'I am, but I just wanted to see how you were getting on.'

Ginny smiled softly. 'All good. I'm home now. Keys have been handed over.'

'Oh, how did that make you feel?'

Relieved. Numb. Indifferent. She couldn't be sure.

'Okay,' she lied. 'I moved out years ago, so it wasn't a big deal saying goodbye to the old place.'

'I guess. As long as you're all right.'

'Yes, I'm fine. Go sell your fish.'

Sophie laughed, crackling the line. 'I'll bring you up a nice bit of tuna on my way home. I'm sure your cat will appreciate that.'

Ginny agreed. 'I'll see you later. And, hey, thanks for checking in on me, chick.'

'Love you, Gin.'

'Love you too.' Ginny hung up, feeling her appetite return. She stuffed one corner of her sandwich into her mouth, then headed for the front door to see who was knocking.

A male delivery driver, wearing headphones and not taking much notice of her, walked off while pointing down at the parcel he'd left on her doorstep.

Ginny frowned. 'Yes, thank you,' she mumbled, bending to pick it up.

Lucky curled round her feet.

'You can get in, missy, before—'

169

A loud crash came from the builders next door, making both Ginny and Lucky jump, and before Ginny had a chance to close the street door, the kitten flew out towards the narrow road.

'Lucky, come here,' called Ginny, rushing to the pavement, but the skinny little thing was already over the other side, cowering by the edge of the drop.

Great!

She quickly went back to the kitchen to fetch some cat treats, hoping shaking the box would encourage Lucky away from the clifftop. It wasn't the biggest drop in Cornwall, but it was still a fair way down to the shingles, and the last thing she wanted was the death of her first rescue animal on her hands.

Lucky murmured in the grassy verge.

'Come on, you. I've got your favourite.' Ginny gently shook the box of treats, but the kitten wasn't moving.

A gust of wind pushed into them.

Ginny was so pleased she still had her boots on as she scrunched in the earth made soggy by the recent snow. If only she had her coat as well. Her fingers were already starting to numb.

She tossed some treats down. 'Come on, Lucky, before we both catch our death.'

Lucky crept a little bit closer, still looking unsure and afraid.

'I won't let anything happen to you. I promise.' Ginny smiled, crouching lower, prepping to rugby tackle if need be.

Another loud crash came from Lottie's house, as something metal was tossed into the skip.

The hairs on Lucky's back shot up along with her legs, and she darted in the direction of the drop.

'No,' yelled Ginny, making a grab for the kitten.

Lucky was too fast, zigzagging from left to right, not knowing which way to turn. Her little paws scampered at the edge of the cliff, flicking up dirt and mud as she almost toppled over the edge.

Panic filled Ginny as she tried so hard to reach the nervous moggy. Her foot slipped in sludge, her legs buckled, and her nails gripped into the grass as she grabbed Lucky, flinging her out of harm's way. But as she quickly turned to flee the scene, part of the clifftop crumbled and fell down to the rock pools below, taking Ginny along for the ride.

CHAPTER 21

Will

'Might have some more work for you, Will,' said Shaun, entering Lottie's back garden.

Will glanced up from clearing away some plastic packaging. 'That'll be great, thanks.' He figured the more to keep him busy while he sorted the tearoom the better.

Over the last few days, Will had really sorted out his head, knowing exactly what path he was going to take. Doing a bit of hard graft, even though most of it was him being the dogsbody, helped keep his fitness levels up.

What with it coming up to Christmas, Will assumed the job would be in the new year. 'Is it local?' he asked, slinging a rubbish bag over his shoulder.

Shaun grinned, placing a gloved hand close to his lips. 'Samuel's bought next door. It's a surprise for Lottie, but we'll make a start next year.' He muffled his laugh as he added, 'Another one to knock through.'

Will stared over at Ginny's fence as Shaun went back to work.

Someone asked him to make a cup of tea as they passed by, which was a welcome relief. The air was turning bitter, and he still hadn't got over his rotten cold, quite sure it had moved to his chest.

Clearing his throat, Will set about making a brew for the workers. The new kitchen cabinets were at different heights, making life easier for both Samuel and Lottie, and now Will, as doing anything on the lower worktops gave him backache.

Paint charts were on the side, so he had a nosey, thinking he needed to be as creative as Lottie. She seemed to have her home all figured out. What a shock she would get once Samuel hit her with the news he'd bought Ginny's. Lottie would have to start over with her decorating plans.

Perhaps Will could get her input for his shop. He knew gingham would be involved, and something with coastal vibes. Never mind he spent twenty-two years of his life as a sailor, he couldn't copy Ginny's café.

Will placed down as many mugs that would fit on a tray, then walked around the house, handing out the tea.

'Ooh, lovely, thanks, mate,' was his feedback.

He nipped to the loo to spend a minute coughing his lungs up, then washed his hands and went into one of the quieter bedrooms; his head was aching. Perhaps it would be best if he cut his day short. Not only was he feeling rough, he was sure the others wouldn't want to catch his germs, especially just before time off to spend Christmas with their families.

I need to buy some presents.

The thought had completely slipped his mind. He was definitely going to buy Mabel a little something, as she was so good to him, and seeing how he was having dinner at the pub with his new friends, he'd have to buy them a gift too, but what?

Chocolates?

It was always an easy buy but lacked thought. He went to the window to stare out at the sea. Perhaps he could buy starfish keyrings or something from the RNLI gift shop.

Not a bad idea. I could . . . What on earth?

Across the road, by the cliff edge, was Ginny. What she was doing, he couldn't say. She appeared to be on her knees, stretching out an arm.

'What are you doing, woman?' He breathed out a laugh, watching her for a while. Then he noticed the black cat. 'Ah, I see.'

The wind blew up, flapping a piece of green netting on the scaffolding.

Will thought he'd better report to Shaun that it needed securing, but just as he went to turn away from the view, his heart plummeted as he witnessed Ginny tumble over the cliff.

'Ginny!' he cried, hurtling down the stairs and running out the house. 'Call 999,' he yelled to Shaun as he passed him at the front door. 'Ginny's fallen over the edge.'

Shaun said something, but it was lost in the wind.

Within seconds, Will was lying flat, peering over the drop. Every single part of him locked into rescue mode. The last thing he expected to see was Ginny hanging on to the side of the cliff. He was certain her lifeless body would be down in the rock pools. The tide was out, but he knew, even if in, she'd be in trouble if she slipped.

'Ginny, hold on. Don't you bloody move a muscle.' He heard a whimper, but she didn't look up.

Will checked over his shoulder to see Shaun talking on the phone while heading his way. At least the emergency services were on their way, but sod them. He couldn't wait. 'I'm coming down to you, Ginny. Don't move, okay.'

Ginny didn't move an inch. Her fingers were practically part of the rock, her grip was that tight, and her boots were wedged into small crevasses.

Will carefully lowered himself over the edge, knowing full well how dangerous it was without a safety harness, but he couldn't think about that. Ginny couldn't fall.

Each slow and steady move brought him closer to her shaking body. He could hear she was crying, but he had to stay focused on where to place his hands and feet next. He was so pleased the cliff had many nooks and crannies, making a rock climber's life so much easier. Any other time, he'd be in his element.

'Hey, love, you come here often?' he joked, reaching her side.

'Will?' It was as though she'd only just realized he was there.

'I don't know about you, but I'm freezing my arse off on this rock. How about we go home and make some hot chocolate?'

Ginny's breathing was shallow and her lips blue. It wasn't good. Will knew he had to move fast.

Shaun called over the edge. 'Will, I'm throwing some ropes down. They're secured this end.' And with that, two sturdy ropes came tumbling his way.

'Ginny, I want you to use one hand to hold the rope.'

Her head moved the tiniest bit.

Will had strong upper-body strength. Years of training had served him well. With his feet secure and a good grip with one hand, he used the other to tie the rope around his waist, then he moved so his body was touching hers.

'I can't move,' she mumbled. 'Please, don't touch me.'

'It's okay, love. I've got you. You're not going anywhere but up.'

'We're going to fall.'

Will started to loop the second rope around her arm, as that was the only gap he could see. It would have to do. 'I happen to be a skilled rock climber, thank you very much. No one falls on my watch.'

'Will . . . I can't . . .'

'It's okay. What I want you to do is look at your right hand.'

That slight shake of the head was back.

'Come on, Ginny. You can do it. Just look up at your right hand.'

It took a second, but she looked up.

'That's great. Now, you see that dip in the rock just above it? I want you to place your hand there.'

'I can't.'

'You can. It's called rock climbing. All you have to do is find the gaps.' He placed one arm around her back, leaning in as if to hold her up.

'What about my feet?'

'Once you have a good grip with your hands, you can slide one foot up and feel for something you can use as a ledge.'

Ginny started to cry again. 'I can't move.'

'Okay. It's okay. How about you let me slide this rope under your other arm? It'll make a good harness.' Before she could respond, he started to move into her, working slowly while she shook on his body. 'Here we go. Nice and secure you are now.'

'I don't feel it.'

'Did you just laugh? I heard a chuckle. You're just messing with me, aren't you, love? I bet you have a rock climber's badge tucked away indoors with all your other adventure awards. I know your type. Adrenaline junkies.'

'Will, I want to go home.'

He glanced up to see Shaun's head dipped over the cliff. 'That's exactly where we're going. So, remember what I told you. One gap in the rock at a time. No fuss. No frills. Just you, me, and the cracks. It's like climbing a ladder.'

'A ladder?'

'Yeah, you can do that. I know you can. So, right hand first. Go for it. Touch it. Test it. That's it. Solid, yeah?'

Ginny looked only at her hand. 'Yes.'

'Good. Try and find somewhere to place your foot. Give it a little test. Make sure it holds.'

'Found one.'

'Good. Okay, now let's start climbing. Don't think about anything other than the next hole in the wall.'

'Oh, I moved.'

Will smiled, really wishing he could cradle her into his arms, but she needed to be free to climb, and the cliff was perfect for a novice.

The sea whooshed close to the rock pools and shingles below, and light snow fluttered around them in the icy wind. Sirens suddenly filled the air at the same time a helicopter flew over.

'Keep going,' yelled Shaun, holding both his arms down. 'You're almost at the top, Gin. You've got this.'

Ginny was shaking terribly, but she was moving up, and that was all that mattered to Will. He could hear muffled voices and knew the helicopter was on standby.

'Don't pull so fast, Shaun,' Will called, seeing Ginny edging away from his care. 'Slow and steady.' He came face to face with Ginny. 'Don't want you covered in scrapes, do we?' He could already see marks on her cheekbones and forehead.

'I'm climbing a cliff,' she muttered.

'That you are, love, and doing a fine job of it too.'

'Not sure I want to do it again.'

Will grinned. 'Ooh, I don't know. With these skills, you would make a good teacher. Just next time use the safety equipment, yeah?'

'I knew I forgot something.'

Will laughed, then his chest tightened, causing a major coughing fit. He gripped the rope, feeling himself being pulled upwards. It seemed like Shaun had no more patience, either that or the firefighters had gained control of the only harness Will had.

'Will?' Ginny's voice was filled with panic.

'I'm okay,' he lied, moving her a little faster in case his chest infection took over again.

Whoever was up top, heaved Ginny the rest of the way, leaving Will to help hoist her up from below, and before he knew it, he was lying by her side on the grassy verge.

'You're a hero, mate,' said Shaun, patting his shoulder, but no, Will was simply relieved.

He sat up, looking around at the flashing lights, mounds of people, and paramedics surrounding Ginny. The hovering helicopter flew off as Samuel pushed his way through the rescue workers.

'You all right, Will?'

Will scrambled over to Ginny, but the medics had her on the gurney and were taking her over to the ambulance to check her over.

Lottie whizzed to the vehicle. 'Is she okay? Please tell me.'

'I'm fine, Lott,' said Ginny, just as Will reached her side.

'Does she need stitches?' he asked the female paramedic.

'It's not deep. A butterfly stitch will do.'

Ginny tried to touch her head, but the medic lowered her hand.

'Let's get you cleaned up,' said the paramedic.

'Can I go home?' asked Ginny.

'She lives right there,' said Lottie, pointing at their houses. 'I can look after her.'

'Me too,' said Samuel, holding Lottie's shoulder.

Will started coughing his guts up again, gaining attention from another paramedic.

'I need to look after Will,' said Ginny.

'I'm fine,' he called, being checked over. 'Just a cold gone to my chest.'

He was told he'd need to see the doctor for some antibiotics, and when he said he hadn't signed up with a local surgery yet, Samuel got on the phone immediately and arranged for a private doctor to come to his house within the hour.

'Well, that's one sorted,' said Lottie. 'Can we take Ginny home now, please? I want her snuggled on the sofa in her PJs for the day.'

Ginny climbed out of the ambulance as soon as her head was patched. 'Honestly, I'm okay. Just shaken, that's all. Lottie's right, I need a bit of peace and to settle down for the day.' She turned to Lottie. 'Have you seen Lucky?'

Lottie gestured towards Ginny's house. 'Yes, she's inside, where you should be. Come on.'

Will watched Ginny head towards her house with Lottie and Samuel. Shaun was informing the police about the accident, and half of Port Berry was racing up Berry Hill to find out what the pandemonium was about.

He flopped to the kerb, cupping his aching head. He could do with his PJs and a snuggle on the sofa as well.

Jed sat to his side. 'You okay, son? You're the talk of the village already.'

Will wasn't sure how he felt. It was all such a whirl. How he had just climbed down a cliff without protection was beyond him. 'I know I was stupid—'

'You weren't stupid. You were brave. And you saved our Ginny.'

He met Jed's serious eyes. 'I just couldn't wait.'

'It's okay. It's over now. Don't you let any what-ifs take over. You saw danger, and you did what you've been trained to do. Mission complete. Now, what you sitting here for? Go see the woman.'

Will looked over at the crowd dispersing. 'I think the police want to talk to me.'

'Come on. I'll go with you.'

Shaun approached as they met the police. 'I've explained what happened. Just let them know what you saw.'

Will turned to the waiting officer. 'She tried to save her cat but slipped.' He pointed back at Lottie's. 'That's what I saw from the window.' He started coughing again, and Jed took over with the chatter.

It took a while for the emergency services to clear out, and Shaun told his workers to call it a day.

Samuel came over just as Will was about to head off too. 'Hey, no you don't. The doctor is on his way. I told him to come to Ginny's. Come on, let's get a hot drink inside you, if nothing else.'

Will was too tired to argue, plus Jed had already gripped his arm, leading the way.

Inside Ginny's living room was Sophie and Alice snuggled on the sofa with Ginny. Spencer was on his knees lighting the fire, and Robson, Matt, and Lottie were in the kitchen, making tea.

'Everyone's gone home,' said Jed, entering the warmth.

Ginny shot upright. 'Where's Will?'

He raised a hand her way. 'I'm here.' He glanced at Samuel, who walked in behind him. 'Waiting for a doctor, apparently.' He went to say something else, but Ginny flung herself at him, wrapping her arms and legs around his weary body.

Sophie waggled her hand. 'Okay, everyone in the kitchen. Let's give them a moment.' She quickly herded her friends and grandfather, then closed the living room door.

'Thank you so much for saving me.' Ginny's mouth was squashed into his neck. 'I was so scared.' She started to sob.

Will held her in place as he sat on the sofa. 'It's all right. It's over.'

'But what if—'

'There are no what-ifs. Only the present moment.'

Ginny sniffed, pulling her head back, and Will swiped away her dark hair so her covered wound was clear. Their eyes locked, and his heart slowed.

'You're safe,' he added quietly.

'I feel safe with you.'

'Yeah? I feel a bloody mess when I'm with you.'

Ginny smiled softly, then cupped his face. 'I don't know what to say.'

'You just need to rest. Your shock is wearing off.' He smiled back. 'How you feeling?'

'Bruised.'

'You'll heal.' He started to cough, slipping out of her hold to move away from her face.

'You need to heal. The doctor will be here soon.'

'I could do with my bed.'

Ginny placed his face back into her palms. 'You can get into my bed. I'll make you some soup.'

Will assessed her eyes. She looked as worn out as he felt. 'I'd like that, but I don't want you to catch my—'

Ginny pressed her lips on his, pulled away slightly, then kissed him again.

Will kissed her back as much as he could before another round of coughing interrupted.

'Stay with me tonight, please, Will. I'm sorry I was mean to you. I'm sorry for the row about the tea shop. I'm sorry for—'

'Whoa, whoa! Forget about all that. It doesn't matter now. Besides, I'm the one who should be apologizing to you for not coming to see you after your mum died. I wanted

180

to, but I was sure you hated me, and I didn't want to make matters worse for you. I didn't know what to do for the best. And I want you to know I would stay with you every night. You never have to say please. But, Ginny, I haven't the energy to—'

'I don't want us to do anything. Just sleep, like when we were at the hotel.'

He smiled. 'Best sleep ever.'

'I agree. So, will you stay?'

'I don't have my things, and you shouldn't be sitting on my work clothes when you have nice clean pyjamas on.'

'I can put on another pair, and I can get Mabel to bring you some bits over. She's probably heard what has happened by now. Everyone will know.'

'Okay. You got yourself a deal.'

Ginny smiled and snuggled into his chest, pulling a blanket from the arm of the sofa to drape over them. 'We'll stay like this until the doctor arrives, then I'll sort Mabel and your food. We can spend the rest of the day watching telly in bed.'

'Ooh, yeah. There's a good film on tonight about mountain climbing.'

Ginny laughed, then started to cry again, and Will held her that little bit closer.

'It's okay. You're safe.'

'Will?' She raised her head, revealing her bloodshot eyes and sad expression.

'What is it, love?'

'I wondered if it was karma or something.'

He narrowed his eyes. 'Karma? For what?'

'Not being good enough.' She lowered her head, but he tipped her chin back up.

'You are good enough, Ginny Dean. You're so much more than that, and don't let anyone tell you any different.'

'I'm tired, Will.'

'I can see, but you're going to be all right now.'

She snuggled her head back to his chest and sighed deeply. 'I want to say something about the tea shop. How I overreacted. I've been talking with Jan, and I came to realize that the real issue wasn't with you, it was with my mum. All my life she'd tear down my dreams, snatch them away from me. So when I had the tearoom idea, and you came along and just got on with it, it was a trigger. I felt like someone had stolen a dream, just like she used to. It's hard to explain, but that's the gist of it, and I had planned to come see you and explain.' She sighed, and he took her hand in his. 'I am sorry, Will. You didn't deserve how I spoke to you. The way I've been treating you.'

Will's heart went out to her, and he was pleased she had been talking with Jan and clearing her head. 'I will admit, it didn't make sense to me at the time, but now you've said that, I understand why it affected you so badly. Thank you for sharing that with me.'

'I'm sorry, Will.'

Will pressed his mouth onto her hair. 'It's okay. Everything's all right, love,' he whispered.

Because I'm going to make it so.

Muffled voices came from the hallway, the living room door slowly opened, and in slinked Lucky, making her way straight to the rug by the fireplace.

Will tipped his head back, closed his eyes, and told himself to relax. Ginny was safe. He was staying the night. All was right again in his world. He just hoped it would stay that way.

CHAPTER 22

Ginny

Making up Christmas food parcels in the Hub was keeping Ginny busy all morning. So many people had come in to collect and donate.

Alice was also rushed off her feet, so Ginny plopped her onto a seat in the storage room so she could take a break, knowing her friend's pain levels had been at level five for the past hour.

Ginny smiled as Spencer entered, carrying two large shopping bags filled with children's selection boxes.

'I just cleared the shelf at the supermarket.' He raised both arms as though doing weight lifting. 'Let's get these added to some parcels.'

'Ooh, I can do that,' called Alice.

'Drink your tea,' said Ginny, shaking her head at Spencer. 'She's taking a minute.'

Spencer understood and set about getting involved himself while singing along to the Christmas music playing on the radio.

Ginny went to the front door to adjust some fallen tinsel, then smiled as a woman around her age approached.

'Morning, chick,' she said, swinging the door open, letting in the icy air along with the woman. 'You want a cuppa?'

The woman shook her head. 'No, ta. Just came to grab some bits.' She smiled at Ginny. 'How you getting on since your fall? You look a lot better.'

There was no way Ginny wanted to go over that moment of her life again. It was Christmas Eve now. Mince pies were on the table, wrapped chocolates hanging on the small Christmas tree by the window, and festive cheer in the air. The time for misery and worry was over.

'I'm good, thanks. Come and have a treat while you're here.' Ginny pointed at the tin of assorted sweets.

Spencer tugged on a Santa hat, then handed the woman a small red card. 'Take that to Sea Shanty Shack and swap it for a chicken. Just let Sophie know if you need small or large.'

Ginny was pleased the subject had been well and truly changed from her cliff horror story. The memory still had the ability to cause a shiver to run the full length of her spine. What would have happened if Will hadn't climbed down to her side?

'Would you like a selection box as well?' asked Alice, poking her head around the door to smile over at the waiting woman. 'Oh, hi, Janine. Didn't know it was you.' She turned to Spencer. 'Janine's got two girls, so make sure you pop a couple of those in with her parcel.'

Spencer did as he was asked and handed everything over. 'Merry Christmas.'

As soon as she left, another woman entered, swiftly followed by two men and an elderly couple.

'Need an extra set of hands?' asked Will, closing the door behind him.

Every part of Ginny beamed. Ever since he saved her, she'd not wanted to spend a second away from him, making sure he spent each night in her arms.

'Here, stick this on.' She placed a pair of reindeer antlers on his head, then tipped her own to tickle his chin while his head was bent.

184

Will lifted her mouth to his for a quick peck. 'Where do you want me?'

Ginny bit her bottom lip as she grinned, knowing exactly where she wanted him.

He gave her a knowing look, then gestured at the small gathering taking up half the Hub.

'Help Alice in the back room,' she suggested. 'Then see if you can bring any more carrots down from Lottie's.'

'Excuse me,' said a meek voice from behind her.

Ginny turned to the middle-aged woman matching her height. 'Happy Christmas, chick. How might I help you on this crisp winter morning?' She followed Will with her eyes, then paid full attention to the lady.

The woman pointed at the ceiling. 'I heard upstairs is going to become an office for the Les Powell Trust. Is that right?'

'Yeah, that's correct. Did you want to see Samuel about something related?'

'I wondered if he might need a cleaner.'

Ginny slid the plate of mince pies towards her, offering one. 'I reckon he'll need one. Let me check for you. Have you got a minute to wait?'

'Got all the time in the world, me. My husband passed away this year, and I don't know what to do with myself. Someone suggested a part-time job might help. I'm okay for money, not rich but comfortable, so it's more for my mental health than my pocket.'

Knowing how much work helped her own mental well-being, Ginny nodded. 'What's your name?'

'Rita Callaghan.'

'Pleased to meet you, Rita. I'm Ginny.'

Rita nodded. 'Yeah, I know who you are. You're that lass who fell off the cliff. Saw you on the news.'

Great!

'Let me just make that call.' Ginny raised a hand to Spencer, gesturing towards the kettle.

Spencer made Rita and some others a cup of tea, then went back to handing out food parcels and chicken vouchers.

Ginny went in the back room to call Samuel, pleased he said he'd pop down to the Hub in about five minutes. She stole another quick kiss from Will, gaining her a smile from Alice, then went back to let Rita know Samuel was on his way.

The morning was flying by, and the need for two days' worth of food plus extra treats for the holly jolly season had failed to ease.

'I wish we could do more,' said Alice, once the Hub was clear.

Spencer nodded. 'I know we're trying to keep everything upbeat here, but blimming heck, it's so sad seeing people needing this kind of help.'

'At least that Rita lady got a job with Samuel. Another win for the Hub,' said Will.

Ginny agreed. 'Will's right. We need to focus on the positives, no matter what. People come in here for help, so we can't cry, and yes, I'm looking at you, Alice Dipple.'

Alice lightly dabbed under her eye with a tissue. 'Sometimes it gets to me.'

Spencer held her shoulder. 'Gets to us all, Al. I'm just so glad we created this place now. The more help we can be, the better. It'll come in handy having the Trust's headquarters upstairs as well. Although I'm not sure how Samuel will cope once he's run out of jobs to hand out.'

'We can still help with work,' said Ginny. 'We know when jobs come up around here before the job centre.'

Everyone laughed. It was true. The Port Berry community had its own methods.

Will put his arm around Ginny, and she happily snuggled into his side, absorbing an overwhelming feeling of contentment.

Spencer raised a finger, moving it in circles. 'So, is this a full-on thing now?' He gestured at the blissful couple.

Oh, how Ginny hoped. Having someone at her dinner table each evening, then in her bed at night was fulfilling on levels she couldn't explain. The company, the friendship, and the love all made her feel she belonged somewhere in the world. It was so much better than she had imagined, and since Will had been sleeping over, she hadn't had one nightmare.

'This is an everything,' replied Will, his words adding to her joy.

'Aww,' said Alice, hugging her hands. She glanced up at Spencer. 'Can't believe you don't want something like that, Spence.'

He frowned as he grinned. 'I'm good, thanks. Anyway, since Lottie's accident, I've changed.' He quickly raised his finger again. 'Not that I'm saying I want to settle down. It's just, well, I don't see the point in casual relationships anymore. Got better things to think about.'

Alice sat up. 'Ooh, like what?'

Spencer tapped the side of his nose.

The street door opened, and Matt walked in with a tray of small poinsettias. 'Lottie gave me these earlier to hand out to any customers wanting to take one home. Thought I'd bring some in here.' He placed them on the floor by the Christmas tree. 'How's it been in here? We've had loads in for chickens. Three cheers for the Berry Buoys raising money for those, eh?'

Will fist bumped the air as he cheered, making everyone laugh. He sang a couple of lines from a shanty, then bowed.

Matt clapped. 'Good to see your lungs are back to normal.'

Ginny patted her chest. 'Thanks to me nursing him back to health.'

Will grinned. 'That and the antibiotics.'

Ginny nudged his ribs, and he kissed her cheek, causing their antlers to tangle.

Alice stood, widening her arms. 'It's all about love and mince pies in here, Matt. Feel free to join in.'

Laughing, he took a treat from the table. 'Every time I drop something off to someone today, they feed me something sweet. I'm starting to know how Father Christmas feels.'

'Yeah, well, you just mind how you go on those rooftops,' said Spencer, pointing over at the harbour. 'Mind you, if you do fall down a chimney, we can always send Ginny to the rescue now she's a pro rock climber.'

'Oh, ha-ha.' Ginny shook her head. 'The only thing I'll be climbing from now on is the ladder to success.'

Spencer laughed. 'Oh, is that right?'

They could laugh, but she had plans. Harbour Light Café needed no help whatsoever to bring in the punters, so all she had to focus on was bringing her new home to life in the new year. That was where her success story lived, thanks to Mr and Mrs Henshaw.

She gazed at Will as the others set about helping the next flood of people entering the premises.

'What's with the stare?' he questioned, raising one eyebrow and quirking his lips to one side.

'How would you feel about helping me with my farmhouse?'

'What do you need?'

You.

'Oh, just a chicken coop, some fencing, a few enclosures, probably a new kitchen . . .' She started laughing. 'Everything.'

His smile warmed her heart. His words even more. 'Count me in.'

'You could even stay at mine while you're still looking for somewhere to live. Got to be better than the B&B. Although don't tell Mabel I said that.'

He lowered and nudged her nose with his own. 'I'd like that.'

'Really?'

'Oh yeah.'

There was way too much fizz swirling around her body for her to think straight. All she wanted to do was take his hand and go home. She thought of telling him she loved him, but she daren't utter the words. Half the time when she looked his way, she worried he might be a dream that would one day fade away, leaving her all alone once more.

Will gently kissed her mouth, wiping her mind of all anxiety. 'You've got me, love,' he whispered on her lips.

A need surfaced. 'Promise me you won't leave.'

He took a moment, seemingly studying her eyes, then his expression softened, and he gently kissed her once more. 'I promise.'

That was good enough for whatever made her say that out loud. Just being in his presence settled her no end, and now she was as relaxed as could be, until Spencer called out for some more cardboard boxes.

'Hey,' whispered Will, tugging her to his arms as she went to get back to work. 'I've got to go see Babs after you and me have had ourselves a cosy lunch, but are we still on for Christmas Eve dinner tonight?'

'Yes, I got some salmon from Sophie. But I did say I'd join the others at the pub for a drink afterwards. Is that okay with you?'

Will nodded. 'Sounds like a plan.'

'I know another one.'

'Hit me.'

'You waking up at mine Christmas morning.'

A slight twitch of a grin hit the corner of Will's mouth. 'I would say I'll pack a bag, but most of my things are already at yours, so I guess you've got yourself a date.'

'Just a date?'

He shook his head slightly. 'No. You get everything.'

Ginny pulled him in for a heated kiss, feeling every part of her being melt into him.

CHAPTER 23

Will

Will sat in the communal lounge at his grandmother's care home, staring out at the Christmas lights in the back garden. Cheerful music was playing quietly in the background, and all staff members were in festive tops and party hats.

'Have a mince pie before they all go,' said Clare.

He smiled at his gran's carer and took the treat, even though he was still full from the large lunch he'd shared with Ginny at the café.

'Doesn't she look lovely?' said Clare, nodding towards Babs.

Will had to agree. The young lady adding the finishing touches to his grandmother's hair had done a grand job, and Babs was smiling, which was the most important thing.

Clare tapped the back of his chair. 'Best go make some more tea.'

He watched her skip off, then glanced back at Babs, now having a hand massage from one of the spa ladies volunteering for the day.

The other residents looked just as refreshed as they were pampered and fussed over, some even standing for a slow dance for all of one minute.

It was a lovely atmosphere, and one Will was glad to witness, even if it was from the corner of the room. He wished so badly he could sit with his grandmother, talk all things Christmas, and perhaps give her a hug. Babs was on top form, so there was no way he was going to risk triggering her by showing his face.

It no longer mattered how often he visited; he would always have to view her from afar, as not to scare her. For some reason, Babs just couldn't take to him, often welling up and yelling for help.

Willard was her husband's name, and it was triggering, so Will soon learned to keep his mouth shut, but it was hard. If he stayed in the background sometimes he'd catch a rare smile aimed his way, but it was polite, or maybe she was looking straight through him, he couldn't be sure. It was just nice to see her relaxed.

Clare popped another mince pie in front of him, but he declined, asking if he could help out at all, as it was better than sitting there twiddling the foil the shop-bought mince pies came in.

'You could play dominoes with Ted, bless him. Look, he's just sitting there not wanting to be manhandled, as he calls it, by the spa ladies.'

That was an easy yes, and something that would help pass the time.

'Oh, sent you over, have they?' said the elderly gentleman, bobbing his head at the seat opposite him.

Will flashed him a friendly smile. 'Well, I'm not getting pampered either, so Clare thought we could keep each other company.'

'Go on then, park your arse.'

Will started setting up the game. 'Do you fancy a mince pie, Ted?'

'I fancy a pint, but that's unlikely. They won't even let me have a fag, and I really miss smoking.' He wrinkled his nose in Clare's direction. 'Reminds me of my Sally. She was always watching my health as well. Fat lot of good that did me.'

191

'Why do you say that? Look how long you've lived.'

Ted frowned. 'Not exactly a blessing, son, when you're stuck in here. I want to go out and watch the footie. They shove the telly in front of me in here. That's no good to me. I want the atmosphere.'

'We all have to slow down at some point.'

Ted scoffed. 'Not me. I've always been fit as a fiddle, then one day, bosh! My legs decide to give up the ghost. I have to use that stupid thing.' He tipped his head towards his walking aid. 'I feel like I'm part trolley now.'

Will tried not to laugh. 'So, how long have you been in here?'

'Just over a year. Still, mustn't grumble. They're not a bad bunch. I just prefer to cook my own breakfast, you know? I don't care what anyone says, there's nothing wrong with fried sausages every morning. Not killed me yet.'

'There's nothing wrong with some porridge either, Ted.'

'Oh, porridge smorridge. You eat it.'

Will couldn't help but laugh as he moved his domino piece in place.

Ted glanced around. 'My Sally would've liked all this. Loved a bit of fuss did that one. Never a hair out of place and always faffing with her nails.' He swiped over his own. 'That girl over there asked if I wanted a manicure. I'm ninety-two years old. Never had one of those in my life. Not about to start now, thank you very much.'

Will glanced at his own hands. 'Mine could do with a clean-up.'

'Well, that's the trouble with you young'uns. Focus on all the wrong things.'

'What should I be focusing on then?'

'Love, son.' Ted pointed his way. 'If my years on this planet have taught me anything, it's love matters most.'

Ginny sprung to mind, warming Will immediately.

'How long did it take you to know you loved Sally?' Will asked.

192

Ted smiled. 'Straight away, son. I took one look at her and I just knew. Funny thing, eh?'

'Do you believe in love at first sight then?'

'Happened, so yeah. We were a good fit, then she had to go and ruin it by dying on me.'

Will's heart sank for the man. He'd already fallen so deeply for Ginny, the thought of never seeing her again destroyed him. 'How long ago was that?'

'About ten years now.' Ted looked at the ceiling for a second. 'Blimey, has it been that long?' He turned back to Will and smiled. 'Dying's not so scary now I have her waiting for me.'

'It's great you had a long life together, as long as you were happy, that is.'

'Ooh, we were, son. Had our moments, like anyone, I guess. But we worked. Not much else to add. People you meet can be a blessing or a curse. They're not all nice out there, but I was lucky. I found a nice woman. Kind.'

'Maybe it's pot luck who we end up with.'

Ted scoffed. 'Nonsense. You don't have to stay with someone if they're horrible to you. You leave. Find a better life. That's what I told my daughter when she found herself stuck with some lowlife. All he did was find ways to disrespect her. Rotten excuse for a man. Ought to be ashamed. His parents should be.'

'I've never been in a toxic relationship with a partner, but whenever I didn't like something about my life, I found ways to change my situation. Until you said that, I'd not really thought about it before. I just got on with it.'

Ted nodded. 'That's good. That's how it's done. Move on, find what works. It's not rocket science.'

'To be fair, change isn't easy.'

'No, but it's doable.' Ted folded his frail arms. 'My little girl is with a lovely man now. Happy as anything she is. Wouldn't have had that had she stayed with the coward.'

'Coward?'

Ted nodded. 'Any man who raises a hand to a woman is a coward. I let him know that when I smacked him one.'

Will breathed out a laugh. 'You hit him?'

'Wouldn't you if that was your daughter?' A cheeky glint filled the man's beady blue eyes. 'I got a rap on the knuckles for it, but it was worth it.' He shook his head as though he were talking to himself. 'You've got to protect the ones you love, son.'

There wasn't anything Will wouldn't do to keep Ginny safe. He could see the sadness in her eyes, feel her pain, and recognize the healing she needed. It wasn't too dissimilar to his own. But he had reached a stage where she came first, and if helping her build a farm made her smile, then so be it. Ted was right about one thing, change was doable, and he could see quite clearly that both he and Ginny had always somehow managed to find things that worked for them.

Being in the navy cured a lot of ills. It was when left to his own devices that things built up in his mind.

'You got someone special, son?' asked Ted, leaning closer as though studying him.

Will nodded. He liked to think so. 'Her name's Ginny.'

'You be kind to each other. That's how you get a good life.'

'I wouldn't hurt her for all the tea in China.'

Ted smiled. 'Sounds like you were raised right.'

'I raised myself.'

'Then good on you, son, for turning out so well. Got no one to thank but yourself. Well, isn't that something to be proud of, eh?'

Will had never thought of it that way. He just got on with life, putting one foot in front of the other, always trying to find some form of happiness.

'You know what, Ted? I'm glad I sat with you. You've certainly brightened my day.'

'Cheers, son.' Ted gestured at Babs, still having her hands massaged. 'Not easy, is it?'

Will watched Clare ask Babs if she could give her a hug, wishing he could do the same. It was nice to see his grand-mother receiving affection.

'Can't remember the last time I got a hug,' said Ted, looking wistful.

Will grinned, then shot out of his chair to wrap his big arms around the old man.

'Get off me, you great lump.' Ted wriggled but laughed, even more so when Clare sprinted over to join in the cuddle.

'Aww, I've been wanting to do that since we met, Ted,' she told him.

Ted straightened his shirt with one hand while flapping them away with the other. 'Yeah, yeah, that's enough of that.'

Clare winked at Will, who smiled her way. 'He totally wanted that hug.'

'Be off with you, girl, and make me a cuppa. I'm parched.'

'I'll make you one too, Will,' said Clare, putting one of Ted's domino pieces in place.

'Too much fuss.' The slightest of smiles still broke free from Ted's stern expression.

Clare plopped an elf hat on Ted's head, then skipped off, and Ted left it in place, proving he was only in half-grump mode.

'Looking forward to a nice bit of Christmas dinner tomorrow, son. Got the kids popping over as well. What you got planned for the big day?'

'My friend owns a pub, so there are a load of us going there for dinner. Should be good.'

'It's always good when you're surrounded by love. Remember that. Love is what makes this whole journey bearable.'

Will thought about Port Berry. He really had found something special. The old-timer was right. Love certainly made a difference. Meeting Ginny Dean had changed everything. The past could stay there. He had a future to prepare for, and that included making sure the woman he loved knew just exactly how serious he was about her.

Ted knocked on the table, bringing Will out of his trance. 'Head in the game, son. Not in the clouds.'

He wasn't wrong.

Will decided he'd talk to Ginny about them becoming a more secure couple. He'd already promised he wouldn't leave, so something solid in place could help seal the deal. Could he really ask her to marry him? Would she agree? Was it a wise move? He was sure Ted would think so, but would Ginny?

He stared through his domino pieces, only seeing Ginny's face. It was quite surreal finding love. All those years, he'd kept women at arm's length for fear of getting too close and then being tossed to one side, and now his love was stronger than his fear.

Glancing over at Babs made him wonder what would happen to him down the line. What if he forgot Ginny one day? The thought stabbed at his heart. He had to hold on to what they had now. Wrap himself fully in each and every moment. The best thing he could do was live for the now, and that meant coming clean with Ginny about just how strong his feelings towards her were.

CHAPTER 24

Ginny

Ginny was having the best Christmas of her life, and she'd only been awake for five minutes. There had been no clattering on the rooftop last night, but there was definitely some clanking going on downstairs in her kitchen.

What a glorious sight, and it wasn't the rose petals scattered on the table. Just seeing Will pottering around in the morning, humming along to the festive music playing quietly on the radio and looking completely at home gave her every gift she could have asked for.

She hopped straight over to the freshly brewed tea and took a quick sip while eyeing up the small gift box with the silver bow.

'And Merry Christmas to you too, Miss Dean.' Will glanced over his shoulder, offering a cheeky wink that hit her straight in the heart.

'Happy Christmas, chick. Is this for me?'

Will chuckled as he approached to kiss her head. 'Go on then, seeing how you can't wait till I dish out the bacon rolls.'

'Ooh, brekkie too. Best Christmas morning ever.'

'Yeah, mine too,' he said softly, sitting to her side.

Ginny leaned over to plant a kiss on his lips, then excitedly turned to her gift, her unwrapping skills giving any eager child a run for their money. 'Oh, I love it.' She beamed happily at the donkey in a snow globe. 'It's brilliant.'

'Thought you might approve.'

'Wait, let me get yours.' She hurried to the cupboard in the hallway to fetch a bundle of red foil. 'I had a bit of trouble wrapping it. I won't buy that paper again, that's for sure.'

Will looked it over. 'It's a fine job. You missed your calling.'

Giggling, she nudged his arm. 'Go on. Open it.'

Will teased her lack of patience by tearing away the smallest piece of sticky tape.

'Hey,' she urged.

'Okay, okay.' Will fumbled with the strong foil for a moment before managing to rip it apart. 'Ha! I like your thinking.' He held out the navy top to reveal the white embedded words, *Berry Buoys*.

'Do you like it?'

'I love it.' Will beckoned her towards him. 'Come here.' He kissed her mouth and smiled.

'You know, we're running late this morning.'

Will frowned, pulling her in for another kiss. 'I didn't know we had a schedule today.'

'Christmas dinner at the pub. I said we'd be there for twelve.'

'Ah, we've got plenty of time.'

'Ooh, yes, to eat our breakfast and—'

'Enjoy a long hot shower together.'

Ginny laughed. 'This day just keeps getting better and better.'

A thump on the wall broke their embrace.

'Happy Christmas, Ginny,' yelled Lottie from the other side.

Ginny grinned at Will. 'Oh, I'm going to miss living next door to her.' She called back her own seasonal greeting while watching Will get on with breakfast. 'Hey, do you think Samuel has told her about this place yet?'

Lottie's voice was muffled through the old thin wall, but they still heard the delight in her tone as she yelled, 'Sam bought me your house. Thanks, Gin.'

'Guess so,' said Will.

'Come on, let's get on with our morning, then we can pop next door and walk down to Robson's with them.'

* * *

The walk to the Jolly Pirate was fresh and filled with cheer. The sea salt in the air mingled with the aroma of roast dinner wafting out the opened doors of the pub, and Ginny and Lottie couldn't stop talking about moving homes and new beginnings, leaving Will and Samuel discussing which seafood starter they fancied.

Tinsel and fairy lights decked the long bar, and foil decorations hung from the ceiling. Party hats and streamers were scattered everywhere, along with Christmas crackers and wrapped chocolates. Music played, and Alice was already bopping away with her mum, Lizzie.

Sophie squealed with delight as soon as Ginny entered the pub. 'Look. Look!' she cried, flashing her engagement ring.

Ginny took her hand for a closer look at the diamond. 'Oh, Soph, congratulations.' She pulled her in for a hug, then turned to do the same to Matt, now receiving hefty pats on the back from Samuel and Will. 'This is so exciting.'

Sophie gushed a thousand times over, 'I'm so happy.' She flapped her other hand in front of her face. 'Ooh, sorry. I keep crying.'

Matt pulled her in for a hug, and Ginny's heart warmed watching them so in love.

Robson came over with a tray of glasses, offering a choice of champagne, lemonade, or orange juice. 'To the happy couple,' he announced, handing out the drinks.

Spencer held his glass high. 'May they always be as happy as Jed is when fishing.'

Everyone laughed as Jed cheered.

'And here's to a blimming good year,' said Sophie. 'We opened the Hub, the food bank, helped so many people, and we're still going strong, especially now Ginny's café is up and running for free meals some evenings.'

'And we're starting a repair service for clothes,' said Luna. 'We'll sort that at Ginny's in the new year.'

Will nudged Ginny's arm. 'Looks like you'll be busy.'

With the thought of setting up a farm, she was sure she would be. Had she taken on too much just at the time in her life she found herself free? Thinking about it, it didn't feel the same as when she was tied to her mother. All the things she had going on in her life now sparked joy. She loved the fresh start she was creating and couldn't wait to move to the farmhouse in January.

'We'll have another good year next year as well,' she said, saluting Sophie with her glass.

Robson gestured at the dining area of the pub. 'I'm fully booked so best get on.'

'I'll help serve,' said Alice, stepping forward.

Ginny turned to Will. 'Robson's pub is booked out every Christmas, so we all help lighten the load for his staff, then we get to sit and have our dinner.'

Will nodded. 'That's okay. I'm still stuffed from breakfast. Plus, I've got my eye on that seafood platter if I get a bit peckish beforehand. So, where do you want me?'

Ginny snuggled under his arm. 'Back in the shower with me. Or here's good.'

He chuckled as he kissed her head and clinked glasses. 'We'll do that later, but right now, here's good for me too, and if all hands on deck are needed, then I'm in. Give me some orders.'

Ginny pointed her glass at the bar. 'Grab a tray and find some empties. I'll go help serve some starters.' She tugged him close as he went to slip away. 'And don't forget to kiss me each time we pass.'

'Well, now, that's the best order I've ever had.'

Ginny practically skipped off to get on with her task.

A few hours later and the customers had been fed and were in full festive swing over by the bar. The music had been turned up, and the kitchen staff had slowed to eat their own dinners while Robson and Alice got busy looking after their own group.

'This table has certainly got longer this year,' said Robson, looking over at Matt and Samuel, then Will.' He grinned at Spencer, who was sipping on some bubbly. 'Hmm, let's see. Who will Spence bring to dinner next year?'

Spencer almost choked on his drink as everyone laughed.

'Aww,' said Lottie. 'You leave my big brother alone. He can't help it if he's afraid of women.'

'I'm not afraid of women.'

Sophie laughed. 'More like afraid of falling in love.'

Spencer swiped up some roast potatoes from a nearby bowl to place on his plate. 'I'm not afraid of that either, thank you.' He rolled a finger around in a circle towards Alice. 'Pick on Al. She's single too.'

Alice frowned as her nephew Benny laughed. 'Hey! I have other things to concentrate on.'

'I might bring someone,' said Lizzie, earning her a few glares from her daughter.

'And who's that, Mum?' asked Alice.

'You dating, Nan?' asked Benny, chuckling into his glass of orange juice.

'No, she's not dating,' said Alice, before Lizzie could speak.

Luna pulled a Christmas cracker with Jed. 'Nothing wrong with my daughter dating. She's not dead yet.'

Lizzie's blue eyes twinkled with mischief. 'There's life in me yet, Alice.'

Alice frowned. 'So, who is he?'

Lizzie shook her head. 'I've not met anyone yet.' She turned to Robson. 'I was just saying it could be me adding to our Christmas table next year.'

Spencer raised his glass to her. 'Good for you, Liz. At least it won't be me.'

'It's not a bad thing, Spence,' scoffed Sophie, snuggling into Matt, who was trying to plate up some veg. 'Look what happened to me this year. It just goes to show. You never know what's around the corner.'

Matt leaned her way to kiss her cheek, making everyone coo.

'Maybe I just enjoy my own company,' said Spencer, going back to his food.

'Nothing wrong with that,' said Jed. 'But if love does happen to find you, son, don't you shy away. It's a hell of a thing is love. You don't want to miss out.'

Spencer frowned. 'Can we change the subject? Talk about turkeys or something.'

Sophie nodded. 'Well, whoever is at our table next Christmas is in for a real treat.' She looked at Matt, who smiled her way.

'Go on, then. Tell them,' he said. 'I knew you wouldn't last five minutes.'

'Tell us what, Matt?' asked Lottie.

Sophie beamed. 'We've already decided to have a Christmas wedding next year.'

A round of applause and cheer filled the air.

'So you see,' added Sophie, standing to take a small bow, 'we'll have another wonderful year next year, and in all the years to come. Here's to the Happy to Help Hub's team.'

'Happy Christmas,' yelled Robson.

Ginny had never felt so alive before. She had miserable Christmases as a child, always believing Santa must have hated her guts, especially the time he put an actual piece of coal in her stocking. Growing up and making her own festive cheer with her friends made so much difference to the time of year she had little affection for.

Will was chatting merrily away to Samuel and Matt, and Ginny knew she'd turned a corner. The past was over, and she had no room for regrets or ghosts. All her focus needed to be on the here and now so she could enjoy life and build something for the future. Hopefully, one with Will.

Sophie was flashing her engagement ring again, this time to Luna, who looked to be casting some sort of spell over it, and Lottie was holding Samuel's hand while she faced the other way, talking to Lizzie.

Ginny absorbed the love surrounding her, counting her blessings and thanking the determination she had to make the changes needed. It was all a little too overwhelming, so she excused herself and headed for the bathroom to roll back her happy tears and settle her overjoyed heart for a moment.

As soon as the two women in the toilets left, Ginny gazed at her face in the mirror above the sink, then gave herself the thumbs up. 'Look at you, knowing what real love feels like,' she whispered.

It was the most incredible feeling, and one she couldn't quite believe belonged to her. For so long she had dreamed of a soulmate, believing him to exist. How she'd stare out to sea, sending love and well wishes to wherever he was. Knowing now he was on a warship somewhere all that time was quite mind blowing, and she couldn't help but laugh.

'What you laughing at, love?' asked Lizzie, walking in.

'Oh, just my crazy life.'

Lizzie nodded. 'Gets you like that sometimes.'

'It's been a really eventful year.'

'Yep, those tend to pop up every so often.'

'I'm not sure whether to laugh or cry, if I'm honest.'

Lizzie reached over and lightly tapped Ginny's arm. 'Smile. That's all you need to do from now on, girlie.'

Ginny breathed out a hushed laugh. 'I wish I could read the tarot like you and Luna. At least then I'll know what's coming next.'

Lizzie grinned. 'You know it's just a guide, right? You still get to choose which path you take.'

'Sometimes I feel I need a guide.'

'Okay, well, in that case, I can tell you something for free.'

Ginny braced herself. At least when Lizzie had some fortune telling at hand she didn't make it cryptic like Luna.

Lizzie gave her hand a gentle squeeze. 'You found him, girlie. The one you've been searching for. Now it's time to breathe.'

'Thanks, Liz. I do feel happy.'

'That's good, love. Now, excuse me, my bladder isn't as strong as it used to be. Flipping menopause.'

Ginny laughed as Lizzie made a dash for the cubicle. 'I'll see you back outside,' she called.

The sensation of sheer bliss hit her as soon as she stepped through the door. She was just about to turn the corner when she heard Will talking, and just like that everything about her happy vibe flushed straight down the loo.

'I'm just so glad Ginny's smiling again after the terrible life she had with that abusive mother of hers,' he said.

'What?' came Alice's voice, filled with as much shock as Ginny felt wash over her.

'I'm sorry,' said Will. 'I thought you knew.'

'No, she bloody well didn't,' snapped Ginny, stepping out from her hiding place.

'Oh, Gin,' said Alice, raising a hand to cover her mouth.

Ginny pointed at her. 'Don't.' Then she turned her anger on Will. 'How dare you tell my secret.'

Will's gulp didn't go unnoticed. 'I'm sorry, I thought—'

'You thought wrong. No one knew about me but you. So thanks for that.'

He stepped forward, reaching out a hand, but Ginny stepped back.

'Don't touch me.' Every part of her felt on fire. Desperately trying to find some air, she shoved him out of the way to head towards the main door.

'Please, Ginny, don't leave,' he called.

She turned abruptly, showing him nothing but the rage in her eyes. 'No, that's right. You should leave. This is my home, these people are my family, and you have no business here. So sod off, and don't come back. I never want to see you again.'

Will's mouth sagged for a second, then he gave the smallest of nods and walked away, leaving the pub altogether.

'No,' said Alice, sprawling her arms in opposite directions. She looked at Ginny. 'You need to talk, that's all. Don't let him leave. He thought I knew about you.' She dropped her arms and furrowed her brow. 'Why didn't I know about you? You're one of my best friends. You can tell me anything. Any of us, Gin. Whatever happened to you with your mum could have been shared with us. I would have helped you.'

'Me too, love,' said Lizzie, leaving the bathroom.

Without her consent, Ginny started to cry. 'He had no right calling my mum abusive.' Just when she thought she could have one Christmas without her mother ruining it in some way, there she was.

'But was she, love?' asked Lizzie, curling an arm around Ginny's shaking body.

Ginny sobbed into Lizzie's Christmas jumper. 'Yes.'

Alice leaned in for a group hug. 'Oh, Ginny. We've got you. It's going to be okay.'

Nothing felt one bit okay. Will had blurted out her deepest secret, now all her friends would know her backstory, and she'd just basically told him that wherever he belonged in the world, it wasn't Port Berry.

CHAPTER 25

Will

The venom in Ginny's words stung, crippling Will in a million ways. All he could do was flee the scene as quickly as possible. Air was what he needed. Sea salty air to remind him of freedom and what his only family looked like.

There had been times Will had stood on deck of a warship, staring out to sea, wondering what else was out there for him. A home, a different job, love. He never saw too far past the Royal Navy, always staying within the moment, feeling it a safer place for his heart. His shattered, worn-through heart was with the sea once more.

The water lapped against the limbs of the short pier. An eerie but comforting sound, and before Will had a chance to assess the cold bitterness of the dark liquid below, he jumped in.

He'd always loved cold water swimming, and knew his body could handle the temperature for a while.

'Sanctuary,' he muttered, lying flat on his back, watching a thousand stars peering down from an early-evening black sky.

Even with the shore close by, Will stayed put, enjoying the peace the sea brought him.

The face of his mother flashed before his eyes. Babs had her picture in a frame at the care home, alongside one of her late husband. Where was the picture of her one and only grandchild? Lost somewhere in her memories, that was where. But it didn't matter that he knew the reason. It still hurt. Once more, he was missing from their family. Just as he had been banished from Ginny's.

Port Berry had brought him nothing but misery. Worse, it gave him expectations. Something he knew as a child not to have. If only he had stayed that way. It wouldn't hurt. It just wouldn't hurt.

How had he allowed possibilities to appear? What was he thinking buying a shop, selling everything he owned in Wales, and more importantly putting all his eggs in one basket labelled Ginny Dean?

Seawater lapped at his ears, deafening him at every roll of a wave. It was getting colder by the second, and if he didn't get out soon, someone would have to drag his deadweight from the shoreline if the tide was kind enough to herd him in that direction.

Will knew if the RNLI was called to rescue him, having got wind he'd jumped into the sea on Christmas Day, there was no way they'd let him join their crew. Not that he'd blame them.

But there was something serene about his surroundings. The peace, the stars, the feeling of insignificance in such a vast open space. He wondered if anyone would miss him if he floated away, not that he had any intention of doing so.

It was a strange face to see first, but Mabel came to mind. She'd been kind to him since his arrival in the fishing village. Telling him the gossip, helping him find his feet, even kick-starting a new beginning for him on his behalf.

Will's blue lips twitched into a smile.

Jed appeared next. Setting him up with village life, making him part of the team.

Then came Alice's smile. Inviting him places, showing him friendship.

One by one, the locals entered his weary head. Their voices, comments, offers of kindness, a community. He never had that in Wales. Just a lot of moving around and a few people he knew here and there.

'I did find happiness,' he spluttered, spitting salty water.

And just like that it hit him all at once. Port Berry wasn't a curse. It was a blessing. Did he find what he was looking for when he arrived? Not exactly. He got his answers, none of which he'd expected, but now he had something else.

It didn't matter what Ginny said or thought. He did belong, and not because he was born there. He fitted. And he'd be damned if he was going to move around ever again.

'Not this time,' he told the dark sky.

The sea was freezing, and Will's body was almost powerless, but through sheer bloody determination alone, he rolled over onto his front and started to slowly swim towards the shingles.

The ice in the air chilled him to his core as he trudged over to the B&B. How he could stand, he didn't know, but something was holding him up, moving his legs, and keeping him alive.

Mabel wasn't about, and his key was hanging out with the fish, so he grabbed the spare from the little cupboard behind the reception desk and headed to his room to defrost.

* * *

Thump, thump, thump. Will was sure his ears were ringing too. He opened his eyes, realizing the banging wasn't in his dream at all. It was coming from his door.

'Will, you awake?' called Mabel.

That was odd. She didn't normally wake him. Nobody woke him since his navy days when Call the Hands would let him know it was time to rise and shine, swiftly followed by the

Standard Operator Checks. Ginny's body wrapped around him were the only other times, but that hadn't been often. He hoped Mabel hadn't witnessed his moment of madness at the pier. How long had he been asleep anyway? The last thing he remembered was taking off his wet clothes and flopping to the bed.

He turned to his phone on the bedside cabinet, then groaned as he remembered it had drowned. Maybe it could be repaired, but he wasn't holding his breath. Nope, he'd have to buy a new one.

Oh, what was I thinking?

Mabel knocked on the door again.

With heavy heart, and even heavier limbs, Will got up to see what was so important. The light blaring in the window told him it was daytime, so maybe he'd slept in late and she was worried because he hadn't shown his face. At least someone thought of him.

'Morning, Mabel. Everything all right?' He stretched his aching right arm up to the back of his neck.

'No, lovey, it's not.' Her pale-blue eyes held nothing but dismay, and Will wondered what was wrong with the B&B.

'What's wrong, Mabel? Do you need to sit down?' He moved towards her, but she placed her frail hand on his.

'It's Meadow House. They've been trying to reach you all morning. They called here.'

Every fibre of Will's being woke. 'Is Babs okay?'

Mabel slowly shook her head. 'I'm sorry, lovey. She passed away in her sleep last night.'

He was sure that was what she said, but it took a moment for her words to sink in fully. Not knowing what to say or how to act, he just stood there, lifeless.

'It's okay, Will. I'll help you.' Mabel gestured at his room. 'You get yourself ready, and we'll pop over there in a jiffy. See what needs to be done.'

As he seemed to be unable to make any decisions himself, he followed orders, only feeling his senses return when they stepped foot inside the residential care home.

Clare came rushing forward, flinging her arms around him tightly. 'I'm so sorry, Will.' She pulled back, offering a warm smile. 'She was one of my favourites. I'm going to miss her so much.'

Mabel thanked her, as Will stayed silent. 'We thought it best to come over. See what you want us to do.'

Clare shook her head. 'Oh, there's nothing to do. It's all sorted.' She moved closer, lowering her voice. 'Her body has already been taken, and I'm not sure if you're aware, but Babs had made her own funeral arrangements a while back. Bought some package deal at the local funeral directors. I can put you in touch with them.'

'Yes, please,' said Mabel, as Will went over to a nearby chair to sit down.

From the moment Ginny tossed him out of her life to the second his backside met the plump seat in the foyer of Meadow House, it all seemed like a never-ending nightmare. Had he been the one who died? Did the Grim Reaper play tricks?

Alive or dead, Will had no one anymore. Babs was his past. Ginny no longer a future. He didn't need to make arrangements for his gran, like a normal family member, because even that had been taken away. So he just sat there, feeling alone.

'Come on, lovey,' said Mabel. 'Let's get you home.'

The drive back to the B&B seemed to take longer, and Mabel going on about Boxing Day dinner went in one ear and out the other. What day it was no longer mattered.

Mabel stuck the kettle on as soon as they entered the warmth of her kitchen, but Will wasn't in the mood for chit-chat or sympathetic smiles. He made his excuses and left, and not just for his sake. Mabel needed to be back in her own life, not worrying about him.

He waited in his room until he heard her go off to her friend's house for dinner, then he popped back to the kitchen to grab something for his empty stomach.

Mabel had left him a note, stating there was a plate of turkey and stuffing sandwiches in the fridge with his name on them.

Will unpeeled the foil to check he had the right grub, grabbed a bottle of water, then headed off to his new shop.

It was cold inside, reminding him to call the electricity company soon. Sheila had cleared the place, leaving nothing but a small toilet and a back room suitable for a kitchen.

Shaun had promised to start renovations in a couple of weeks, so that was something at least. There wasn't much to do in the grand scheme of things, but it certainly felt over-whelming as Will sat on the hard floor, going over the to-do list.

He bit into a sandwich, hoping it would help settle the swirl in his gut.

Paint charts caught his eye. He still hadn't decided on a main colour. Something to do with the sea was winning the race, but Ginny's café had the harbour theme well and truly in place. Perhaps aquamarine gingham for tablecloths and awning. Maybe the tearoom could look beachy, rather than harbour. Flip-flops and buckets and spades. But there wasn't anywhere in Port Berry to make sandcastles.

'Hmm.' Will glanced around. 'Speak to me.' He stood, eating his sandwich as he approached the window to stare out at the empty street.

Ginny would be with her friends, enjoying Boxing Day, or not, seeing how he'd embarrassed her in front of them. There was no point thinking about how much she hated him. He'd had about as much self-pity as he could take.

'Ah,' he said, mouth full, pointing towards the lighthouse in the distance. 'Could go red and white like that.' He shook his head, as candy canes came to mind.

A seagull cried outside, gaining attention. Will knew he'd have a war on his hands with that lot come summer.

Harbour Light Café hit all the right notes for the fish-ermen, but what if the tearoom focused on the pirates of Cornwall? Surely that would make the customers smile. He'd noticed there was something about a pirate at every turn since he arrived. Why shouldn't the tearoom join in with the sto-ries? He wouldn't be able to fly the flag, as Robson's pub already had one behind the bar, but he could have parts of a ship, make it more light-hearted so kids would tug their parents inside to plop on a hat and eat a skull and crossbones cupcake.

Will laughed at the thought.

The staff could wear costumes, and the menu could be filled with pirate puns.

'Am I going overboard?' he asked the mooching seagull.

Pastel lemon on the paint chart caught his attention, taking his mind to a rustic farmhouse with animals and warmth. Ginny.

Will smiled. He knew exactly what to do.

CHAPTER 26

Ginny

'I can't believe it's January already,' said Ginny, handing over two slices of her own handmade lemon drizzle cake to Samuel.

'I know, and what a year last year was.' Samuel took the cakes over to the couple by the window in Ginny's café.

Tell me about it!

She was hoping the new year would bring less chaos and more stability, especially as she had a farmhouse to move in to.

Samuel came back to the counter and took a swig of water. 'They're the last two for the evening.'

Ginny glanced at the clock. It had just gone seven. She went to speak but smiled instead as Samuel's staff came out of the kitchen to head off, having finished their shift. She thanked them all, then saw them out, turning the sign on the door to *Closed*.

'How's it been?' asked Samuel, following her around the counter.

'It's okay. Two nights a week is manageable for me, but honestly, I wasn't expecting to see that many in need of a free meal. Don't get me wrong, I know how many food parcels we hand out at the Hub, but still, I was surprised.'

Samuel nodded. 'It's like that at The Food Bank Café. I know we're set up for exactly that purpose, but it's still shocking to see so many people in need.'

Ginny stole a peek at the couple by the window. They were chatting quietly while enjoying her cake and seemed happy enough. 'This is one of the problems we face at the Hub,' she whispered to Samuel. 'Sometimes it just breaks our hearts.'

'Yeah, I know.'

'I'm glad you asked me to do this with the café. I know two evenings a week isn't much, but it all helps.'

Samuel gestured at the front door. 'Especially during this dreary month.'

'I always find January a good month for baking.'

The couple stood, waving a goodbye and saying their thanks as they left.

Ginny went to clear their empty plates away. 'And my cakes are going down well.'

'Speaking of which,' said Samuel, pointing at the window.

Ginny followed his eyes to see Sophie standing out in the cold, holding a large white box.

Samuel opened the door, then stayed there, letting the chilly air in.

Ginny stopped wondering what he was waiting for and turned to Sophie instead as she entered. 'All right, chick. We were just about to head home.'

'I know. That's why we're here.' Sophie placed the box on a table and beamed, confusing Ginny even more.

'Oh, about time,' said Samuel, looking down the street.

Ginny stepped closer to him. 'What are you talking . . .' Her words drifted off as soon as she saw Lottie, Spencer, Robson, Matt, and Alice heading towards her café.

'Surprise!' yelled Sophie, lifting the lid off the box.

Ginny whipped her head around, then approached her excited friend to see what exactly the squeal of joy was all about. 'Oh!'

'Happy birthday, Ginny,' called Lottie, entering the warmth.

Not being much of a fan of the day, Ginny had hoped to let it pass without an audience. Her friends didn't normally make such a fuss, and it was obvious why they'd upped their game this time.

She so wished everyone would stop making sure she was okay. Ever since blabbermouth Will let out her secret, her mates had become clingy and melodramatic.

Robson put the radio on, Samuel produced a cold buffet from the fridge that one of his cooks had secretly prepared, and Alice filled glasses with fizzy wine.

'Now, we know you don't like presents or any sort of fuss,' said Lottie, whipping out a wrapped gift. 'But we figured a little something for your new home would be okay. Here, check it out.'

Ginny smiled, knowing she was blessed to have such love in her life. She unwrapped the balloon-patterned paper to find a set of coffee mugs with a farm animal print. 'Aww, I love them. Thanks.'

Lottie grinned. 'We've actually got you a few more, but they're back at mine, so you can get them later.'

'Four is enough,' said Ginny, raising the box.

Sophie chuckled. 'Not for when we all come over.'

'Which will be in a couple of weeks when we move your things,' said Spencer, taking a prawn sandwich from a platter.

'It's all happening so fast,' said Alice, handing Ginny a glass of bubbly. 'It's so exciting.'

It was and it wasn't. Ginny had the silliest idea that Will might just move in with her and they'd live happily ever after like the Henshaws. Oh well. It wasn't as if she had a healthy relationship with luck.

Robson and Matt started singing along to the radio, raising their arms, adding an impromptu dance.

Lottie was inserting candles into the birthday cake, and Sophie faffed with crockery.

All Ginny could do was smile, realizing she had something good in her life, so maybe luck liked her in a small way. She flopped into a chair and picked at the food on the plate in front of her. There was no way she was going to shoo her friends out the door, so she decided to join in by making a start on dinner, seeing how hungry she was.

Lottie manoeuvred to her side. 'Thirty-five now, lady. You feeling it?'

Ginny laughed. 'I've been feeling fifty since I turned twenty-one.'

'Aww, well, at least you only look about thirty.'

'There's not much difference.'

Lottie rolled back her shoulders. 'You're only as old as you feel.'

Ginny laughed. 'Fifty it is then.'

Lottie dipped her head and voice. 'How are you, really?'

'I'm okay. You lot need to stop fussing.'

'But we love you, Gin. You had such a mad year last year.'

Ginny nodded. 'Which is why I'm determined to make this year better, even if it didn't start off well.'

Lottie leaned closer. 'What do you mean?'

They knew everything else about her life, there was no point hiding things anymore.

'It's Lee.'

Lottie folded her arms in a huff. 'What's he done now?'

'He went and scattered Mum's ashes without me.'

'He did what?' yelled Lottie, making everyone turn.

Robson was the first to join the table. 'What's happened?'

'Lee scattered Birdy's ashes without Ginny,' said Lottie, before Ginny had a chance to draw breath.

Sophie wrapped an arm around Ginny's shoulders. 'Ooh, I never liked him, little runt.'

'Why did he do that, Gin?' asked Spencer.

Ginny shrugged. 'He said it didn't matter who was there. It was just the ashes. He didn't even put her where she wanted to be.'

'Where did he put her?' asked Alice.

Ginny thumbed towards the door. 'Up his way. Some memorial ground.'

Sophie clenched her fists and growled. 'Ooh, that horrible git.'

'It's okay, Soph. I'm not going to stress over it.' Ginny sighed, smiling gently at her concerned friends. 'I'm going to put up a birdhouse at my new place, and that will be in memory of my mum.'

'I don't mean to be rude, Gin,' said Matt, 'but I'm surprised at how good you are about her.' Sophie nudged him, and he frowned. 'I'm not trying to say anything out of line here, but after finding out about your upbringing, I'm just a bit . . . I don't know. I don't really talk to my mum, so I guess I'm just going by me.'

Ginny glanced over at him. 'It's okay. I know she didn't deserve my love, but she was still my mum, and in all honesty, I just wanted her to notice me. To love me the way she loved Lee. I'm coming to terms with it all now, thanks to Jan helping me, but it's a slow process.'

'I think you're doing brilliantly,' said Sophie, giving Matt another nudge.

'Me too,' said Matt.

'And we're all here for you every step of the way,' said Robson. 'We're even going to help you eat that birthday cake, that's how good we are.'

Everyone laughed, and Ginny waved them away.

'Go on, get some food in you.' She snaffled a sausage roll.

'Here, drink your fizz,' said Alice, sliding a full glass across the table.'

Ginny wrinkled her nose. 'I'm not feeling it, Al. I did have a cuppa on the go. Not sure where that's got to.' She stretched her neck towards the counter.

'Ooh, I could go for one,' said Lottie.

Alice beamed. 'How about I make us hot chocolate?'

Lottie lightly clapped. 'Now you're talking.'

Ginny laughed. 'Do you even know how to work that fancy gadget back there?'

Alice scoffed. 'Please. I'm going to boil some milk in a pan, the normal way.'

'Wait, wait,' called Sophie, lighting the candles on the cake. 'Let's sing to Ginny first.'

'No, we can skip that part,' said Ginny.

Robson kissed her cheek. 'No chance, chick.'

She sat back and watched them flailing their arms while belting out her least favourite song in the world when it was aimed at her, but out of politeness, she threw in a little cheer along with a clap.

Alice made the hot chocolate, Sophie sliced the cake, and Robson upped the volume on the radio, pulling Ginny to the makeshift dance floor.

'You know you're my best friend, right?' he said close to her ear.

Ginny pulled back and grinned. 'Yeah, why, what you after?'

Robson crinkled his brow. 'Moi? Nothing, thank you very much. I just have some birthday advice.'

'Is that a thing?'

He nodded and grinned. 'Is now.'

'Come on then. Hit me. What you got?'

'It's about Will.'

Ginny lost her smile. 'I don't want to talk about him, Rob. You know what he did.'

Robson nodded. 'Yep. He put his foot in his mouth. Happens to the best of us.'

'Well, it bloody well hurt.'

'I think it hurt him too, Gin.'

She dropped her arms from his. 'So you're on his side?'

'No. Yours. Always yours, no matter what.'

'Funny way of showing it.'

Robson narrowed his eyes, but still the piercing blue went straight through her like a laser. 'I happen to know he thinks the world of you. I don't want you to walk away from that, because you deserve happiness. All kinds of happiness. You, my beautiful mate, deserve the world.'

His words melted her heart, but also scared her. What if she had just tossed out the best thing that had happened to her? Did it really matter? She'd spent her whole life holding her own hand.

She glanced down. She was holding her own hand now. 'I've got more to think about now, what with the farmhouse.'

'Let him in,' said Robson, taking her hands. 'That's my birthday advice.'

Ginny needed to do something. Her heart ached for the sailor. But that was the problem. Just like her mother, he too now had the power to destroy her.

'We're going to his gran's funeral in a couple of days,' added Robson. 'Why don't you come? It's not as though you didn't know Babs.'

'He didn't exactly show up for me when my mum died.'

'Wasn't that because he thought you hated his guts?'

Ginny gave a half-hearted shrug. 'I think it's best I stay away, Rob. Just focus on my own life now.'

He gave a small nod, then pulled her back for a slow dance to the upbeat music playing. 'You know what's best for you.'

Ginny scoffed. 'Since when?'

'Ooh, I don't know, since you moved out of your mum's, since you set up your own business, since you bought a farmhouse, since you go after all those dreams of yours.'

'I didn't complete my tea shop dream.'

Robson nodded. 'Well, let's just focus on that then.'

Ginny nudged his side. 'I'm just saying.'

'You could always go ask Will for a Saturday job at his tearoom.'

'Oh, ha-ha.'

'Hey, sometimes what you want comes at you from a different angle to what you expected. You used to blow kisses out to sea, then a sailor came to town. You wanted a tea shop along the front, and now we have one. Well, when it opens. The point is—'

'I need to read the small print when I make wishes.'

Robson laughed. 'You, my lovely, need to open your eyes and see just how magical you truly are.'

Magic or no magic, Ginny had decided she was only going to focus on the good things in her life, because the past wasn't going to own her any longer. Plus, she had something else coming her way to add into the mix of her new beginning. Something she hadn't shared with her friends just yet. But they'd find out soon enough. Everyone would, including Will. So, sod Lee, and her demons. A whole year was ahead of her, and she was determined to fill it with nothing but happiness.

CHAPTER 27

Will

Will was blown away by the support he received from his new friends in Port Berry. He hadn't expected many to turn up for his grandmother's funeral. Perhaps a couple of her carers, maybe Ginny, seeing how she grew up next door, but Jed had rallied the troops, and Robson had laid out a small spread at the Jolly Pirate.

Sitting in the corner of the pub by the open fire, Will stared at the crackling flames and wondered if Ginny hadn't turned up because she no longer wanted reminders of Sweet Cherry Lane. He hoped that didn't include him. Could his existence make her think about that house?

It was all such a mess. He had an idea what to do to make things right with Ginny, but the surprise he had in store was a long shot, he was sure.

'Hey, how's it going?' said Spencer, joining him. 'You've got the best seat right by the fire. It's always cosy in here this time of year, and a little quieter, but that won't last long, what with the big birthday bash we have here on the twentieth each year.'

Will lowered his cup of tea. 'Oh, what's that for?'

'I'm surprised Jed hasn't mentioned it. It's his birthday, so he normally tells everyone.'

Will glanced over at Jed propped up at the bar. 'Ah, there has been a lot going on.'

'Doesn't normally stop him. He's like a big kid on his birthday. Anyway, the reason it's a big to-do is because it's not just his birthday that day. It's also Luna's and Robson's.' Spencer leaned back and smiled. 'So you can see why we go all out.'

'Just when you think the present buying is over.'

Spencer laughed into his glass of lemonade. 'I know, right. January needs to be a time for peace and quiet and nothing going on.'

'Doesn't help your business much.'

Spencer circled a finger in the air. 'Had a few funerals this month already.'

Will nodded. 'Thanks for the flowers you made for Babs. They were really nice.'

'No worries.'

'Have you always wanted to be a florist?'

Spencer shook his head. 'It was my aunt's place, so Lottie and I just carried on with it after she passed away.'

'Makes sense.'

'What about you? Did you always want to be a sailor?'

'Not really. I didn't have much going on in my life, and a mate told me about Sea Cadets he went to, so I joined that and went from there.'

Spencer looked over at the doors that led to the front beer garden. 'Even though I grew up by the sea, it never called to me.'

Will was glad he had memories of a home on a ship. He often felt the freedom of the open sea calmed him, and he was glad whenever Jed offered him a short trip around the harbour. 'Might have to consider buying my own boat.'

'Good luck with that. I'll stick to flowers.'

Will smiled and sipped his drink. 'As long as you're happy, that's all that matters.'

Spencer leaned closer to the table. 'I've got some other plans for this year.'

'Okay, now I'm intrigued, especially as you're whispering.'

Spencer laughed. 'I haven't told anyone yet, that's why. Lottie will make a big deal out of it, and I'd rather just stay under the radar, so to speak. No doubt she'd ask me to do one of her interviews for the Hub's website. Hey, you could do one about life at sea. Although her chats are usually well-being related, but I'm sure there's an angle there.'

'Mental health and the military. I'll speak to her. But meanwhile, what's going on with you?'

'Ever since Lottie had her accident, it made me think about working in mental health care. She's a really positive person, but even she had her moments in the beginning when she found out she'd never walk again.' Spencer wrinkled his nose. 'I haven't got much in the way of exams under my belt, as I didn't take school very seriously, so last year I started an evening course in mental health care for kids at a local college.'

'Good for you, Spence.'

'Thanks. It hasn't been easy keeping it a secret. But with help from Debra at the Sunshine Centre, I managed to get a work placement there.' Spencer glanced over at Lottie sat by Samuel sharing a plate of chips. 'My sister started going there for art therapy, and I told Debra I'd like to help out, and she was the one who pointed me in the direction of the college.'

'So what will you be doing exactly? Working at the centre?'

'Only part-time. I'm still needed in the shop, and I like my job at Berry Blooms. But I used to help out at Scouts, so I thought with my clean police record and the mental health care certificate, I could focus more on the kids that attend.'

Will nodded. 'I've already signed up there for summer activities. You know, the adventure stuff.'

Spencer bit his lip as he chuckled. 'Rock climbing.'

The thought of Ginny trapped on the side of the cliff had a shiver run the full length of Will's spine. He was sure he'd never get over that day.

'Sorry,' added Spencer. 'I shouldn't joke.'

'Ah, it's okay. At least we survived.'

'Bloody hell, mate. What a nightmare.' Spencer sipped his drink. 'I might have to go climbing with you myself.' He sat up straight, shifting closer again. 'This is the type of stuff I want to do with the kids. The ones there won't join the Scouts. Debra told me. No confidence or their anxieties get in their way. So I want to work with them and see if I can get them outdoors building camps, mixing with people, that sort of thing. I know they've got it in them.'

Will agreed wholeheartedly. He'd witnessed first-hand what the members of the Sunshine Centre were capable of, and the younger ones too. 'Emotional support goes a long way, Spence.'

'It certainly does. So that's what I'm currently working on. I need some sort of set-up that works well for the group Debra has in mind.'

'I can always help with that. You just let me know if and when you need a hand, and I'll square it with Debra.'

Spencer raised his glass to clink it with Will's mug. 'Cheers, mate. Oh, and keep this between us for now. I will let Lottie know, but I just want to wait until I've got some more cover for the shop. The last thing I want is for her to think I'll leave her to it alone.'

Will gestured over at Samuel. 'I don't think your sister will ever be alone, judging by the way he makes eyes at her.'

Samuel raised his head to look over their way. 'Why do I get the feeling I'm being spoken about?' he called.

'Because you are,' said Spencer, grinning.

'Saves everyone else from being gossiped about,' said Lottie, flicking a chip over at her brother.

'Oi! No throwing food,' boomed Robson from behind the bar.

Lottie wriggled a hand in the air. 'Sorry.' She narrowed her eyes at her brother. 'What are you saying about the love of my life?'

Samuel beamed, snuggling into her arm. 'Yeah, what you saying about me?'

Spencer winked at Will. 'Oh, just how gorgeous those golden eyes of yours are.'

Will laughed as Samuel fluttered his eyelashes.

'They're amber,' said Lottie. 'And they're mine.'

Samuel whipped his head her way. 'Oh, is that right?' She giggled as he tried to tickle her before leaning in for a kiss.

Spencer shook his head as he turned back to Will. 'What a load of old mush.'

Will breathed out a laugh into his tea. 'Do you know what they all say about you?'

Spencer frowned. 'No, what?'

'That you're allergic to love.'

'Oh that, yeah, it's true.'

'Seriously?'

Spencer nodded, grabbing a cheese sandwich from the plate Sophie brought over. 'I'm happy on my own.'

'So he says,' said Sophie, sitting next to Will.

'I am.' Spencer tapped his chest. 'There is nothing wrong with single life . . . Oops!' He swallowed his food and apologized to Will.

'What are you saying sorry to me for?'

Sophie leaned into his arm. 'Because of you and Ginny.' She glanced at the door. 'I thought she would've come today,' she mumbled.

'It's okay,' said Will.

'Oh, you two are as daft as each other,' snapped Sophie. 'Go and find her, Will. Go on. Make this right. We've got the big birthday party soon, and I want to see the pair of you dancing together.' She narrowed her eyes as she tipped her head to stare up at him. 'Did you know it was Ginny's birthday the other day?'

'No, but I would have liked to.'

Spencer shook his head. 'Don't worry, mate. She doesn't like a fuss.'

It wasn't the point. Will wanted to spend such a day with her. He loved her. There was so much he wanted to share with her.

Right! That does it. I've had enough of this.

Will abruptly stood. 'Where is she?'

Sophie shrugged. 'Could be at the café.'

'Or packing her last bits,' said Spencer. 'We're helping her move into the farmhouse soon.'

'She's there now,' called Lottie.

Spencer turned in his chair to face his sister. 'What have you got, super-hearing or something?'

Lottie poked her tongue out at him.

'Do you know where it is?' Sophie asked Will.

He sure did, thanks to Jed pointing it out during a car ride over to one of the Berry Buoy's houses one night.

'So what are you waiting for?' said Sophie, standing to push his elbow. 'Go get your missus.'

Will had only planned to go to his grandmother's funeral, then pop into the tearoom to see the new partition Shaun had built. But, as usual, Ginny found a way to occupy his mind and take over.

He climbed into his pickup truck and pulled up at the base of Berry Hill. The sea looked cold and dangerous, even the gulls were quiet. What was he doing going on some hopeless quest when he should be back at the B&B, looking for somewhere to live?

Ginny had made it quite clear he didn't belong in her world. Was it really down to him to make the first move?

Will huffed at the steering wheel. The least he could do was apologize again. He knew she was troubled, and he knew how important it was for her to have peace and stability. It was something he wanted as well.

The heating started to pump out of the air vents, warming his fingers. He glanced at the tight hold he had with the wheel, then loosened his grip and inhaled deeply.

'Okay, Willard. What advice would you give to a mate right about now?'

He mulled it over as a gust of wind blew a nearby shrub, catching his eye.

'Go tell her you're sorry. Tell her you love her. Show her what you did for her. Lay it all on the line. Today.'

It seemed like good advice, and definitely what he would offer, so why were his knees rattling as much as the bush outside?

Will bit his bottom lip and breathed out a quiet laugh.

Oh, you silly bugger.

With that, he turned the wheel and headed straight for the farmhouse. One way or another he would find out where his next destination would be. He just hoped Ginny was part of the journey.

* * *

The old farmhouse looked about as rustic as it could get, and Will knew immediately she would need help fixing up the place.

He sat at the end of the drive for a bit, assessing her new home. The Henshaws were at the front of his mind, and he could almost hear them cheering him on.

Pulling out his phone, he did a quick check online for their hotel. Perhaps if he could see it one more time, it would help shift his butt down the driveway.

Nothing came up, which was strange. Surely their hotel would be advertised.

'Oh, what am I doing?'

A sudden desire to see Ginny took over his foot, causing it to press down on the accelerator and get the vehicle moving to where it was supposed to be.

Ginny opened the front door and stepped onto the porch before he'd even had a chance to turn off the engine.

Will tentatively got out of the truck.

'I was wondering when you would drive down,' she said, hands on hips. 'Sat up the top long enough.'

Will realized his mouth was sagging, so snapped it shut.

'Cat got your tongue?' she asked.

'Actually, I have got words to say, thank you.'

Ginny tipped her chin up. 'Let's hear them then.'

It wasn't quite how he expected the conversation to start, but here he was.

'I'm sorry for having the biggest gob in Britain. And I'm sorry I hurt you. It was never my intention. Alice and I were talking, and the way the conversation was going, it suggested she knew about you and your mum. I was wrong. And I'm truly sorry. You'll never know how much.' He waited, but she didn't speak.

Part two. Say the next bit. Go on.

Will took a calming breath. 'I love you, Ginny Dean, with all my heart, and I want you to know that too.'

Her arms loosened, so did his chest.

'And there's one more thing.' He motioned to his truck. 'But it means taking a short ride with me. You up for that?'

It seemed like forever until she moved towards the front door to lock up.

Will opened the passenger door for her, chewing the inside of his cheek so not to grin as she passed him to clamber inside without making eye contact.

The silence on the drive to Harbour End Road wasn't as unnerving as he thought it might be. Just the fact she was sitting by his side was settling.

He parked outside the B&B and went to open the truck door, but Ginny touched his arm.

'Will, there's something I want to say.'

'What is it?'

'I want to apologize for how I spoke to you on Christmas Day at the pub. I was out of line.'

'I was the one who put my foot in it, sharing your secret.'

'I know, but I could have handled it better. Again, it was more about my mum than anything else. Having therapy has helped me see these things now.'

'I'm still sorry for opening my mouth about your business.'

She smiled softly. 'I'd like to move on from all that now.'

'Me too.' He pointed at the window. 'Follow me.'

Ginny got out the vehicle and went to walk towards Seaview B&B.

'No, this way,' said Will, gesturing towards the tea shop, with a roll of the arm.

She didn't look too impressed when she came to an abrupt halt outside his new business. Okay, so it wasn't finished, but the sign was up, even if covered by tarpaulin.

'Now, hear me out,' said Will, pointing at the dust-covered window.

Ginny folded her arms and shivered, and it was at that moment he noticed she didn't have a coat on. He quickly whipped off his dark jacket and draped it over her shoulders.

'Right,' he added, trying not to shiver himself. 'You once had a dream about owning Harbour Light Café, right?'

She didn't respond. Her eyes fixed only on the window of the shop.

Will continued. 'Okay, well, then your dream changed, but before you could do anything about it, I came along with my own tearoom idea.'

Still no response.

'So, here's what I have in mind,' he added. 'See what you think.' He moved away from her side to go over to the door, then with one robust tug on a rope, he pulled down most of the tarpaulin, as some of it refused to budge, not that it mattered. What he wanted her to see was clear enough.

Ginny gasped, and he hoped it was one of delight.

'Erm, so . . .' Will swallowed hard. 'Here's my proposal. A swap. I take the café, and you have this place. Obviously the café is worth more, so I'll pay the difference. So that's my idea. I get to have a business that pretty much runs itself, which is what I wanted, and you get to have your dream.'

She was still staring wide-eyed at the sign. 'Ginny's Tearoom,' she read aloud.

'That's just so you get the idea of where I'm coming from.' Will cleared his throat. 'You can call it what you want.'

Watery eyes met his. 'I love it,' she whispered, shivering into his jacket.

'I love you, Ginny. I want you to be happy.' He also really wanted her to be warm. 'Sit back in the truck. It's cold out here.' Before she could respond, he bundled her inside and switched the engine back on.

'Thank you,' she said quietly.

'That's okay. Your lips were starting to turn blue.'

'No, I meant for thinking of this. Of me. Swapping shops.'

Will smiled. 'You take your time and think it over. There's no—'

'But the answer is yes. I don't need time to think. I like your idea. I love the sign. I want to do this, Will.'

He shuffled in his seat so he could face her full on. 'This is a big step. I need you to be sure. You made that café your life for a long time.'

'Yeah, well, my life has changed.' Ginny reached over and placed her cold hand on his, making his heart jump to attention. 'I want to do this with you.'

'Okay,' he managed.

Ginny smiled softly, and he so wanted to kiss her mouth. 'But first I want you to take me back to the farmhouse, as I have something else I want to say.'

'Can't you tell me here?'

She shook her head slightly. 'I want to talk there.'

'Okay, buckle up. Let's go talk.' He side-eyed her as she pulled on her seat belt. It felt so good to be by her side again, even if it was to talk business.

CHAPTER 28

Ginny

Ginny already had the heating on in the old farmhouse, so it was nice and warm as she entered with Will. Ever since she took ownership of the place, she had wanted to show him around. 'We can walk and talk,' she said, removing his jacket from her shoulders to place on the coat hook by the front door.

Will was eyeing up the walls and ceiling. 'It's higher than I expected.'

'Bigger too.' She pointed down the hallway. 'It goes quite a way back.'

'What did the surveyor say?'

'It's in pretty good shape. There's nothing that would cost too much to fix.' She glanced over her shoulder as they walked up the stairs.

'That's good. I can help with anything you need. I'm not sure if I'll be any good as a handyman. Not really tested those skills, but I'm always up for trying.'

Ginny smiled. 'Thanks. I'm someone who likes to call in a professional, but there is one thing I'd like you to do for me.'

'What's that?'

She motioned for him to follow her into the main bedroom at the back of the house. 'Look down there.' Pointing out the window, she waited to see his expression.

'Oh wow! That's a nice bit of land you have there.'

'That's for the animals.'

Will's eyes smiled along with his mouth as he gazed her way. 'You definitely doing that then?'

'I've got a meeting tomorrow with an animal welfare centre to talk all things chicken.'

He glanced back at the field below. 'So an enclosure is needed, and a henhouse.'

'That's what I'm going to find out. They're going to teach me everything.' She hesitated, debating whether to include him after all, but seeing how he'd declared his love and offered a business swap just to make her dream come true, she wanted to be totally honest. 'Would you like to come with me?'

'Yep.'

His quick reply had the corners of her mouth twitch into a small smile. 'I was hoping you'd say that.'

'I told you. I love you. I want to help, even if you only want me as a friend now.'

'I . . . It's just . . .'

Will touched her hand. 'It's okay, Ginny. I get it. I messed up, and I hurt you.'

She huffed out a breath, then nodded. 'I accept your apology. We've moved on from that, right? In fact, I've moved on from a lot. I don't want to live a life where my past gets to control me. So I made the decision to wipe the slate clean and just focus on what I have here and now and what I can build for a better future.'

'I made that decision too.'

Ginny smiled, staring down at their linked fingers. 'It's refreshing, isn't it?'

'Oh yeah.'

'You know, for a moment, I thought you would leave Port Berry.'

232

Will grinned. 'What, because you tried to run me out of town?'

Ginny dropped her gaze. 'Yeah, sorry about that. I shouldn't have—'

'It's done. We've moved on, remember?'

She shot her head up to meet the warmth in his eyes. 'Yes.' She turned to the large empty room. 'So, this is the main bedroom. I . . . Would . . . I . . .'

His brow lifted as he shook his head. 'Spit it out, love. You're killing me here.'

'It's just, well, I had this other dream where we lived happily ever after.'

'You and me?'

Ginny nodded, all the while thinking she was making a right pig's ear of explaining her feelings. 'I just . . .' She lowered her head, and the next thing she knew, Will had dipped to peer up at her.

'Talk to me, love.'

'I'm a little scared, Will.'

'Of?'

'How vulnerable I feel.'

He lifted her chin. 'I feel it too.'

'I don't want the past to guide me, but it's hard to shake off the trauma. With my mum, all I wanted was for her to love me, and I don't want to feel that way again. I don't want to have to fight for something that should be given freely, and when I look at you, I worry I might spend the rest of my life needing your love and suffering for that want.'

Will sighed quietly. 'I'm with you all the way with that, because I always craved the love of a family as well, but I need you to know that you won't ever have to fight for my love. It's yours. I'm yours. I want to walk this journey with you, Ginny.' He raised their joined hands. 'I came here searching for a home and I found you.'

Water filled her eyes as she took a steady breath. The last thing she wanted was to cry, but his words were meaningful and wrapped around her like a comfort blanket.

His fingertip met the escaped tear rolling down her cheek. 'Hey, it's okay,' he whispered.

'I always believed you existed.' She blinked away the dampness and sniffed. 'You helped get me through some tough times.'

Will bent to kiss her cheek. 'We're a team, you and me, and even though we're at the start of our journey, I can tell we're going to have a long and happy one.' He pulled back and grinned. 'Just like the Henshaws.'

Ginny giggled at the thought. 'I blimming love that place.'

'Well, I would take you back there, but I can't find the website.'

'Oh, they must have one.' She pulled out her phone from her dungarees. 'Look.' Humming quietly while flicking through her search, she came to realize he was right. 'But I'm sure . . .'

'Wait, let me get the map up, now I know where we were stranded.'

Ginny snuggled into his side as she peered down at his phone.

Will kissed her head, then laughed. 'There's nothing there.'

'There has to be. We were there.'

He faffed about with the map some more, showing a street view that only offered trees and fields. 'It's not there, love.'

'Why isn't it showing up? That's so bizarre.' She put her phone on the windowsill, widening her eyes. 'Ooh, what if it's one of those magical places that only appears once every so often?'

Will grinned. 'And it just so happened to appear for us?'

Ginny laughed. 'Yeah, because we were stranded in a snowstorm. The magical Henshaws knew we needed help.'

'And maybe not just in travel?' Will chuckled. 'Well, whoever they were, they accepted my credit card, so at least my bank account will prove we weren't imagining things.'

'Oh, Will, do you think the universe has been working in mysterious ways to bring us together?'

He laughed. 'I honestly don't care. I'm just grateful I met you.' He took an obvious breath as he stepped back, holding her at arm's length. 'So, Ginny Dean, tell me straight. From this day forward, is it going to be just you and me joining our dreams and building a life?'

There had been many moments in Ginny's life where she wished for the happiness she could feel flooding her whole being. She prayed it would stay that way after her next sentence.

'No, Will,' she said softly, gauging his expression. 'It won't be just the two of us, because we two are now three.'

He frowned, lowering their arms. 'What does that mean?'

Ginny stroked over her stomach. 'I'm pregnant.' He didn't respond, so she added, 'We're having a baby.'

A beat passed. Will's eyes widened. His mouth sagged, then finally he spoke. 'A baby?'

'Yep. It's early days. I've not long found out, but it's true. Pregnancy confirmed.'

'I don't know what to say.'

'That makes two of us. I was going to tell you about this even if we weren't together. I want you to know that, but right now, I'm still getting my own head around it.'

Before she could say another word, Will pulled her in for a hug. 'Ginny, a baby?'

'Yes,' she mumbled into his shirt.

'I wasn't expecting this when you brought me here. I honestly thought you were going to ask me to help with the chicken idea.'

Ginny giggled. 'We have our own little chick to hatch.' She pulled away so she could see his face. 'How are you feeling about this? I know it's a shock. It was to me too, but are you happy, mad, sad, or something else altogether?'

'Oh, I think the latter, because I can't describe to you just exactly how over the moon I am with my life right now.

Ginny, love, I came to Port Berry to find answers, and I've ended up falling in love, settling down, and now I'm to be a father.' Will's smile dropped, and he flopped to the worn-through tweed carpet, slapping a hand to his head.

Ginny kneeled to his side. 'Will, are you okay? Do you feel faint? Should I call a doctor?'

He reached out to her hand hovering by his forehead and held it. 'I'm fine. I'm just having a moment.'

'What kind of moment?'

Their eyes met. His filled with nerves. Hers with concern.

'How am I supposed to know how to be a dad? I never had one.'

Ginny snuggled into his side, trying to find a comfy position on the hard floor. 'Nor me, but I don't think it's about the way others raise or don't raise their kids, it's about how we do it, and if anyone knows that children need love, it's us. We can do that much. We might not be experts, and I'm sure we'll get loads wrong along the way, but as long as our kid knows it's loved and wanted, everything should be okay, right?'

'You asking or telling?'

'Both.'

Will placed a hand over her stomach. 'We certainly can give love.'

Ginny met his eyes and smiled. 'I love you, Will,' she said slowly.

They shared a gentle kiss, neither moving for a while.

'We have a busy year ahead of us,' said Will, standing and helping her up. 'We need to get this home fixed up for you and the nipper.'

'And you too, Will.' Ginny took his hands. 'I want you to live here with us. I know we haven't been together long, but it feels as though we've been a couple forever, and now with a baby on the way, and rescue chickens, I want us to be all in. The businesses, our home, this relationship. No halves, no maybes, no uncertainty. Just a normal, everyday couple, doing normal, everyday stuff.'

'With rescue animals.'

Ginny laughed. 'I know you said you love me, and I know you're a good man who would never let his family down, and we are one now, but I need you to say it out loud so the corners of my mind understand.'

Will nodded and shuffled closer. 'Okay, well, listen up, Ginny's brain, I, Willard Pendleton of the sea far and wide, do hereby solemnly swear to be everything you need and more. I love you. I'm here for you, and I'll never leave you, because you, Ginny Dean of Port Berry, are my world, my family, and every inch my happiness.' He tipped his head and winked. 'How was that?'

'Perfect.'

They kissed once more, then turned to face the acres of land belonging to them.

'Our farm needs a name,' said Will. 'What do you say, love?'

Ginny twisted her lips to one side. 'Hmm. How about Happy Farm?'

Will's head bobbed. 'Straight to the point. I like it.'

Ginny nudged him. 'I like you.'

'A minute ago, you loved me.'

'You can love someone and not like them.'

Will smiled. 'Ah, I see. So I get both.'

'You, chick, get everything.'

Their hug tightened as they continued to stare out at the cold January day.

'You never know where you're going to find happiness, do you?' said Will quietly.

'Maybe it finds you.'

Will kissed her head. 'All my life I wondered what home looked like.' He cupped her face and smiled. 'Now I know.'

Ginny smiled back. Peace filled her heart, and joy her mind. 'All my life I wondered what happiness felt like. Now I know.'

Will nudged her nose with his own. 'Now we have everything, love.'

'We do. Except for one thing.'

'Oh, what's that?'

'A nice cup of tea.'

Will laughed. 'Come on then. Let's start the way we mean to go on.'

Ginny held his hand as they left their bedroom. 'By having tea?'

'No, by being a normal, everyday couple.'

'Except we'll have a donkey.'

'I knew I came to Port Berry for a reason.'

Ginny grinned into his arm as they walked side by side down the wide stairway. 'You came to find happiness and a home. See, wishes can come true.'

THE END

ABOUT THE AUTHOR

Hello, I'm K.T. Dady. I'm the bestselling author of the Pepper Bay series. Also bringing to you the delightful small-town romance stories of Port Berry. I'm also a chocolate lover, mum to a grown-up daughter, and a huge fan of a HEA. I was born and raised in the East End of London, and I've been happily writing stories since I was a little girl. When I'm not writing, I'm mostly reading, baking cakes, or pottering around in my little garden in Essex, trying not to kill the flowers.

I love hearing from readers, so please get in touch over at my website or sign up for my newsletter and receive a free Pepper Bay short story that you won't find anywhere else.

Newsletters go out once a month and often contain free gifts, previews, and writing tips amongst the news. Head over to my website at ktdady.com

If you enjoyed reading my book, please leave a rating or review on Amazon or Goodreads. It really helps to bring the story to more readers. Thank you so much.

You'll also find me on my social media accounts.

Instagram: @kt_dady

Twitter (X): @kt_dady

Facebook: @ktdady

ACKNOWLEDGEMENTS

This story is dedicated to everyone on a healing journey. You are powerful, resilient, problem-solving masters who know how to survive the deepest, darkest pits of hell. Remember that next time you doubt your strength.

Sending a huge thank you to former care worker Claire Sparrow for help with Babs's care home and dementia storyline. Birdy's care home was based on one I visited a long time ago. Hopefully, they are all now as lovely as the one Babs was in. Also, sending a massive thank you to former Petty Officer Ben Green for the Royal Navy information. Thanks for your service, Ben.

Huge thanks goes out to the Choc Lit/Joffe Books team for their help, support, and encouragement for the Port Berry series and my author journey. Much appreciated.

I'm also sending a cheer to my readers who are a constant support. I want you all to know that I'm so completely and utterly grateful to each and every one of you.

As always, sending lots of love and light your way. Keep reading. It's good for the soul.

THE CHOC LIT STORY

Established in 2009, Choc Lit is an independent, award-winning publisher dedicated to creating a delicious selection of quality women's fiction.

We have won 18 awards, including Publisher of the Year and the Romantic Novel of the Year, and have been shortlisted for countless others. In 2023, we were shortlisted for Publisher of the Year by the Romantic Novelists' Association.

All our novels are selected by genuine readers. We are proud to publish talented first-time authors, as well as established writers whose books we love introducing to a new generation of readers.

In 2023, we became a Joffe Books company. Best known for publishing a wide range of commercial fiction, Joffe Books has its roots in women's fiction. Today it is one of the largest independent publishers in the UK.

We love to hear from you, so please email us about absolutely anything bookish at choc-lit@joffebooks.com.

If you want to receive free books every Friday and hear about all our new releases, join our mailing list here: www.joffebooks.com/freebooks

www.choc-lit.com